REUSED

Robin Tidwell

Rocking Horse Publishing, St. Louis, Missouri

First printing, December 2012
Second printing, September 2014

ISBN 10: 0988493322
ISBN 13: 978-0-9884933-2-2

Cover design by Shannon Yarbrough, St. Louis, Missouri
Cover art by LeAnn Areford, St. Louis, Missouri

The characters and events in this book are fictitious.

www.RockingHorsePublishing.com

BOOKS BY
ROBIN TIDWELL

REDUCED
REUSED
RECYCLED
SO YOU WROTE A BOOK: NOW WHAT?

DEDICATION

To my good friend, Alison. Um, Laura. Uh, Whatshername?

Without her research and enthusiasm, this book would not have been possible. Or the next one . . .

ACKNOWLEDGMENTS

I'd like to thank my editor, Peggy Linhorst, for her unfailing attention to my errors and omissions, as well her endless supply of, er, amusing and entertaining commentary down the side of the manuscript.

I'd also like to thank author Shannon Yarbrough, for answering so many stupid questions that I asked him, over the last nine months or so, and for his unwavering ability to keep from laughing in my face.

And of course, my very, very patient family, for being mostly understanding when dinner was late. Or burned. Or missing altogether.

I would be remiss if I didn't also mention my dear friends from camp—yes, THE camp—thank you for your inspiration, your support, and your abiding friendship. I know that you'll always be there for me, as I will for you.

Finally, big thanks to my friend LeAnn Areford, whose photo made the cover of this book. It's beautiful and perfect, and exactly right to complement the concept of my book.

To all my readers: Thank you, thank you, thank you!

Chapter One

"At ease, Major Blake." The older man lowered himself carefully into a chair and turned to study the younger officer. As Colonel Barton's recent replacement in St. Louis, he was familiarizing himself with the new command and had requested Major Blake, specifically, for this detail. He busied himself for a few moments with a stack of papers on his desk, while covertly watching the newer recruit for any signs of recognition or remembrance.

Finally, he spoke again.

"Major, we have a very important mission for you. There are still pockets of rebels out there, somewhere, even after all this time. One would think they'd have accepted the status quo by now, but. . . " The colonel shrugged. "Perhaps not. Colonel Barton was remiss in not following through on our original plans which, I suppose, is why I am now here.

"Please, Major, have a seat. We have much to discuss." He shuffled the papers on his desk again, appeared to have found what he was looking for, and continued. "So, Brad, if I may address you as such?"

"Yes, sir!"

"It appears that you have had, in the past, some knowledge of these fringe groups, yes? And that you may still possess some familiarity with some individuals so involved?"

"Yes, sir. I know where to find them. I know them, I know how they operate. And I have every desire to bring them to justice, sir, if I may say so."

"I'm sure you do," murmured the colonel, barely audible. "And I assume that, given specific direction, you will be able to take out these insurgents, without any qualms whatsoever? Even supposing there are, say, a woman and a young girl among them?"

"No, sir. No reservations whatsoever. My time among those people was a poor decision on my part, and I cannot forget the things to which I was subjected during those few years." Brad's face was inscrutable. The colonel continued to watch him closely for any signs of a breakthrough, any signs of wavering in his duty or, in his own case, of identification. There were none.

"That is as it should be. Very good, Major. I see we are on the same page and, if you are able to finish what was begun five years ago, you will indeed be rewarded.

"Your immediate territory will be to the south of the city, as far south as is needed. You will work with a handpicked squad and you will have much discretion as to how you perform your. . . er. . . duties. You will report only to me and, in matters of urgency, the code word "Pops" will get you through to me immediately."

Brad's face showed nothing, not even a tiny flicker of memory. The colonel handed him a file and rose from his seat.

"Dismissed."

Colonel Clarence Hoefer walked around the desk and closed the door. Now, his real work could begin.

For years, Co-opCom had struggled with the whys and wherefores of VADER. Why were some individuals targeted, and others seemed to be immune? More specifically, why were there so many for whom the profile was inaccurate? It was supposed to have worked a whole lot better than it had.

VADER had been developed some two decades earlier, by the Ultratron Corporation in conjunction with the new government, the Cooperative Commonwealth. The purpose was to target certain groups of people, those who were opposed to Co-opCom's heavy-handed takeover and, in effect, stop the protest. In other words, terminate them.

The remaining population would support the government, as the government would support them, and all threats would have been eliminated. Those who now occupied certain key cities throughout the US were as sheep—as long as they were fed, sheltered, clothed, they required nothing more than an occasional sacrifice of freedom.

Guns or other weaponry were outlawed entirely, except for the military. Travel was heavily restricted from zone to zone—in fact, none was allowed at all. Speech was monitored, everywhere, all the time; one wrong word would get a person locked up for months at a time with no contact, let alone a trial or even official charges filed.

When VADER was unleashed, the plan had indeed worked on much of the population—95% of it, which was slightly more than intended. It decimated the military, which was to be expected, but Co-opCom had been prepared with a mercenary force. No civilians had yet volunteered in this new regime.

Yet, it wasn't a perfect system, to remove the dissidents in order to construct this so-called utopian rule. Many of Co-Op Com's supporters were eliminated and a few, a very few, of its detractors not only lived but now were threatening the new government by their very existence.

When one could be found, and terminated, they were that much closer to their final vision of a monarchy. And that was Pops' promotion, based on his success in the field nearly eight years ago combined with the gross ineptitude of a certain Colonel Barton.

The years Pops had spent down at the camp with Abby and little Juliet and all the others was etched in his mind as one of the most difficult assignments he'd had to date. He'd known some of those "kids" since they actually were children, and yes, he did care about them, in his own fashion. And Millie. That had almost been his undoing.

But they were all hell-bent on making their own way, on opposing everything this new regime stood for—and he couldn't let that happen. He had his own life at stake, his own dreams. Hell, he wasn't that old yet. He was waiting for the right time to retire, and then he'd have anything he wanted. Anything at all.

Chapter Two

Abby straightened up and stretched, rubbing her aching back. Feeling much older than her 39 years, she finished banking the fire for the night and looked around for the girls. Juliet and EJ were curled up on a blanket, and Juliet was telling EJ a story about when she was a little girl, living nearby with Abby and Emmy and all the rest of them. EJ was silent and enraptured.

"Come along, EJ, bedtime!" Abby lifted her daughter, swinging her as high as the ceiling of the cave would allow. "Let's get your hair brushed out and your pajamas on. Perhaps Juliet can finish her story then?" She looked questioningly at the older girl.

"Of course," said Juliet. "I have to brush my hair too, EJ, then we'll get all snuggled up again. Winter's coming soon, isn't it, Abby?"

Abby shivered a bit at the thought. It was hard work, keeping the wood supplied, the fire burning, food on the table. The girls helped a lot, especially Juliet who, at 16, was almost as tough and strong and capable as Abby herself. EJ tried to emulate them, bless her little heart, but was often more hindrance than help.

She thought less often about their circumstances than she did about what the future might hold, for both of the girls. Juliet was like a daughter to her, but the girl certainly remembered her parents as well; she'd been so young when they died, barely four years old, younger even than EJ was now.

What was next? Keep living here until they died? Or until she died anyway. That was more likely to happen, that she'd be gone and these two would have to manage on their own. Not that they couldn't, certainly; she'd trained Juliet well, and EJ was learning rapidly. But this was no real kind of life for any of them.

For nine years they'd lived here in this cave, up on the hillside in the abandoned camp near St. Louis. First Abby and Juliet, and then Noah. Always, Noah was in the back of her mind, sometimes urging her on, sometimes cautioning. She knew it was her imagination, but sometimes it helped. Sometimes.

And then there was EJ. Born in the woods, raised in a cave. Abby thought there was probably a song in there somewhere, but she couldn't really sing. Whistle at the birds, yes, back and forth. That was about her limit. At any rate, EJ was thriving. She had a wonderful role model in Juliet, sweet Jules who'd been through so much in such a short amount of time. She'd lost her parents, her grammy, and Noah who'd been like a father to her.

And Emmy. Stalwart, never questioning, always willing to help. Abby missed her friend so much sometimes that she physically ached. Ten years she'd been gone, yet sometimes it seemed like yesterday. Abby couldn't forget that last day: the noise, the bombs, the terror. Emmy's last words to her, screaming, "Run, take Juliet and run!"

She'd occasionally wondered if she could have done something, anything, to save Emmy, but she knew it wasn't true. Emmy had been so close to the old infirmary when that last strike hit, and Abby was starting up the hill with Juliet. Noah had shoved them both out the door when the first round came streaking down, and Emmy had stayed back with Pops. Abby knew, too, that she'd never forget any of them.

Cal and Pops, dead before the building collapsed; Noah barely escaping. Emmy and Ted, lying dead outside. And all the others, gone before that: Meg, Sandy, Lorie, Zoe, Janey, Brad. Gone. Abby sighed. She tucked in the girls and Juliet smiled up at her.

"You've been doing this a long time, Abby," she said. "Remember my first night? That nightmare when you came running, gun drawn? I'm not sure what scared me more, the dream or your gun!" She laughed. "But I haven't been scared since!"

Abby smiled back, too tired to laugh, too lost in thoughts of the past. She kissed EJ's soft cheek, still full and babyish, and wondered for the millionth time how she, Abby, had ever given birth and raised not one, but two wonderful girls.

Settling down with a blanket and a cup of coffee, Abby watched the low flames flicker and begin to die. She questioned the wisdom of caffeine at this hour; she didn't sleep particularly well these days as it was. It had been too long since they'd seen anyone, or heard any news at all. She assumed that things were heating up in St. Louis. A few days ago, during one of her evening sky checks, there had been a black formation far off to the northeast. And she knew.

Thinking back, it had been what? Two years ago? Probably. That was the last time Abby had seen anyone, and it was just a couple, poking around in the debris in town. No one had ever bothered to finish the demolition or clean anything up; it was fair game for anyone to scavenge. They hadn't seen her, though. She was still careful. They were probably harmless, but Abby wasn't going to take any chances.

She finished putting out the fire and went back to the cave, crawling into bed after checking on the girls. Tomorrow she'd have to make a list of supplies and go into town, see what she could find and maybe even plan a longer trip, up to the outskirts of St. Louis. Something to think about, anyway.

Chapter Three

Alison stood in her small apartment, hands on her hips, surveying the mess in front of her. She had to finish packing and get a move on here. The chopper would be landing any minute, and she'd been ordered to St. Louis to help out a Colonel. . . yes, Hoefer, that was his name. She sighed and grabbed a bottle of tequila, stuffing it into her bag.

Goodbye, Chicago. While it certainly wasn't much of a town, she'd been here for most of her life, since well before VADER made its appearance. Since then, she'd been plenty busy fielding questions, putting out fires—figuratively, not literally—and handling all the petty issues that came from within a huge bureaucracy. Not a lot of time for socializing, even though, as one of the new regime's top cities, Chicago offered quite a lot of entertainment options.

Besides, most of the country's programming came from the Windy City, from supercomputers to news networks (or propaganda farms, as Alison sometimes silently referred to them) to military frequencies. Chicago was the hub of the Midwest and St. Louis just a blip on the radar.

No, Alison wasn't happy about this new assignment. The perks and promotions came from Chicago. All the top officials were located here rather than the capitol itself, which hadn't had much left to offer after VADER was contained. Seems there was more culling to do there than anywhere else which, she figured, wasn't too surprising. Everyone there had something to hide, but no one could hide from VADER. It got rid of the undesirables, or it was supposed to. Sure, a few unlucky ones had contracted it as well, but mostly she knew the right ones were affected. Ha. The right ones. That was funny.

She did sometimes wonder, though, how so few had survived. The word was that 95% of the population was dead, but she knew that official numbers had to be correct, since prior to VADER only about 40% should have been targeted. Chicago said there were 30% left, so that must be right. Chicago was never wrong.

Still, sometimes she wondered.

Packed and ready, she called down to make sure her car was waiting. It was, and she left, carefully locking the door, the thought of not returning never crossing her mind.

Her driver saluted, and Alison returned it, settling into the back seat of the Lincoln for the drive to O'Hare. She closed her eyes for a few minutes, knowing that, even with the diplomatic flags fluttering from the hood of the black sedan, it would take at least thirty minutes to arrive at the helipad.

She awoke with a start. Damn. Strange dream. She shook it off, realizing the car had stopped. The young corporal opened the door, and she scrambled out and took her bag from him. She strode purposefully towards the waiting chopper; it wouldn't do to show any kind of weakness even though her legs were trembling a bit. Taking a deep breath, Alison climbed into the seat and strapped herself in, willing the dream to disappear as she focused on what lay ahead.

By the time her chopper landed, and those escorting it had veered off back to the north, Alison was more composed. A short drive later, and she was meeting with Colonel Hoefer.

He sized her up; she returned the favor. Neither particularly liking what they saw, they moved on to the business at hand.

As the senior officer, the colonel spoke first. "I have a particular assignment for you. In the field. You'll be working with Major Blake. I assume this isn't an issue?"

Alison merely smiled. "Of course not. Assuming you're referring to the field position, and not Major Blake? And no, I don't have an issue with this Major, either." She couldn't quite pin it down, but she already was actively disliking the colonel. And she definitely could use a drink. Field position? What the hell?

"Good," said Pops. A moment later, the door opened and in walked, Alison presumed, Major Blake. Tall, good-looking, maybe a year or two older than she. Blank expression. Then again, he was in the presence of two superior officers. Hmmm. Maybe he didn't get along with Colonel Hoefer either. Either? C'mon, she told herself, you just met him. Cut him some slack.

So she tried. But it wasn't easy; something about the man just irritated her and set her on edge. Then she realized he was speaking again, outlining the details of the mission. She sat up straighter, giving him her full attention while trying not to notice Major Blake seated next to her; he was awfully close, and it seemed a bit warm in the room.

"So," continued Pops, "you will leave at 0600 hours and proceed south. You will find and either bring in, or terminate, any groups you encounter outside the protected radius of the city. You will communicate only as absolutely necessary, and not return until you have accomplished the initial goal.

"Captain, Major Blake will brief you on the more intimate details after you have left the area. Dismissed."

Alison blushed. Brief me on the what? Oh. Yes. She composed herself, saluted the colonel, and took her leave, along with Major Blake. Outside, the man silently handed her a piece of paper with information on their rendezvous point, saluted, and left her alone.

Back at her hotel room, the first thing she unpacked was the bottle of tequila.

Chapter Four

Abby awoke in a pool of sweat, yet shivering. She glanced over at the girls, both still asleep, then fumbled for her watch. Five o'clock. No wonder it was still so dark. She quietly got up and moved farther back into the cave where she splashed her face with cold water from a bucket and brushed her teeth. After dressing warmly, as near-winter was beginning to settle in, she went outside and stirred up the fire. Before long, they'd move it just inside the cave.

She put on water for coffee and dug a crumpled pack of cigarettes out of her jacket pocket. She really should quit, but at least she'd cut back to just a few a day. After a few minutes she felt awake enough to start her day, pausing only to brush out her long, blond hair and re-braid it. She poured a second cup of coffee and began to make her list, distracted by the dream she'd had last night.

Choppers, more of them, a strange woman. And oddly enough, Brad. She hadn't thought of Brad for years, it seemed; she tried, not always successfully, to avoid remembering the old days. The days when they were all here, or even before that, back when they were kids. Huh. Weird.

Abby finally shrugged off her thoughts and, list complete, went to wake the girls. They stumbled outside and Juliet poured herself some coffee. EJ tried, but a stern look and a raised eyebrow from her mother foiled her plans. She settled for a cup of milk instead; the last of it, Abby noted.

"Juliet, I'm going into town shortly. You're in charge, keep a good eye on EJ, and if you see anything—anything at all—unusual, you know what to do. Right?"

Juliet rolled her eyes, as only a teenager could do. "Yes, Abby, I know what to do. Same thing we always do: crawl all the way back into the hiding space and let whoever do whatever. 'Stuff can be replaced, but we can't.'"

Abby resisted the temptation to roll her eyes as well and merely said, "Yep." She hugged them both, and set off down the hill, shouldering her pack and, when her back was turned, rolling her eyes anyway and shaking her head. She figured that must all be something innate, things that all teenagers did to drive older folks crazy. Then again, she realized, she was still doing it, so maybe it was more nurture versus nature.

It was a beautiful fall day, as the sun finally rose. The leaves had turned; some were beginning to fall. Abby realized, as she uncovered the old black truck, camouflaged neatly at the base of the hill, that it was about time to move it across camp. She'd be lucky to get in one more trip this year, but she wasn't too worried. She generally made the journey only once every few months.

With the briefest hesitation, the engine coughed and turned over. She idly wondered if she should start looking for another ride. Surely there were other suitable vehicles sitting abandoned along the roads. Last time she'd left the camp, there were still plenty of them sitting in the ditches and parking lots, rusting out and probably worthless, she guessed.

She pulled through the gates and carefully closed them. Not that that would keep anyone out, but it might make them think twice. If anyone ever came down this road, that is. Still, better safe than sorry. The undergrowth had crept closer to the road, rising higher, each time she came this way. The trees, in spite of losing leaves, were beginning to hang low enough to occasionally scrape the roof of the cab. At some point in the last few months, the creek had covered the low-water crossing and left quite a lot of debris behind. The old truck slogged through it, and Abby continued on.

Reaching the old gas station where, back when, they'd usually begun their scavenging, she stopped. A quick check was all it took to confirm that the place had been cleaned out. Must have been that couple she saw last time, or maybe someone else finally in the area. She resolved to pay closer attention and, at that, whipped her head around and stared out at the road.

She really had lost her edge. She blinked. All those cars and trucks, parked haphazardly along the way, were gone. Cleaned up, cleaned out. Why? And when? She counted backwards. Yes, it had been late August, right after Juliet's birthday. That was the last time she'd been here. And they were there then, all of them, best she could remember.

Back in the truck, she crossed under the highway. This store, too, was cleaned out and cleaned up. She pondered for a moment, finally deciding to head north a bit. Normally she'd go south, as the farther she went from St. Louis, the better. The skies were clear, it was still early, and she really needed to see what she could find. She turned left on Highway 67, chuckling to herself as to how old habits die hard as she checked for traffic first.

A few minutes later, she reached Barnhart. The road had been clear, but had been for some time, and there were still a few cars on the shoulder. Fewer, perhaps, but it was hard to tell. There was a small store, closed up, but Abby stopped in the back and pried off the boards covering a window. She climbed inside and shined her flashlight around, .357 in hand. She wasn't taking any chances.

No human presence, and little evidence of anything or anyone else. She breathed a sigh of relief and began searching the shelves for anything usable. It seemed as though the place had been boarded up and closed for quite a while. There were canned goods and paper products; the coolers were about half full. A lot of miscellaneous items, like batteries, fishing line, camo gear, and even some boxes of ammo behind the counter. Abby started making a pile near the back door, listening intently for intruders or worse. . . choppers.

She and the girls had managed quite well over the years, but there were still things that were hard to obtain. They lived simply and frugally, depending on little from the outside, but there were still products that they couldn't make and, sometimes, a little luxury was called for. Like beer, thought Abby. And maybe some soda for the girls, a little candy. She was very particular about sweets, given the lack of dentists these days, but a treat every few months was perfectly acceptable. She grabbed a couple cartons of smokes, too, vowing yet again that she'd quit for good. Someday.

There wasn't much in the coolers that wasn't spoiled, but she did find some packaged goods that hadn't been chewed on by mice. Ready at last, she was just about to start loading the truck when she heard the choppers.

Out of habit, she clicked off the flashlight and crouched behind a display, gun at the ready. The sound became louder. After a few minutes, Abby let her breath out in a rush. The sound faded as they circled and flew away. Taking a moment to relax her clenched muscles and steady her breathing, Abby realized the damn things had been hovering directly over Barnhart. She wondered if they'd seen her truck, if they'd noticed. Surely they'd picked up her presence, through infrared if nothing else. Then she remembered: that didn't work, for whatever reason, on VADER survivors.

Nevertheless, she quickly loaded the truck, ducking low. She secured everything in the bed, filled the cab, and took off, gravel flying. When she reached the underpass, she stopped.

The last few years, Abby had mostly scavenged to the south, tiny towns like Mapaville and Knorpp, even down to Valles Mines. None of those had been destroyed, but were ghost towns now nonetheless. After her last venture into St. Louis and the surrounding county, she wanted no part of it. Once or twice, she'd taken Juliet and EJ along, after being fairly sure that the coast was clear.

Now, though, nothing seemed safe since they appeared to be stepping up the patrols, the flyovers. She'd noticed that, sure, on her twice daily-checks, but had never seen the choppers hovering. Not until today, when she was directly below them. She had considered moving all of them south, and even further west. There was a lot of empty country both directions, but they had a decent setup where they were now. It was familiar and, so far, safe.

But now? Abby wasn't sure. She got back on the road and headed for the camp, still thinking.

Juliet and EJ helped unload the truck and haul everything up to the cave. Juliet stowed most of it herself, as EJ was too busy announcing each acquisition with glee—especially the popcorn, which she loved. Abby finished concealing the truck and smiled when she saw her girls working together. She gently directed EJ to help Juliet a bit more, while she herself settled down with yet another notebook, this time to record her observations on the trip. Abby smiled when EJ brought her a rather sloppy peanut butter sandwich and a Pepsi. Over lunch, Juliet filled Abby in on the morning they'd had, detailing EJ's lessons for the day.

Abby lit up a smoke and told the girls that they needed to talk. She said she knew that Juliet had seen more choppers lately and, while she didn't want to scare them, they had to be told about the incident today. EJ looked more puzzled than scared, but Juliet was all for them packing up and moving further away from the city. She jumped to her feet, ready to get started.

"I do not," she said, "repeat, do not, want to lose anyone else!" She stamped her foot, her long braid swinging wildly. Abby stared at her.

"Relax, honey, it's okay. Nothing to worry about yet. We just have to talk and come up with a plan, and see what's what." Abby tried to be calm and conciliatory, but Juliet was having none of it.

"Fine!" she shouted, and stomped off.

Abby sighed. Teenagers. Obviously, it was a universal thing, nothing to do with peer pressure. So much for that theory. She shrugged.

"EJ, bring me the radio, will you? Let's see if we can fire this thing up and hear any chatter out there."

EJ handed the radio to Abby. "Mom, what's wrong with Jules? She's crabby today."

"All morning? Or just since I've been back?"

"All morning," said EJ. "It started after I went to get dressed, and she came rushing inside, all distracted. And she kept watching the sky. Like, the whole time we did lessons." The little girl plunked down beside her mother.

"I see," said Abby. "EJ, why don't you go find Juliet and bring her back here? Let's see if we can get anything on the radio here." She fiddled with the dials as EJ ran off to the cave.

After some tinkering, the radio sputtered to life. Abby turned another dial. . . . "10-4, I see it and I'm going in for. . . ." Then static. Then nothing. Just as the girls sat down by the fire, the radio crackled again, then BOOM. More static. Voices. "Got it! Last one, we're out of here!"

"Where to, boss?"

"South."

Abby hastily turned off the radio and sat back, thinking furiously. Couldn't be. That had sounded exactly like. . . Brad. But he was dead. Surely she was mistaken. After all, she hadn't heard his voice, let alone over a radio, for what? Eight years? Seven?

She glanced over at the girls. Juliet had turned white; EJ clung to her, not knowing what was happening but frightened by the look on her mother's face. "Jules. . . ."

Juliet threw off EJ's arm and leaped to her feet. "I'm not doing this again!" she shouted. "I'm not!" She turned and stumbled into the cave, her long braid swinging wildly. She reappeared just minutes later, loaded for bear, quite literally.

Her waist was encircled with not one, but two leather ammo belts. She carried her shotgun as well as Abby's, and her knife pouch was strapped to her thigh, fully loaded. Her eyes were wide, but her actions were now under control. "Here." She tossed Abby's Mossberg to her and reached for EJ's hand. "I'm ready."

Abby remained calm. She caught the gun easily, lowering it carefully to the ground. She tried to send a reassuring look towards EJ who, at this point, was stoically attempting to emulate her mother and just barely managing to hold back tears. "Ready for what, Jules?"

"Why, to go after Colonel Barton, that son-of-a-bitch!" Juliet exclaimed. "Come on, Abby, we're not going to sit around waiting for him, are we?"

"Jules!" Abby was shocked. "Language!" EJ giggled, more so at Juliet's comment than at her mother's rebuke. It wasn't as though it was the first time she'd heard something like that.

"Oh, Abby, really? Like I haven't heard you say the same thing?" Juliet tried not to smile, in spite of the earlier craziness she'd displayed.

Finally, Abby shrugged. The girl had a point after all and, truly, she herself wanted to shoot that son-of-a-bitch too. Maybe more than once. "Okay, fine, I get it. Now, before we go off all half-cocked, let's sit down and discuss this. And," she added, seeing the look on Juliet's face, "make some plans."

Chapter Five

Alison lost her footing a few times in the dark, earning a glare from Major Blake each time she made too much noise. Honestly, the guy was weird. Blank expression, blank eyes for heaven's sake, totally creepy. At last they stopped to make camp, and Alison sank to the ground, rubbing her tired feet. Thank goodness they had a big enough entourage to take over so she could rest for a few minutes.

Damn. Now he wanted a conference. She slowly stood up and walked over to the fire already burning. Ignoring yet another glare sent her direction, she defiantly took a swig out of her flask, making a face at the taste; straight tequila would get her through, by God, but she'd much prefer the whole margarita. No such luck out here in the boonies.

"Captain, I am in charge of this mission under special assignment. You will please follow protocol."

"Yep," said Alison, stifling a hiccup. "Yep, sure will, Major. Now, what's going on? Do I finally get clued in here or what?"

"Just over that ridge," said Major Blake, pointing slightly to the west, "is the encampment that is our target." An aide held a lantern over the map spread on a table nearby. Alison took a quick look. They were very near the confluence of the Missouri and Mississippi rivers. She glanced longingly north, wishing she were back in Chicago. It had been a long time since she'd been in the field, and she wasn't too thrilled about it all.

"Our orders are to terminate; we will take no prisoners."

Alison struggled for a moment to keep her face as carefully blank as Major Blake's. She hadn't signed up for this, not really. She knew what the government did; after all, she was part of it, but so far she hadn't been right on the front lines like this. She shrugged. She supposed she could do what was necessary and, well, if this was deemed necessary, then so be it. The rebels probably had done worse; in fact, she knew they had. She'd seen the reports.

The Major laid out his plan of attack and Alison watched disinterestedly until she heard her name. "Captain, you'll start the party from here. Once you open fire, there should be enough confusion for the team to move in and begin rounding up the insurgents. We will, of course, want to be sure that all are accounted for prior to termination."

"Excuse me, Major, but how is my sharpshooting going to cause enough distraction?" Alison was rather proud of her marksmanship and confident that she could surreptitiously take out the enemy without causing undue panic.

"Oh, you won't be using your rifle, Captain. An operation such as this calls for maximum terror. You'll be armed with an M72."

Alison took a quick slug from her flask. Seriously? He wanted her to use a rocket launcher? Was he trying to kill her off first chance he got? She considered that for a moment. Well, yes, probably. She shrugged. "Okey-dokey then, Major. I'll let 'er rip for you." If the Major was looking for fear or panic, he had the wrong woman in mind.

Just before sunrise, Alison climbed the hill. The rest of the team was scattered strategically around the area, all weapons pointed into the draw where the rebels were camped. As the sky began to lighten, Alison could make out the shadows of the tents below; she swung the cumbersome weapon to her shoulder and aimed for the very center of the hollow.

Taking a deep breath, then letting it out slowly, Alison squeezed the trigger.

BOOM!

The rocket arced into the air, then turned, plummeting towards the earth.

BOOM!

The impact, centered so closely in the camp, flattened the half-dozen tents and sent unsecured gear flying. And then the screams began.

For a few moments, all that Alison could see was clouds of dirt and smoke; as that began to clear, and the sky lightened, she watched dumbfounded as the rebels scurried to and fro, calling to each other, pulling comrades out from under the flimsy structures. Within a minute, Major Blake and the rest of the team had descended and were firing upon the survivors. To Alison, it looked like a scene from hell itself and she fervently wished she'd brought her flask.

Mentally shaking herself, she remembered that it was, after all, well before noon anyway, and so she joined the others, half-sliding down the ridge into the campsite.

What she saw upon her arrival was horrendous.

There were seven bodies being lined up, side by side. Two of them were children.

As the smoke began to drift away and the sun rose higher, the smell became stronger. The metallic smell of blood was heavy and, Alison noticed, her stomach clenching, a few body parts seemed rather detached from their owners. She turned abruptly and vomited into the charred grass.

She had done that. The M72, her finger on the trigger. Kids. Babies, really, they weren't more than seven or eight years old. She staggered away from the hellish scene as others began to scavenge underneath fallen canvas, and sat down at the base of a tree.

After a few minutes, Major Blake appeared to notice her and came to stand over her, arms crossed and scowling. At least, Alison thought, he wasn't quite as creepy when he was annoyed.

"Captain, is there a problem?" Major Blake was tapping his foot, waiting for her answer. Alison peered up at him, beginning to be annoyed herself, wondering at his complete lack of. . . well, lack of any feelings at all!

She scrambled to her feet, still a little shaky. "Did you know there were kids down here? For God's sake, babies!"

"Doesn't matter," answered the Major. "I was told to remove the insurgents, and that's what we did. Toughen up, Captain. We've only just started." He turned and walked off, directing the rest of the squad to finish up so they could move out.

Alison just stared at him.

Chapter Six

Two days later, they'd finished packing for the move. A temporary one, Abby hoped. Still, they closed up the cave as best they could, storing what wasn't already in the truck and camouflaging the entrance. They'd leave at dusk which, Abby squinted at her watch, was in about half an hour or so.

She'd made the decision, in spite of pleas from Jules to go into the city and see what was happening, to move the girls to another location. She hadn't been out to Franklin County in many years, even before. . . before it all happened, but she was familiar with the area. It could be their best chance, for now, to avoid whatever was coming next and to have time to make further plans.

EJ was excited, understandably so since she'd seldom left the camp itself, and was bouncing up and down the trail as they finished loading the truck. Jules was more subdued, but Abby could tell she was excited too; especially since they were, in her words, "doing something" besides just waiting. With everyone buckled in, Abby drove across the camp to where she'd hidden the extra fuel.

Finally, they were on the road itself, heading out of the camp. Abby drove slowly and cautiously, knowing that running without lights was a sure way to end up stuck in a ditch, in spite of Jules' impatient fidgeting. EJ tried desperately to see out the tinted windows, but soon gave up. She sat back with a sigh, reaching for a blanket as she realized that, until dawn, her sightseeing would have to wait.

The girls traveled west on Sandy Creek Road, winding up and down hills, moving slowly. Three hours later, after stopping twice to clear the roads of fallen trees, they reached the town of Pacific. Or what used to be Pacific. Seems that Colonel Barton's forces had reached here as well; even the overpass at Highway 44 had crumbled and, even if it weren't dark, Abby suspected that there would be no view of the amusement park back against the hills.

EJ was sleeping, and Abby hesitated to wake her up. She knew, though, one of the foremost rules drilled into her during her time out west was to eat and drink whenever you had the chance. You never knew when the next chance would come along.

After the brief stop, Abby restarted the truck and they began to move north, turning to the west an hour later. Hills and trees, but at least there was plenty of cover. Abby wondered what had happened to those who'd lived out here. . . before. There had been a few large homes, but mostly just modest dwellings on an acre or two. A few tumbledown trailers and some old barns. And a few tiny towns, nestled in those hills, which is what Abby was counting on—even if there were no people, there might still be standing structures. Livable ones.

They pulled into Labadie around 3:00 a.m.

It was difficult to see much in the dark; sunrise wouldn't be for another few hours. Abby pulled the truck through an almost-too-small opening in the brush and trees on the east side of the town, and didn't stop until she'd left the road nearly half a mile behind. She killed the engine and turned off the dome light before opening the door and getting out to stretch. Both girls were asleep.

She walked around a bit, shivering in the chill night air, listening carefully for any untoward sounds. She heard nothing but the quiet rattle of leaves, making their last hurrah before soon falling. It was early November, and before long there would be little cover in the woods. She hoped that they'd find something in town in which to take shelter. Finally, she crawled back into the truck, wrapping herself in a blanket, and fell asleep.

Abby dreamed of Emmy, as she often did, and the dream ended as usual: Emmy screaming, the sky falling, Abby running.

The lightening of the sky brought Abby fully awake, cramped and achy after sleeping in the truck for just a few hours. The girls were beginning to stir, so she handed them water bottles and granola bars and cautioned them to stay where they were until she returned. Wishing desperately for a cup of coffee, Abby began to walk towards the town, watching the skies as much as the terrain.

She stayed just inside the tree line as she approached Front Street, pausing to orient herself. To her right, just a couple blocks north, was a small, man-made lake; most of the buildings should be directly across Front Street and beyond, but there were several vacant lots, too, if memory served. And a field just past the grove in which she waited and watched.

Abby saw no signs of life, so she finally crossed the street and ducked into the shadows of the old Hawthorne Inn. The front porch railing had mostly fallen down into the dirt and some of the windows were broken, randomly, it seemed. She crept around the back, listening hard, but hearing nothing.

There was an alley of sorts behind the remaining few buildings here, and she walked along it, pondering her choices. The town itself felt very exposed, after having been in the woods and cave for so long. She'd been hoping for something more substantial than that, a barn, maybe; but for that she'd have to go outside the town.

She turned right at the next street, still staying behind the small houses, and walked until she reached a field. This, then, was where the town faded away into farmland, except for the homes that spread out north, towards the lake. Proximity to water was a good thing, of course, but not too close—they would be expecting that. She made her way through a string of trees to the dead end of Academy Street, then into a wide swath of forest. Abby immediately felt safer and less exposed.

A quarter of a mile later, she came to a cleared area and stopped. Looking across, and through more trees, Abby saw what she was looking for: a small house, surrounded by woods, with a barn nearby. And an access road. It wasn't far from the lake, but there appeared to be several ways to get in and out, which meant more places to hide if that became necessary.

She looked up at the sky, then at her watch. Hurry, she told herself. Not much time before it became full light but, thankfully, it was proving to be another cloudy day. Abby skirted the clearing and approached the house warily. She stopped to observe.

The roof seemed mostly intact, the outside weathered but in decent condition. The windows were dirty but unbroken. No signs of life. Abby went to the back of the house and climbed the creaking steps, pausing at each noise. Nothing. The door was unlocked, and she twisted the knob and swung it wide, .357 at the ready.

There was no electricity, of course, but no holes in the walls either, and the structure seemed sound. Abby shone the flashlight around in each of the four rooms on the ground floor before ascending the stairs. Two bedrooms, cluttered with old furniture and assorted junk. She idly wondered what had happened to the owners, or anyone who was there after. . . She quickly put those thoughts out of her mind, and went back downstairs.

The woods came up to the house, but Abby caught glimpses of the barn; she'd have to wait, however, to examine it more closely. It was time to collect the girls and their gear and get back here before the sun rose any higher.

Robin Tidwell

Chapter Seven

Colonel Hoefer drummed his fingers impatiently on the desk. It was well past time that Brad should have checked in from the camp. He hoped fervently that there had been no untoward setbacks, either in the mission or in Brad's memory.

He left off the drumming and opted to pace the confines of his office.

Alison was getting the heebie-jeebies again. Most of it had to do with Major Blake, of course, the guy totally creeped her out, but part of it was because of the territory they were in now. They'd moved southwest after that horrendous demolition of the rebel campsite, and were closing in on their new target, an old state park at the far west end of St. Louis County.

Their forces were grouped just beyond a ridge, and on the other side was a collection of shanties and tents. Scouts had fanned out over the rest of the area, and one had brought back a report of a hidden cache in a small cave. Major Blake had frozen for a split second when he saw some of the items that had been retrieved; his face paled, and he began to sweat. He quickly recovered, and returned to barking orders, most of them directed toward Alison.

She sighed and settled herself more comfortably against a tree. This was going to be long and, in the end, what did it matter? She'd be ordered to slaughter more people, people who weren't necessarily rebelling—as far as she could see—but who simply wanted to live life on their own terms, not those of the government.

Her thoughts were interrupted as Major Blake approached.

"Captain, you will accompany the first wave over the ridge, armed with the M72, and proceed as discussed."

Alison rolled her eyes. "Yes, sir!" she snapped, jumping to her feet. A quick salute, and she was off to catch a few hours' sleep. Maybe. If she'd stop dreaming about that little girl, whoever she was. . . .

Three hours later, a groggy Alison was taking aim with her rocket launcher. There was barely enough light to see and she preferred it that way. Less chance of actually hitting something, although, she mused, with this baby there was an even chance of blowing something. . . or someone. . . to smithereens, regardless of aim.

The quiet of the early morning was shattered by screams.

Alison jumped, nearly losing her hold on the M72.

Wait, that wasn't right. She hadn't fired yet. She whipped her head to the right and saw Major Blake. He was silhouetted against the skyline, standing tall on the ridge. Screaming.

Well. Orders were orders, and she'd deal with Major Creepy in a moment. She fired.

In an instant, the squad swarmed over the ridge and rained more terror down on the hapless people, just emerging from flaming tents and shacks and what they had thought was a secure night's sleep. Alison laid down her weapon and ran toward the major who, thankfully, had shut the hell up.

Ignoring protocol, she grabbed his arm and pulled him down. Unlike the last time, these folks were fighting back and slugs whistled around them. He landed on his back, staring up at Alison and, for a brief moment, his eyes were clear and the blank look disappeared.

It was gone in seconds, but she knew she hadn't imagined it. Weird. At that thought, Major Blake roused himself and struggled to turn over, grabbing his field glasses. Alison was dumped unceremoniously off him and rolled onto the ground.

"Captain, whatever you think you were doing will be discussed, at length, this evening. Now, kindly get yourself down that hill and do your job."

"Fine. Sir." Alison huffily got to a crouch and made her way down to the carnage. She'd be damned if she would participate any further in the ongoing bloodbath. Major Creepy could just deal with it.

Soldiers were lining up the bodies. Thankfully, Alison noticed no children this time. She hauled sheets of plywood and personal belongings to the pile to be burned, and tried not to watch as the soldiers added an extra bullet to the heads of the victims, just to be sure. At last, the cleanup was complete and the squad packed up, prepared to move to the next location.

Back on the road, the black SUVs traveled south.

Colonel Hoefer clicked off his radio. He sat back, smiling, satisfied. He had suspected that Major Blake would do a fine job. He had also smelled trouble the minute that Alison character had walked into his office. He wondered. . . he needed her to keep an on Brad for the time being, especially for this next stop on their trail, but he believed that after that. . . well, she was expendable after all. The top brass had mentioned it already in the initial communications with Chicago.

He had no idea what they were thinking, but it wasn't his job to know that. He didn't like her, hadn't wanted her here, but was determined to use her until he was told otherwise. Well, he'd been told already, but the time wasn't quite right. He'd wait and see how things went, and then. . . good-bye, Captain!

The convoy drove down Highway 55, heading past the county line. They stopped for a break around noon, and Alison stretched and tried to make herself look halfway presentable. She irritably wished for a drink, knowing she'd finished off her stash several days ago, and settled for trying to untangle her hair and rub some of the dirt off her face. She quickly did up an auburn braid and flung it over her shoulder, out of the way, before gratefully accepting a sandwich and a bottle of water from a young soldier.

She looked up. Great. Here came the major. What now?

Brad stopped and stared at Alison. He blinked. He started forward again, and stumbled, nearly falling to his knees. What the devil?

Abruptly, he stood straighter and continued his deliberate stride. "Captain, I need you to ride with me. We have things to discuss." He turned on his heel and took his leave.

Lovely, thought Alison. I get to spend more time with a guy who seriously seems to be losing his mind. She shrugged and dusted crumbs off her hands. Finishing her water, she followed Major Blake to the front of the line and climbed into the SUV beside him.

"Okay, boss. What's up?" The major glared at her. "Oops, I mean yes, sir! With what can I assist you?"

Major Blake sighed and spread out a map. "Shortly, we will arrive at another camp. This one has a security fence, condition unknown. You and I will proceed inside, alone, while the squad remains with the vehicles outside the gates.

"There are two females present, as per our last intelligence, and both must be removed. Terminated," he added, in case there was any doubt.

Alison held her breath for a moment. She wondered, briefly, if this was his chance to get rid of her. Alone with the major? Huh. And wait a minute. . . terminate? Two of them? This could get ugly.

"What else do we know about these people?"

Major Blake rifled through a folder. "They are armed. The older one is the head of an area-wide rebellion planned to restore the government to an earlier state; she is skilled in combat, camouflage, and weaponry. There are reports of explosives being manufactured and stored. They are both responsible for many deaths and for most of the destruction in St. Louis that occurred six years ago."

Alison mulled this over for a minute. She wondered how the major had come up with this intel. It sounded a bit unlikely, that these people had been hiding out for so long while still orchestrating a rebellion. And how could just two of them be responsible for the destruction she'd seen in the city? Perhaps they were the last ones left alive? If so, they weren't much of a threat, not to the government anyway. Maybe to two people, going in alone, to try to take them. . . .

She glanced at the major. He was staring out the window and his hands were shaking, rattling the papers he gripped so tightly.

"Sir. Major?" Alison nudged his arm and he turned to face her.

She was startled by the expression on his face: sad, scared, and shaken, all at once.

"You remind me of someone," he said.

Then he blinked once, twice, and resumed his usual stoic demeanor.

The convoy traveled on, turning off the highway onto a narrow, paved road. They stopped in front of a rusty iron gate with stone pillars. Alison and Major Blake stepped out of the SUV, and the vehicle backed slowly down the road, leaving them alone.

Chapter Eight

Jules was wary of their new home. She jumped every time the house creaked or groaned, and kept her knife close by at all times. EJ, on the other hand, was thrilled with everything—the doors, the staircase, the walls, and especially the bathtub.

"Yes, little one, I see how you fit so well in there," Abby said for the hundredth time since they'd moved in a week ago. *I do believe she'd sleep there if I'd let her,* she added to herself, *and it might not be a bad idea at that!*

They'd settled into the old house quite well, considering that EJ had never lived in one at all and Abby and Jules had become used to the cave and living outdoors for the last ten years. When Abby thought about it, she couldn't quite believe that it had been that long.

She finished loading up the truck with the assortment of containers they'd collected, and called the girls. As they drove slowly down to the river, EJ chattered on and on about the house until Jules finally lost patience and tickled her to get her to stop talking.

Breathless, EJ tried to continue, only to be pounced upon again by an increasingly crabby Jules.

"Abby," asked Jules again, "why can't we do something? Anything besides sit here—it's just like being back at the camp, except we're in that creaky old house and I feel like we're just waiting to be found. I don't like it. At all."

"Enough," Abby said firmly. "You know we left because they were too close. You know there's not much to be done, since it's just the two of us. Okay, three of us," she relented, as EJ gave an exaggerated cough to make her presence known. "Now, let's get this water loaded up and get back home."

EJ climbed into the bed of the truck and began handing out jugs and tipping a barrel over the side, while Abby and Jules filled them and dragged them back from the river. Then she jumped down and began to lift the smaller containers, moving them up toward the cab to make room for the barrel.

Once everything was tied down, they drove back to the house and unloaded on the porch before Abby parked the truck in the old barn. Exhausted, she was thankful that they only had to do this a couple of times a week, and not every day. She sat down near the fire that Jules had started and gratefully accepted a cup of coffee and pulled EJ close.

"Mom, are we going to stay here for a long time?"

"I don't know, little one." Abby exchanged looks with Jules. "We'll have to see how things go, I guess. But for right now, yes."

"Good," said EJ. "I like it here. I like our house." She snuggled next to Abby, shivering a little in the cold winter air.

Abby smiled. "I'm glad you do, EJ." She hugged her daughter tightly and kissed the top of her head.

After dinner, the girls went inside to get ready for bed and Abby banked the fire. She yawned and stretched and glanced around, mentally checking that everything was out of sight and closed up for the night. At last, she climbed the porch steps and went inside to tuck in EJ, who was nearly asleep but still managed to mumble something about the bathtub. Abby decided that tomorrow she'd see about EJ actually being able to use that tub. Maybe that would end the obsession. Maybe not.

Jules was still awake.

"Abby, I want to go on a mission. Like you used to do. You know, scout out the area."

Abby bit her lip, her shoulders tensing. She'd known this was coming for quite some time. She just. . . she was tired and feeling old. The responsibility, the horror, the loss, all of it, and now Jules wanted to leave. She knew, intellectually, that it wasn't really leaving, but it still felt like it. Then again, the girl wanted to be doing something. . . anything besides waiting. Abby knew how that felt. She remembered.

"All right."

Jules' jaw dropped and she stared at Abby. "For real? You mean it?" Her face brightened considerably, and she would have let out a whoop of glee if she hadn't been so well-trained in survival mode. "When? Tomorrow?"

Abby managed a small smile. "No, not tomorrow. In two days. We need some time to get you ready, and to get me ready as well."

Jules hugged her knees to her chest, barely able to stop from jumping up and down. Abby smiled again, and this time she meant it. Jules wasn't so little anymore, after all, and it was time for her to do the things she wanted. Within reason, of course. Abby wasn't about to let her just run all over the place, unrestrained, on a whim or two. Or six.

She smoothed Jules' hair back and kissed her forehead. "Now, go to sleep. We'll talk in the morning." Abby walked back outside for her nighttime smoke, and to have some time alone to think. And to plan.

That morning dawned clear and cold. EJ had banked the fire, one of her daily chores, and was sitting in the kitchen doing her lessons. She was very studious when she finally stopped running around and got down to business, and her progress with reading and writing was remarkable for a six-year-old. Jules was ready to go, and Abby was giving her last-minute instructions as they pored over a map.

For this first trip, Jules was to stay under cover, keep the radio on, and check on the buildings on Third Street. She was also, Abby emphasized, to return to the house by noon. No excuses. Abby showed her the route to take, up through the woods to the lake, skirting the perimeter, and down Third Street.

Jules, however, was impatient to be going. "Come on, Abby! I'm not a child, and I'm not stupid. I got it, really."

Abby sighed. "All right. Remember to cache whatever you find, and we'll go back after dark to pick it up. And I mean it, Jules, back here by noon." She gave the girl a quick hug as Jules practically danced out the door.

Juliet walked through the woods and around the shore of the lake. Good thing we have the river nearby, she thought, wrinkling her nose at the smell of the brackish water. Not that the river smelled much better, but at least it wasn't green and gooey. Yuck.

She came first to the old church. A sprawling building, with the parsonage around the corner, it was directly across the street from an abandoned trucking company, devoid of trucks. At least that she could see; she supposed there were some inside, but that wasn't her destination at the moment. Staying just inside the treeline, she paused. Waiting and watching, Jules decided it was probably safe—especially since, in a week, they'd neither seen nor heard a single person.

She walked around to the back and rattled the door. It was locked. Shrugging off her pack, she pulled out a thin, metal pick and within a minute, the door swung open. The hallway beyond was dark, but Jules moved confidently along, a penlight in one hand, her Glock in the other. She listened carefully outside doors before entering and inspecting the various rooms.

One was stacked with cot mattresses; one had obviously served as a nursery, with a changing table and two cribs pushed up against a wall. The others were empty, except for some papers on the floors and a few metal folding chairs.

The hallway opened into a larger room. Jules saw a couple of old-fashioned chalkboards, more folding chairs scattered haphazardly, and two long tables. Beyond that, she could see a kitchen behind a pass-through window.

Jules knew better than to open the fridge—this place had to have been without electricity for years, and no telling what had been left behind. Better safe than sorry. She found a few old pots and pans, which she stacked on the counter, and a half-empty box of teabags. That was all.

The last room was the smallest. Apparently, it had housed the church library; the walls were covered in bookcases with a few dusty tomes remaining. She knew that EJ liked to read, so she carried those back to the kitchen and, gathering everything in one precariously balanced load, moved it all back to the hallway near the door through which she'd entered the building.

Slipping outside, Juliet looked around and quickly ducked back into the trees to make her way to the next block. There were two small homes there, and one on the next block, and then she'd be done for the day.

She had no trouble gaining entry to the houses; in the first two, the back doors had blown open and at the last one, the door was closed but not locked. She found a few musty blankets, some rope and a couple fishing rods, and even two packs of cigarettes for Abby. She grinned when she imagined how stale they must be. . . good thing Abby wasn't very picky these days.

Finished with her assignment, which was only to cover this side of Third Street, Jules checked her watch. She probably had time to move back down on the other side, but maybe not. She didn't want to mess this up; she was hoping Abby would let her go again. . . and farther. And longer. She sat down to think, gazing off towards their new home.

Rolling her eyes, even though there was no one around to see her, Jules gathered her haul from the last house and stomped off, retracing her earlier steps. She made a bundle of everything inside the blankets, and went back to the church. Her mood lifted, though, when she thought about this first mission and how, really, it was kind of exciting to be in a new place and see new things. Even if she had to get home now, she was sure she'd be able to come back. She looked up at the sky, grateful for both the warming sun and the distinct lack of choppers blocking her view.

Jules headed back, even relocking the door to the church, her cache safely inside.

Chapter Nine

Major Blake unlocked the gates. With a key. Alison was stunned. The major, however, merely looked puzzled as he slipped the key back into his pocket. Quickly recovering, he swung the gates open and the two of them walked through. Alison followed him silently, and cautiously, wondering why they were simply walking up a road, in broad daylight, if indeed there were two violent rebels to apprehend.

A quarter mile later, the major stopped. Alison stopped. He looked around, furtively, and began to sweat. Abruptly, he sat down.

Alison raised an eyebrow, then knelt down beside him. He might be creepy, but something was clearly wrong. She put a hand to his forehead; no, no fever. She tilted his head up and looked into his eyes. No longer blank, they seemed full of anguish and regret. What the heck?

The major threw off her hand and lurched to his feet. "Captain," he barked. "Just what do you think you're doing?"

Alison stepped back and stared at him. Major Creepy was back from. . . wherever.

Major Blake gestured for silence, then motioned Alison to follow him up the steep embankment and through the trees. He paused every few feet to listen and get his bearings, then continued on, up to the top of the hill. Alison guessed that he'd memorized some sort of map, because she sure had no clue where they were going. She just hoped that the major knew. . . .

They traveled along the ridge, more slowly this time, stopping more often. Alison sneaked a glance at her watch and saw that it was near mid-afternoon. She wondered how much longer they'd be hiking and, more importantly, what they'd find when they stopped. She took a long drink from her water bottle and looked up, seeing that the major had stopped.

Oh, cripes, he was doing it again.

Major Blake was sitting on a log, staring into space. He looked at Alison as she approached, hesitated, then spoke. "What are we doing here?"

"Um, you said, sir, that we were going to, um, terminate two insurgents who were hiding out up here. Somewhere."

"Yes, Captain, I did say that. But why?"

Alison was flummoxed. Why did he say it, or why were they planning to kill two more people, for reasons she herself wasn't too sure about? "Well, sir, I suppose. . . because we have orders?"

"Yes, yes, Captain. You are correct. Orders. So we should go." The major jumped to his feet and began walking, but this time he angled back down the hill, moving quickly and heedless of the noise he was making. Alison followed him. Not much choice, really.

He stopped. She stopped. This time, her hand was on her sidearm. Things were really getting strange.

"Alison."

What? He actually said her name? What happened to "Captain this" and "Captain that?" She raised an eyebrow. "Yes sir?"

He smiled. At her.

What the hell.

Colonel Hoefer was pacing. Again. He almost couldn't stand the suspense, waiting to hear from Brad, wanting to know that the treatments had indeed worked. If everything was on schedule, and he'd last heard from the major when he was at the camp gates, Abby should be dead by now. Or very soon. And that brat she'd taken in, too.

It had been tough during all those years, trying to pretend that he cared, recruiting others to do the dirty work. He remembered his first meeting with Jeff, Cal's ex; he had thought, at the time, that Jeff was the perfect one for the job. At least the guy had some brains. But no, he'd been taken out by Abby—a girl, at that. Carelessness. That's all it was.

And that other guy, what was his name? Oh, yes: James. And his ditzy girlfriend. Suckers, both of them. And dumb as rocks. Well, that was a long time ago. He'd survived, and now he was back. Where the devil was Brad?

He kept pacing.

Major Blake had, in fact, reached the cave. Or rather, he was standing just above it on the hillside, with Alison. Frozen in place, frozen in time.

Alison reached for his arm, but he shook her off. He began to sweat, to breathe heavily, to tremble all over.

"Abby," he gasped, as he tumbled to the ground and lost consciousness.

Wait, what did he say? Alison dropped to the ground next to the major, looking around wildly for. . . someone. Was anyone even here? Did he see something? What the heck was going on?

Alison checked his pulse and made sure he was breathing. Yes, okay, there was that anyway. Now what? Oh, yes. Wake him up. So she slapped him.

His eyes fluttered, but remained closed. So she slapped him again. Nothing. I could get used to this, Alison thought.

The third time, Brad's arm flew up and caught her hand just before she connected. She jumped back, tripping over a hidden log. Brad sat up and rubbed his cheek.

"What the hell did you do that for?" he asked.

"Because you were acting like a. . . " Alison stopped. She'd completely lost her train of thought. This wasn't the major—or was it? Who was he? This guy didn't have that horrifyingly blank look. He had seemed confused a few moments ago, and now he was. . . smiling?

"It's Alison, right?" Brad asked.

"Y-yes, sir!"

Brad waved his hand vaguely. "Forget the 'sir' stuff. It's Brad. I think. Yeah, that's right. No more of this 'Major' crap." He tried to rip the insignia from his uniform. "What the heck do they put this stuff on with, superglue?" At last he was successful, threw his rank aside, and tried to get to his feet.

Alison had managed to get herself upright and approached him warily, hand extended to help. Unfortunately, she was still rather unsteady herself, trying to make sense of this, and she fell onto him in a tangled heap.

Exhausted from the sudden dearth of adrenaline, she simply rolled over and stayed on the ground, staring up at the sky. Brad, too, gave up, and stayed seated, looking at her. "Are you okay?"

"Of course, I'm okay," Alison snapped. "I'm fine! Lovely! I'm stuck in the woods with Jekyll and Hyde, I don't know where we are, I don't know if anyone is coming to rescue us, and you, sir, seem to have lost your ever-lovin' mind!"

"I said to call me Brad."

"Whatever!" yelled Alison. "I don't care who you are, I'm leaving and going to try to find my way back. The rest of the squad probably got to take a nap or something, and here I am with a crazy man." She jumped to her feet and began to stomp off in the direction they'd come.

"I wouldn't do that," Brad said mildly. "You're liable to get yourself killed."

"Oh, and by whom? There's no one here; heaven knows they would have heard us coming a long time ago, the way you tromp around in the woods. Goodbye, Major. Or Brad. Or whoever." Alison took several more steps before Brad spoke again.

"Seriously, if you go back, they'll kill you."

She stopped. "Who? What?"

"The squad." He checked his watch as he got stiffly to his feet and leaned against a tree. "Yep, right about now, they're heading this way to finish the job.

"Come on, let's go."

"Go? With you? I'm not going anywhere with you!"

"Fine," Brad shrugged. "Stay here, go back, your call. I, however, am going this way." He began to climb the hill, his pace quickening as his legs became steadier. "Be happy to tell you a good story when we get there. If we make it."

Alison watched him go.

BOOM!

The shot was coming from the direction in which they'd left the squad. She looked back, and looked at Brad. One more look back.

BOOM!

Closer. She began to climb the hill after him. This was not a good day to die, and she figured she'd take her chances with Major Creepy. At least he wasn't quite as creepy as he had been. . . still, the squad was coming, or so he said.

BOOM!

They traveled along the ridge for an hour, then Brad began to descend into a shallow valley. Alison breathed a sigh of relief, quickly squelched by the realization that they were climbing again. At last he stopped. Alison dropped to the ground, exhausted.

"Now what?" she asked.

Brad sat down next to her. "Now, we wait."

Alison began to shiver as the sun dipped low and the wind picked up out of the north. She wrapped her arms around her knees in an attempt to keep warm. "So, um, Brad. Are you going to clue me in now?" Her teeth began to chatter.

"In a minute." He got up and walked over to a couple of shacks that Alison had noticed upon their arrival, but was too tired and sore and cold to ask about. He came back with two blankets, moth-eaten and musty, but still fairly usable. Alison gratefully accepted one and tried to get more comfortable. Brad sat down beside her.

"I used to live here."

Chapter Ten

"Mom, when is Jules coming back?"

"She should be here soon, EJ. It's almost dark." Abby went to the window for the tenth time. Jules had been going into town for nearly a week now, every day, and Abby had extended her trips to dusk. Things were going well, so far, and Jules had amazingly found all sorts of useful items—including a nearly fully intact bar in the back of the old Hawthorn Inn. Abby guessed that folks weren't too concerned about that when they fled, or died, but probably regretted that lapse at some point.

At last, she heard the door open and Jules came inside, shaking snowflakes off her hood and scarf. "Man, it's cold out there!"

Abby helped her take off the wet outerwear and sent her off to change into dry clothes. The temperature was indeed dropping as snow began to fall faster. The wind was picking up as well, and Abby knew it would be a long night. They were used to the cold, but this would be coming through every crack and crevice in the old house. They had enough firewood for the next couple of days, especially since, out of fear of discovery, they managed with as small a fire as possible.

Abby hoped that Jules had gotten some of the wandering out of her system, because she wasn't sending her out in a storm. And after that, they'd all be cutting and hauling wood for many days. EJ wasn't allowed to use the axe, but she could carry armloads of wood. The real problem would be tracks in the snow, if it didn't let up or melt off by then.

Jules came back into the kitchen, trailed by EJ, of course. She began to unpack her bag; the small items she brought back each trip were eagerly anticipated. "I left the cache at the old train station this time. When do you think we'll be able to go get it?" Jules knew that, with the storm outside, it might be a few days, but she seemed quite anxious to get back to town.

"Guess we'll have to wait and see, Jules," said Abby, "but as soon as it lets up, we need to haul more wood. I'm thinking maybe Tuesday?"

"But that's. . . ." Jules glanced quickly at EJ. "I think we should go before that, Abby."

"Like I said, Juliet, we'll see." Abby turned back to the fireplace, ready to light the small pile of tinder now that it was dark. EJ scooted closer to the fire, not only to warm up but also to be able to see the new book that Jules had brought her. She was soon engrossed in the story, and Jules followed Abby back into the kitchen.

"Abby," she whispered. "Did you forget what Monday is?"

"What? I don't know. Monday, I guess? You know, back before. . . before, everyone dreaded Mondays because it usually meant back to work after a weekend. Ha. Imagine a whole two days to do whatever you wanted!" Abby turned back to the dinner prep, which wasn't much beyond dumping canned stew into a pot.

"Yeah, yeah," said Jules. "'Before.' I get it. I wasn't born yesterday, you know. My point is that Monday is Christmas Eve."

"Oh," said Abby, surprised. Could it really be December already? Late December? Thank goodness EJ was as clueless as she herself seemed to be, otherwise she'd have been bugged to death about Santa Claus. Smiling, she remembered Jules' first Christmas with them down at the camp. About the same age as EJ now.

"Well, then, Sunday it is. Depending on the weather," Abby cautioned. "And let's not say anything to EJ until, oh, Monday?"

Jules grinned. "Of course, Abby. I remember when I was that age—bet I bugged you all the time, didn't I? Especially at Christmas."

Abby smiled and hugged the girl and Jules skipped off to get more blankets.

After dinner, they played cards in the flickering firelight. It was EJ's turn to pick the game, and she chose Go Fish, as usual. Juliet became bored quickly, but Abby surprised herself at her own patience. She soon became lost in thought, prompting several plaintive "Moms" from her daughter.

She remembered how, many years ago—even though it sometimes seemed like weeks instead—that she'd had little to do with small children. Teenagers weren't exactly easy to deal with either, as she'd discovered more and more the last few years with Jules, but back then she'd usually only seen them at their best. What they were like at the end of a school day or basketball practice, she'd had no idea.

Life was a lot simpler then, she mused, even with electronics and the Internet and paying bills. At least one didn't have to struggle to get warm, to find food, or to avoid government patrols. And one could choose to homeschool their children, or send them to a public or private institution, one wasn't forced into it which, Abby considered, was something that certainly had not changed. She just wasn't good, even now, with containing her impatience at trying to teach words and numbers. Stories were her forte, maybe, and survival skills.

Well, yes. That was probably a good thing.

"All right, EJ, bedtime!" Abby scooped up her daughter and took her off to the kitchen for a quick washing. "Jules, do you want the first watch?" she called over her shoulder.

"Sure," said Juliet. "No problem. I want to finish this political history book tonight anyway."

They slept in shifts, not so much for security as to keep the fire burning. Abby guessed it was about 50 degrees near the fireplace, and she wanted to keep it that way. The sleeping bags were warm, and they all wore plenty of clothes, day and night, so there was no real danger in freezing. And it was marginally warmer than the cave.

Abby snuggled up next to EJ. "Now, little one, what kind of story would you like tonight?"

"Mom, can I ask you something?"

"Of course," said Abby.

"Why do we have to keep hiding?" EJ struggled to sit up and looked at her mom. "I mean, aren't the bad people tired of looking for us by now?"

Abby bit her lip. She couldn't keep dodging EJ's questions forever; this wasn't the first time she had asked. She glanced at Juliet, whose nose was buried in her book, but Abby could tell she was listening too. She was silent for a few more minutes, gathering her thoughts, trying to decide how best to tell a six-year-old about. . . everything.

"Back in the old days, before. . . before things went bad," Abby amended. She couldn't avoid that forever, either. "Back then, people lived mostly wherever they wanted to, and a lot of them had jobs to go to every day."

"Like hauling firewood?" asked EJ. "That's what we're doing when the snow stops, right?"

"Well, yes. Maybe like that." Abby smiled. "But then, people didn't usually gather their own firewood, or even use it to cook or heat their houses. Sometimes they'd have a fire just so they could. . . just because, I guess. So, I suppose someone had to gather wood at some point so the stores could sell it and people could buy it whenever they wanted a fire.

"Anyway," she continued, "people would go to their jobs and work all day, then come home. One day, some of us heard about something that the government was doing, something bad. Or it could be bad. We really didn't know much." Abby simply could not go into a lot of detail about everything that was happening back then. Just thinking about Cal was painful, and the things that passed as freedom and rights had been getting more and more restrictive even before VADER. Thankfully, EJ was done with questions for the moment.

"So then. . . then the virus hit. It was called VADER. It. . . it killed a lot of people. Some of us went down to the camp, and we lived there for a long time. But the government, they wanted us to come into the city. They wanted those of us who hadn't been killed by VADER to be tested. And some of us. . . some of us, they wanted dead."

EJ was still silent, thinking.

"And then, everything was gone. Everyone, except Jules and me. And Noah. And now you." She kissed the top of the little girl's head and hugged her. "Now, go to sleep. Although that was a pretty awful bedtime story, don't you think?"

"Mom? They're still after us, aren't they?"

Abby sighed. "Yes. I think so."

"But why? Why don't they stop?"

"I don't know, EJ."

Chapter Eleven

"Sergeant Wilson reporting, sir!" The younger man saluted the older one and waited for permission to speak.

"Yes, Sergeant? I trust you have good news?" Colonel Hoefer knew, since Brad wasn't standing there in front of him, that his pet program had failed. He also knew that the top brass wouldn't really hold it against him, or at least not for long or in any serious way, as the entire thing had been wildly experimental from the beginning. They simply needed better recruits.

"Major Blake has disappeared, sir."

"What?" Colonel Hoefer came up out of his chair so fast that the sergeant flinched.

"Yes, sir. We waited the allotted time, as instructed, and went after them. We followed the map exactly, but they were gone. We tracked them for an additional day, and found nothing. Sir."

"They? You lost them both?" Damn. This was certainly more than the colonel had wanted to hear. This might change the outlook with his superiors.

"Yes, sir. Major Blake and the captain, they've vanished. And," he added, "there were no signs of any others, sir."

"Dismissed." The young sergeant left the room. Colonel Hoefer was stymied. He drummed his fingers on the desk. Where had Abby and Juliet gone? And Brad and that. . . whatshername? Perhaps Abby had taken care of them, for him, like a favor. . . no, likely the squad would have seen or heard some evidence of that. Probably Abby had left before the troops arrived; and assuredly, Juliet was with her.

But Brad. . . and Alison. Obviously, Brad had had a breakthrough and remembered things—or was beginning to remember. And Alison? I knew she wasn't entirely on board, he thought. Just something about her.

All right. It was done. Now, he had to spin this, had to come up with something plausible to explain it all. And he had to find them. All of them.

He began to pace again.

Alison went to sleep cold, and she woke up cold. She sat up and stretched, looking around. The major was nowhere to be seen. Great, he'd dumped her here—where the heck was "here" anyway? She got stiffly to her feet, groaning at the memory of the forced march yesterday.

Hearing her stir, Brad emerged from one of the shacks. "Oh, good, you're awake. Come on, let's go get some breakfast." He began walking towards what appeared to be a severely overgrown trail.

"Wait just a minute, mister. I mean, Major. Breakfast? Where? Here? And where's "here" again and why are we here and what the heck do you think you're doing?" All of this tumbled out of Alison as Brad grabbed her arm and started for the trail again.

"Relax, would you? It's downhill. For now, anyway. Save your breath. We'll talk when we get there."

"But. . . ." Alison gave up. The idea of breakfast sounded good, although she couldn't imagine what he had in mind. She kept up his pace, however, and within a few minutes they'd reached a road at the bottom of the hill. Brad turned left, and Alison quickened her pace to walk beside him.

"This," Brad said, "is where I lived for, oh, five years or close to it. With some other people." He stopped abruptly. Alison wondered if he was going to flake out on her again. "Cal. And Mel, Sandy, and. . . Abby.

"The woman we were sent to kill."

"So you knew her?"

"Yes. For a long time. We were kids together, working down here. We kept in touch over the years, on and off. Then, when VADER came along, we came down here. There were twelve of us. . . who made it this far." They crossed a bridge over a creek and walked another hundred yards down the road. Alison could see a few buildings. A couple of them looked to be nearly falling down; they turned to walk behind one of them, a small cabin, and began to climb another hill. Alison sighed.

Finally, they appeared to have reached their destination, but she looked around and saw nothing except trees. Brad had stopped for a moment, looked around a bit, then lowered himself into a ravine. He motioned for her to follow, and she did, wondering just what she was getting into. Still, the promised breakfast drove her along; she was starving.

Brad bent down to examine the remains of an old fire. It was barely discernible in the dim light; Alison was sure she wouldn't have seen it if she'd stepped right in the middle. Another ten feet or so, and she spied an opening in the looming rocks. Brad maneuvered himself through the opening, and she went in after him.

The cave opened up a bit more once they were inside, but it was still a pretty small space. "This is where Abby lived. After I'd been 'killed' and everyone else either left or. . . at least, that's what Pops told me. Come on."

A narrow opening was on the opposite wall from where they stood. Brad squeezed into in, and Alison followed, trying to fight back claustrophobia. Within minutes, they emerged from the crawlspace into a decent-sized cave. In fact, there was plenty of room to stand up. And in the back, there were bundles stacked against the wall.

Brad pointed toward the ceiling. "This," he said, "was where we were standing yesterday. When, um, when I kind of lost it." He grinned.

"Kind of lost it?" Alison exploded. "You went completely nuts! I had to slap you, um, a few times. And I might just do it again!" She plunked down onto the ground. At least it was a little warmer here than outside. "Didn't you say something about breakfast?"

Brad rummaged in the packs, and on the second try he found some water bottles and a few granola bars. "Start with this," he said, tossing a water bottle in her general direction. Alison caught it handily and slurped down the entire bottle without stopping.

"Thanks," she said, tearing open a wrapper. She started on a second one before adding, "So, talk. Tell me what the hell is going on."

Brad sat down beside her, with extra blankets and more water. "All right, but it's a long story. Get comfortable. I figure we can hole up here until it gets dark, then we'll head out.

"No more questions, not yet," he said, as Alison opened her mouth. "I'll explain everything, then we'll talk about what's next."

"Fine," she snapped. "But this better be good!"

"I already told you that I knew Abby from a long time ago. And that we came down here with some others. Abby used to go on scouting missions for us; sometimes she'd go up into St. Louis. Once, she met a man named Henry. He turned out to be the head of a group of rebels, right in the heart of the city. They arranged for Abby, and any other volunteers from the camp, to come help as needed.

"I was one of the volunteers.

"There were a few battles, skirmishes actually, and I was shot. I vaguely remember being taken prisoner, but after that, everything's fuzzy. And I have no idea what happened down here during the last few years."

Alison didn't quite know how to react to all this. It made sense. . . sort of. At least, that last part about his lacking memory had a ring of truth to it—she knew they'd been working on some kind of special program for a number of years now. In Chicago.

"But I do know this: Abby's still alive, still around. . . somewhere. These are her packs, I know how she organizes things and sets up her caches. She's planning to come back, sometime.

"Of course," Brad continued, "the trick will be in finding her. And I imagine Juliet is still with her, my God, that little girl must be fifteen or sixteen by now. . . ."

"J-Juliet?" Alison had turned white. Coincidence? But surely not. . . Juliet? She tried to calm her racing heart and slow her ragged breathing.

"Yeah, Juliet. She was about four, I think, when Abby found her. She was hiding in some bushes at the house of an older woman who we'd brought back here the day before. We were scavenging supplies and Abby heard a noise, and. . . that's it! That's why you look familiar—from what I remember, she kind of looks like you.

"But that was a long time ago," he added. "Maybe I've just been thinking of her or something. . . " He looked closely at Alison. "Hey, are you okay?"

"Yes. No. Maybe." Alison burst into tears. There was no way. No way. But Alison told her story.

Thirteen years ago, she had been living in Austin, Texas. Her marriage was on the rocks and her career had stalled. She accepted a government job in Chicago and made the move. Almost immediately, her husband stopped answering her phone calls, quit his job, and disappeared. With their two-year-old daughter.

Who was named Juliet.

Alison spent two years looking for them, and a lot of money. Even with her connections, there was no trace. And then VADER hit the country. She gave up, assuming the toddler was dead like so many others. In the last few years, she'd put her past life and her daughter completely out of her mind, struggling not to remember, not to feel or think. She focused on her career, rising to the rank of captain with no end in sight. At least, until her transfer to St. Louis. Now that chapter was effectively finished.

"Tell me. . . tell me what you remember, Brad, please?" Alison got a grip on her emotions, for the moment at least, and took a few deep breaths as Brad began to talk.

"As I said, we were out scavenging one day, early on after VADER, and we'd stopped at this electronics store in town. A couple of us went inside to check things out, and the others were in the trucks. I heard them honking, and came outside to find an older woman pointing a shotgun at them, and the girls aiming at her.

"Once the, er, misunderstanding had been cleared up, we took Millie back to camp with us. And Bob." Brad smiled, remembering Millie's dog.

"The next day, me and Abby and a couple others went in to check Millie's house—she said she had a few supplies we could probably use. What an understatement! The whole basement was fitted out for a doomsday operation—which, come to think of it, was probably accurate.

"Just as we were about to leave, Abby heard a noise outside. In the bushes. It was Juliet. Of course, we didn't know that then, because she wouldn't talk to anyone. She sure took to Abby, though. Wouldn't let go of her. She recognized Millie when we got back, and before long she was chattering up a storm.

"She called Millie 'Grammy,' I think, and I gathered that she spent quite a bit of time at Millie's house. While we were living here, she stayed with Abby a lot too. I kind of remember Millie saying something about Juliet's parents, but I'm not sure."

Alison absorbed all of this in silence.

"Tell me about Juliet when she was living here." She looked up at Brad with her tear-stained face. He took her hand and she clung tightly.

"Well, once she got to talking, she was fine. She wouldn't talk about her parents at all, but before long she was spending most of her days with Abby. Abby taught her how to track, and how to shoot—she had a little Glock, even.

"She was smart, too. Once, when Abby went on a scouting trip, Juliet took off to go find her. Gave everyone quite a scare, but that little girl just kept going until she found Abby." Brad pointed over to Tank Hill. "That's where Abby was. And back over the hill where we stayed last night, that's where Juliet started her hike. A long way, up and down, but she did it.

"Everyone loved Juliet. We made sure she had Christmas, too. That first year, we snuck a tree into her tent. Not sure who was more surprised, she or Abby."

Alison appeared to be much calmer by now, and she let go of Brad's hand. "Thank you for telling me all of this." She let out a deep breath and tried to think.

Could this be Juliet? Or was it just coincidence? How could her husband and daughter have ended up here, in the backwoods of Missouri? She wracked her brain, trying to remember if he'd ever said anything about family in the area, or old friends. Nothing.

Well. Maybe she'd find out. Someday. Probably not.

"So," Alison said, briskly. "Now what? Do we go find this Abby, and do you have any idea where she might have gone?"

Brad looked at her closely. "And Juliet. I'm sure they're together."

"Yes, well. . . the odds are totally against it, you know. Even I know that!" Alison answered. "I mean, I'm sure she's not my daughter. There would be no reason for that dirtbag to have taken her here, and besides, she's probably dead. From VADER. Or. . . something else."

"Okay," said Brad. "but why don't you get some rest now that we're fairly safe, and a little bit warmer? I need to do some figuring. . . as in which way to go and how to get there. And how to find Abby and. . . . Anyway, get comfortable for now. We'll be leaving here as soon as the sun goes down."

Chapter Twelve

On Christmas morning, EJ woke up and rubbed her eyes. She started to roll over and go back to sleep, but she caught a glimpse of something sparkly. She sat up quickly and stared at the little tree that had somehow appeared overnight.

"It's Christmas!" she shouted.

Abby and Jules appeared in the doorway to the kitchen. "I think she's awake," said Jules.

EJ was thrilled with her new knife—she'd finally "graduated," as she stated, to a "real" knife, one with a fixed blade and a leather sheath just like her mother's. Jules showed her how to sharpen and clean it, and how to strap on the sheath. EJ spent most of the rest of the day taking the knife in and out of the sheath and closely examining it. Her lessons would start tomorrow.

Abby had scrounged through an old trunk in the attic and found a beautiful red sweater for Jules. It was a little old-fashioned and a bit long, but Jules loved it; plus, she said, it was very warm—almost too warm for her to be sitting so close to the fire. And she, on her part, had also rummaged in the attic, unknown to Abby. She found a heavy wool peacoat that she painstakingly wrapped in some newspapers and tied with twine. It was a dark green and, unlike Abby's old coat, actually had all the buttons as well as a belt.

There were few other gifts; books, of course, but not much else. Jules had found some glitter and a few candles in a drawer at the church to decorate the tree. Abby had discovered knitting needles and some colored yarn in the kitchen but, since she'd never learned to knit, she merely draped the yarn over and around the tree. Good thing she had other skills, she thought, since she wasn't very domestic.

Abby slept fitfully that night, dreaming of other Christmases. She woke up when she heard crying. Jules had taken the first watch tonight, and was sitting near the fire, her book on the floor beside her. She had her knees drawn up and her arms wrapped around them, and was sobbing quietly. Abby went to her.

"Shh, honey, what is it? What's wrong?" Abby took the girl in her arms and rocked her. "Are you okay?"

"Yes," said Juliet. "I'm sorry, I didn't mean to wake you. It's just. . . it's just that I miss my mom!"

"Oh, sweetie, I'm so sorry. So sorry that all this has happened, and that your mom and dad aren't here." Abby held her tightly and smoothed back her hair. "I know you don't talk about her very much, and maybe that's not a good thing. You were so little when you lost them, barely four years old."

"Two," Juliet whispered. "I was two the last time I saw my mom." She raised her head and looked at Abby. "That house I lived in, by Grammy's house? That wasn't my mom, not my real mom. She came to live with me and my dad after we moved there."

Abby was dumbfounded.

"My dad told me once that Mom had left us and moved far away and that she didn't want to be with us anymore. But I still miss her. A lot." Juliet began crying again.

Abby finally convinced Juliet to go to sleep and let her take over the watch. Her heart nearly broke, thinking of all the girl had gone through, all that she'd lost. She wondered what kind of mother would leave her child like that; she simply couldn't imagine leaving EJ for any reason, except perhaps death.

Dawn came at last.

Brad roused Alison and told her it was time to go. He rolled up their blankets and stowed a few smaller packages inside. They repacked the remainder of Abby's cache, and Alison, silently for once, followed Brad down the path to the road.

They walked for half a mile or so, stopping at an old tumbledown shed. The creaky door opened surprisingly easily, and they went inside. Alison's mouth dropped open. The space was large, but was dwarfed by two dusty black pickup trucks. Brad pulled open the driver's door of one of them.

"Get in," he said. "I'm going to slide open those big doors over there. Drive through and stop, but don't kill the engine."

A few short minutes later, Alison scooted over and Brad climbed behind the wheel. "Where are we going?" she asked.

"To find Abby. But," he added. "here's the problem: she's probably not going north, into the city. If she left here, she had to have had a reason; likely the recent activity drove her to find a safer spot. She probably doesn't have any information on conditions out west or to the south, and I'm betting on her sticking around the area.

"We just have to figure out exactly which direction. . . and where she stopped."

"Um, seriously?" asked Alison, incredulously. "'Problem' is quite possibly the understatement of the century! Factor in all those other qualifications and we have a huge issue!"

"Yep," said Brad. "We do. And we'll have a bigger issue if Pops decides to bomb the whole camp, just be on the safe side. So we're heading out, right now, and we'll figure it out as we go along. Why don't you use some of that woman's intuition or something?" He smirked.

Alison glared at him.

"I'm kidding!" he protested. "Geez, where's your sense of humor? Abby always got me, even that time we. . . ." He suddenly broke off and a frown creased his forehead. "Damn! That's it!"

"What's it?" asked Alison, grabbing for the roll bar as the truck spun in the gravel. "And who the hell is Pops?"

Colonel Hoefer was on the phone, getting an earful from his superior. "Yes, sir," he said, slamming down the phone in response to the same on the other end. "Soldier!"

A young man appeared in the doorway. "Yes, sir?"

"Commence the operation. Pull the plug, push the button, whatever it takes. Do it now."

The soldier saluted, and left the room. Colonel Hoefer leaned back, a satisfied smile on his face. There. The camp was gone, or would be shortly, as well as anyone still hiding out there. Both Brad and Captain Pain-in-the-Rear were history. Now he could turn his full attention back to finding Abby and Juliet.

Ha! Just like old times, the first time he'd met her. She and her friend, he couldn't quite remember the name, had decided to go on an overnight themselves, without staff. A bunch of them had climbed Pioneer Hill, behind their cabins, and even though most of the kids turned back, Abby hadn't. She and the other girl, Emmy—yeah, that was her name—had stayed out all night and gotten lost. He'd been the one who found them.

Now he had to find her again.

BOOM!

Brad struggled to hold the truck on the road as Alison bounced around in her seat, trying to hang on and look out the back window at the same time.

BOOM!

"Told you we had to leave," Brad said. "Now hang on!"

"I'm trying, what else does it look like I'm doing?" Alison snapped. "Keep the damn truck on the road, will you?"

"Can't," said Brad, and he veered off the blacktop into some heavy underbrush, killing the engine.

They sat there, in the darkness, listening to the constant barrage. It seemed like hours. Alison finally pulled her hands away from her ears. "So, hotshot, where do we go from here? Did you figure it out?"

"Actually, yes. I think. But," he added, "we should probably wait here for a bit. I don't want them to pick up the heat of the engine. Let them think we were there when the bombs hit." He cracked his window and leaned towards it, listening.

Alison drummed her fingers on the armrest, waiting impatiently, wishing for a drink. At least, until Brad glared at her. She stopped the drumming, but still wanted the drink. Nothing was going to change that anytime soon.

Finally, Brad started the engine and they pulled out onto the road. They took nearly the same route as Abby had, but made much better time, ironically due to Abby and Juliet having cleared most of the debris out of the way just weeks ago.

Alison was mostly quiet on the drive, listening to Brad as he talked about. . . before. He'd first met Abby when they were both 18 and working at the camp that summer. They'd hung out a lot, with other friends, always in a group. Once, when she was in college, he'd driven up and surprised her and they drove around the back roads all night, talking and drinking beer. They stopped to watch the sun come up, then he took her home. A week later, he left for boot camp.

By the time he got out of the army, Abby had finished school and was bumming around out west somewhere. Brad had started a contracting business here in St. Louis, and one day he went to watch his niece play basketball. And there was Abby.

The two of them had gone on float trips, campouts, and to see the occasional movie, but always in a group. Nothing but friends, in spite of others' speculations. Once, Brad had a made a move, but the look on Abby's face stopped him. Besides, they'd agreed later, it had been like kissing your sibling: weird, awkward, and just plain wrong. So they'd stayed friends, and when all the trouble started, their bond was even stronger. In fact, Abby had introduced Brad to Zoe.

Zoe. He still thought of her a lot; at least he supposed he had when he was under the influence of Colonel Hoefer. And their child, the baby girl who hadn't lived long enough to draw breath after her birth. He took a deep breath and kept driving.

Chapter Thirteen

Shortly after Christmas, Abby gave Jules permission to stay out overnight. She knew the girl was capable; still, she worried. She was more concerned, however, with keeping her occupied and preparing her for whatever may come next, and she knew, too, that the more experienced Jules became, the better for all of them.

She stayed awake all night after Jules left, tending the fire, watching over EJ. And thinking. There had to be others out there, somewhere. And no one had come to find them, at least, no one who didn't want to kill them, so she began to make plans to find those others, to see what was going on. Jules wanted to fight and, Abby supposed, so did she. It's just that she was tired. And more realistic.

Morning brought more snow. What little had come down the week before had melted off into a sloppy mess, but this was covering the ground and seemed like it was here to stay for a few days. Abby set EJ to her lessons, and picked up around the house. At noon, she heated leftover stew for the two of them. One good thing about winter, and that was food preservation. That was the only good thing, really.

Suddenly, the back door burst open and Jules ran inside, rattling the old house as she slammed the door and locked it.

Abby jumped to her feet.

"Someone's here," gasped Juliet. She tried to catch her breath and calm herself.

Abby put a hand on her shoulder, pushing her into a chair, and gripped the girl's hands. "Tell me what you saw."

"Footprints," said Juliet. "Just footprints, but they weren't mine. In the snow, over by the train station. There were two sets."

Abby mulled this over for a minute. No choppers in the area. No engine noises. No sighting of actual people. More than likely, there were indeed just two people out there. Friend or enemy? That was the first question. The second, more ominous, was whether these two were an advance party, or just two survivors. Either way, they were strangers, and needed to be dealt with immediately. If they were allies, well, she'd play the wait-and-see game. If they were enemies. . . she'd killed before and would do it again, if necessary, to protect her girls.

Seeing that Juliet had gotten herself under control, Abby pushed a bowl of stew across the table and told her to eat. "Then," she added, "you can work with EJ on her knife skills, and have her help you get the guns cleaned and oiled. I'll be back by dark."

Within minutes, Abby was dressed and geared up: knife strapped to her leg, .357 in her coat pocket, and Mossberg slung over her shoulder. She kissed EJ and hugged Jules, and left quietly through the back door.

It was too light and too noisy to take the truck, so Abby first walked east and then took the old lake road south into town. She crept through the woods, pausing often to listen, and stopped directly behind the train station, concealed in the brush. There, she waited and watched.

"I don't see why we have to stay in that damn truck all the time."

Abby could barely make out the whispered words. She peered through the bare branches at ground level, where she lay hidden, and saw two figures walking down the road, almost to the corner of the building. In a moment, they'd be out of her line of sight.

The two figures stopped.

"I told you, I want to see if she's here. In the town somewhere."

"If you keep talking that loud, I'm sure she'll know we're here. Two days now, and all we've done is wander around."

Abby tensed her muscles, slowing reaching for her .357. She waited to see what they did next, straining to hear the muffled voices. When she did, the words were faint; the couple seemed to have continued walking past the station. She weighed the odds. Yes, there were two of them; she was pretty sure there weren't any more. At least, there were two of them right now. And she certainly had the element of surprise.

Slowly, she crept from her hiding place and sidled around the back of the building, nearly to the corner. She stopped again.

"So, now what? Any other bright ideas?" It was a woman. Abby knew her fighting skills were superior to most, and she wasn't worried about someone who was already careless about potential ambush. She pulled her knife from its sheath with her left hand.

"Of course. We need to check the area outside the town. I didn't really think she'd let herself get boxed in here, but we had to start somewhere. Now it's done, and tonight we'll start to cover the outlying areas."

Abby blinked. Now that she was within feet of the two strangers, she could hear them clearly. That was ridiculous. Impossible. He was dead, had been for years. Just like everyone else. She mentally shook herself back to the present and the task at hand.

One step. Another.

She could see them, about 15 feet away. They were facing each other, talking, standing still. She stepped out of the shadow, turning the corner.

"Don't. Move." Abby said.

The clean-up team had just finished sifting through the bomb site and Major Landon was reporting to Colonel Hoefer. The colonel had flown down that morning, thinking it was preferable to have to return to the camp one last time and be sure the job was done right than to sit and wait. Or pace back and forth in his office.

"What do you mean, 'inconclusive'?" he raged. "They were either here or they weren't. How can you not find anything at all?" His face was red and he appeared to be just on the verge of a verbal explosion. The major was not happy that he would likely be the target of that explosion; still, he patiently explained again.

"Fine," snapped Colonel Hoefer. "Make sure I hear from you the very minute you obtain any kind of news whatsoever." He climbed into the waiting chopper and indicated that he was ready; the chopper rose and banked, heading back to St. Louis.

"Abby," he said.

Abby shook her head. No, she wasn't falling for this. "Put your weapons down. Slowly." The woman started to speak, but stopped when Abby glared at her. "Both of you. Walk backwards ten steps and sit down. Put your hands on your heads."

She walked towards them, never looking away, and scooped up the two sidearms after sheathing her knife, her .357 never wavering. "All right, who are you and why are you here?"

"Well," said the woman, "if you're Abby, we're here to find you. If you're not, I guess we're screwed."

"And who the hell are you? Besides," she agreed, "probably screwed. Take off your hat and scarf." The woman complied. Abby looked at her face closely. Interesting, but not important; she looked familiar, though.

"Well, I don't know you, so there's certainly no way you know who I am. You, next!" Abby had her gun pointed squarely at the man, having decided the woman was the lesser threat. And she effectively had them both covered and disarmed. Probably.

The man slowly removed his hat, and then his scarf. His eyes never left hers. He spoke again.

"Come on, Ab, it hasn't been that long."

She stared at Brad.

Who was dead. Except he apparently wasn't. But. . . .

"Oh, my God." Abby slammed her gun back into the holster and covered the ground between them in a flying leap, landing on top of Brad. He tried to laugh as the wind was knocked out of him, and was still laughing as Abby began to pound on his chest.

"You son of a bitch, you're supposed to be dead! Where the hell have you been?"

"Hey now, it's not my fault, really!" He was still laughing as he finally managed to grab her arms and stop the pummeling. "Come on, Ab, let me up and we'll talk. Oh, and this is Alison." Alison was still sitting in the snow and the mud, thoroughly bemused by the entire episode.

Abby got up and pulled Brad with her, then held out her hand to Alison. "I supposed you're okay, if you're with him. But you both have a lot of talking to do. Come with me." She led them inside the train station and the three tried to get comfortable on the dusty floor; still, it was better than the snow, and they left the north wind outside, closing the door firmly.

"Okay," said Abby. "Talk."

"Well," said Brad, smirking, "obviously I'm not dead."

"Not yet," Abby responded, punching him in the arm. "So what happened?"

"We were down there at the warehouse in South City, the kids were scattered around, watching the doors. The choppers came in and hovered, and that's when we knew we'd been caught. The first one hit near the back, and I scooped up the closest kid and ran to the front. Those bombs of theirs just kept coming, and before I could get us outside, the whole thing came down.

"When I woke up, someone in riot gear was shooting me again, in the leg, and I was out cold for. . . I don't know how long.

"And then, oh, a couple weeks ago?" Brad looked at Alison. She nodded. She hadn't said a word since they'd come inside the train station.

"Anyway," Brad continued, "a couple weeks ago we were out at the camp and BAM! I guess I just came to my senses."

Abby rolled her eyes. "You expect me to believe that? You're missing a lot of years there, Brad. Are you going to fill me in on the rest?"

"Hang on. I'm trying to be, you know, chronological." He looked at Alison. "Your turn," he said.

Alison took a deep breath. She really hoped Abby wouldn't shoot her. That could be messy. "I was with the government."

"And you're here to help?" asked Abby, sarcastically. She reached behind her back for her gun.

"I said, 'was,'" Alison snapped. "I'm from Austin. I moved to Chicago when I got this fabulous new job. Ha. Fabulous. If you call killing kids and babies 'fabulous.' And blowing people to smithereens. And everything else.

"Then I was sent to St. Louis. Assigned to a Colonel Hoefer."

Abby's head jerked up. "Go on."

"He sent me out in the field," Alison continued, "along with the major here."

"Major? Brad, would you care to elaborate on that?" Abby's tone was icy. Her grip on the .357 tightened.

"Relax," he told her. "Just a minor glitch in the story. Alison, hurry it up, will you? Abby's about to whip out that gun of hers and shoot both of us, just for fun." He grinned. "I know you too well. Only please, make it quick, okay? I might die of starvation before we're done here."

"Huh," said Abby. "Guess you forgot about the false bottom in the truck."

"Damn." Brad looked crestfallen. "We've been sleeping on top of actual food and living on granola bars and jerky. Found your stash, by the way," he added.

Alison was not amused. "Geez, and they made you the major. . . ."

Abby was beginning to like her. "So, getting back to this story, Brad. What happened during, let's see, those missing ten years?" Good heavens, ten years? Had it really been that long?

"When they shot me in the leg? I was out for I don't know how long, then came to in a hospital of some sort. They pumped me full of drugs and kept me sedated. I don't remember much, but by the time I was discharged they had me ready to fight—for them."

Abby was horrified. That they'd done this, without permission, without humanity, without. . . common decency. Then again, she knew firsthand just how much decency this new regime possessed. Zip. Like Alison had said, they had no compunction about killing babies, kids, old men and women. And now drug-induced brainwashing. . . or something like that. And to Brad. The horror passed and fury took its place.

Abby tucked her gun back in her belt and held out her hand to Alison. "Hi. I'm Abby.

"Now, let's get you back to the house. I told the girls I'd be back by dark and it's getting close."

"Girls?" said Brad, giving her a look.

"Oh. Um, yeah. Guess I have a few things to tell you, too."

"So how is little Juliet?" asked Brad, glancing at Alison who seemed suddenly tense.

"Huh. Not so little. She's 15 now and a bit taller than I am; loves history and politics, or what passes for it nowadays. Not fond of math. She can track as well as I can, though, and is a darn good shot. And, well, she's a teenager. You remember what that's like, right?" Abby smiled. She could talk about Jules for a good long while, especially if it meant leaving EJ out of the conversation for a bit. She wasn't quite sure how to go about bringing that up.

"What does she look like?" blurted out Alison.

"Oh," said Abby casually, "auburn hair, kind of like yours." She glanced at Alison again, startled.

"Let's get going. Brad, why don't you go back and get the truck? Alison and I will wait here, then we'll go up and around the lake. I don't want to get too close to the house; the girls will hear the engine and think the worst. We'll walk in the rest of the way."

Brad frowned. "You keep saying 'girls,' plural. How many have you got hidden up here? Any cute ones?" He brightened a bit but, seeing the look on Abby's face, laughed and walked away.

Robin Tidwell

Chapter Fourteen

The truck bounced over the ruts in the old lake road, jarring their very bones, but at least the heater worked. Abby hadn't been this toasty in a month, since her short trips to the river were never long enough to warm up the engine. They stopped at the north end of the lake, pulling into the trees. Brad killed the engine and they got out and began walking towards the house. Abby stopped at the barn.

"Wait here," she said. "I need to talk to. . . Juliet. . . first. She thinks you're dead, after all." She opened the side door for Brad and Alison. "Give me, oh, fifteen minutes or so."

Abby climbed the porch steps and Juliet flung open the door. "Is everything okay?" She looked both frightened and relieved. "What did you find?"

Abby hugged her tightly. "Yes, everything is okay. But we have to talk. Where's EJ?"

"She's ready for bed, by the fire, reading again. She's fine. What do we have to talk about? Is someone out there? Did you see someone?"

"Come on." Abby led Jules into the living room and they sat near the fire. She hadn't yet taken off her coat and scarf and the shotgun was still over her shoulder. Jules looked very worried, still. "EJ, put the book down for a minute." Abby cleared her throat. Best to just say it outright; she'd always done that, plain and simple and to the point.

"Jules, you remember Brad?"

"I do, Mom. He's the one who died saving that boy when they were fighting the bad guys," piped up EJ. Jules just nodded, trying visibly to relax and wait to hear more.

"He's here."

Jules stared at Abby. "But, like EJ said, he's dead. He died!"

"No, girls, he didn't. The bad guys, as EJ calls them, took him and kept him in the hospital for a long time. They gave him some sort of drugs and made him think he was one of them. He did some things that he's ashamed of, but he didn't know any better then. He's fine now, and he's here. Out in the barn, in fact."

"Oh good," said EJ. "I liked him. I'm glad he's not dead and he's not a bad guy anymore. Can he come inside, Mom?"

Abby nearly laughed, but Jules was still trying to wrap her brain around this new information. "Not dead. Really?" she asked.

This time, Abby did laugh. "Yes, really. Not dead. And there's someone with him, a woman named Alison." Jules jerked her head up so fast that her neck cracked, but Abby didn't notice. She was walking to the back door.

Abby opened the door and whistled. In a minute, Brad and Alison emerged from the barn and made their way to the porch. By the time everyone had removed their outerwear, Abby had heated some soup and they took their mugs into the living room. She was a little concerned that Jules hadn't made an appearance yet, but supposed she was still mulling it all over; she figured EJ had gotten distracted by the book, as usual.

Jules was bent over the fire, poking it randomly. EJ jumped up and ran to her mother, ducking behind her. "Hi, Brad," she said shyly, peeking out.

Brad blinked. It was a miniature Abby.

"This is EJ," said Abby, nervously. In all fairness, it was the first time she'd ever had to introduce her daughter to anyone. "And Brad, you remember Juliet. Jules? Come here, honey, and say hello."

Juliet stood up and slowly turned around. On her face was a mixture of fear and hope. Those same emotions were reflected on Alison's face. Nearly identical faces, each staring at the other, the matching auburn hair. . . .

"Hi, I'm Juliet," she said to Alison. Her face had gone carefully blank. She didn't move.

Alison wasn't sure how to react. Should she hug the girl? Was Juliet her daughter? It had been so long, after all. Finally, she held out her hand. "Hi, Juliet. I'm Alison."

Abby glanced at Brad. He could see it too, she knew it. As Juliet and Alison both stepped back, Brad swooped in and grabbed Juliet in a big bear hug.

"Is this any way to greet your long-lost Uncle Brad?" he said, grinning. "Little Juliet, all grown up!" Jules giggled in spite of herself and the tension was broken. Mostly.

They talked long into the night; even EJ stayed awake far past her bedtime. Brad told them about his part in the short-lived rebellion, fearing that his status as both prisoner and experiment might be a bit too much for a six-year-old's ears.

Abby filled Brad in on what had happened after he'd been reported as dead. Just weeks after they'd received the news, the survivors in their group had decided to separate. Martin had already moved his family outside of the camp. Cal and Pops had planned to go. . . somewhere; Abby and Emmy were going to take Juliet up to the cave. Ted and Noah were both striking out their own; west, probably.

When the bombs hit, Abby and Juliet had escaped up the hill and into the woods. The rest, Abby told them, unwilling to provide much detail with EJ curled up next to her, were lost. Except Noah. He came back. She kissed the top of EJ's head, and Brad understood.

"That was my dad," EJ said brightly. "I wish I'd known him. Jules did, though, right?" She looked over at Juliet, who was wiping away tears.

Then it was Alison's turn.

She sat cross-legged, looking down at her hands, and spoke very quietly. Brad kept a watchful eye on her. Abby, however, was more concerned about Jules at the moment. The girl was once again using the fire as a distraction and seemed not to be listening.

"I'm from Texas," said Alison. "Years ago, I took a job in Chicago. My—my family was supposed to make the move a few weeks later, but they. . . disappeared. I tried to find them. For years. I finally gave up. . . ." Her voice trailed off as she tried to hold back tears.

After a pause, she continued. "I worked for the government. Mostly in-office stuff, personnel and so forth. I knew what was going on, but for a while it was easier to ignore it and pretend that things were okay. It's a lot easier when you aren't actually faced with all the terror and destruction every day. Plus, there were perks." She shrugged.

"I did have some friends there, we'd go camping and stuff on the weekends. Out in the country to this campground. They were really into the doomsday thing, prepping and all that. Huh," she added, bitterly. "Who knew they were right?"

"Long story, and a lot of regrets. A lot. But, here I am."

Seeing that Alison had seemed to rally a bit—and Abby knew how anger could turn things around—she said, "Tell us about your family."

Alison bit her lip and glanced at Juliet. "I was married. Things weren't going so well. He took off, somewhere. . . with our two-year-old daughter. Her name was Juliet."

No one spoke. No one moved.

"Hey!" said EJ. "That's the same as Jules!"

Juliet jumped to her feet and raced into the kitchen. The door slammed.

Abby stood up and was starting after her when Alison said, "No. Let me." Alison grabbed her coat and another one for Juliet and followed the girl out into the snow.

"Well, it is the same," said EJ.

"Come on, toots, let's get you ready for bed. Mom and Uncle Brad have things to talk about." Abby scooped up EJ and took her into the bathroom. A few minutes later, she tucked her daughter into her bedroll and put another log on the fire; Jules had just about put the darn thing out, with all her poking around. She motioned for Brad to follow her, and they went into the chilly kitchen, lightly closing the door.

"What the hell?" said Abby. "I thought she looked familiar, and then when I saw the two of them together. . . do you think it's true? That Jules is her daughter?"

Brad sighed. "I think so, Abby. Talk about strange, though. I mean, what are the odds? Like, a billion to one or something?"

"So what happens now? I mean, what are your plans? And what about Alison?" Clearly, Abby was worried, but Brad wasn't too sure exactly about what.

"Plans? I'm staying right here, Ab. Never thought I'd see you again, truthfully. Well, okay," he amended. "Except for that part about me being sent to kill you and all."

Abby smacked him on the arm. "Come on, be serious."

"I am serious. I'm staying right here. With you. And the girls. Boy, that little EJ is just a carbon copy of you, Abby!"

Abby took a deep breath. "Brad. Stop. Let's cover one thing at a time here. You said you're staying, right? And Alison? Is there something there, or am I imagining things?" She raised her eyebrows a bit and looked him dead in the eyes. "Hmm?"

"Um, uh, I don't really know. I mean, yeah, I kinda like her and all, but. . . sheesh, Abby, just last week she was calling me Major Creepy and, well, I don't know!" In spite of his protests, Brad wouldn't quite meet her eyes and he was turning a bit red.

"Uh huh. Okay. We'll leave it at that." Abby grinned at his obvious embarrassment. Then she turned serious.

"And Alison? Will she stay? Does she have plans or. . . anyone that might be waiting for her?"

Brad nodded towards the back door. "I think the answer to that last question is yes, and I think she found her." Abby slumped into her chair.

"But," he continued, "I certainly don't think Juliet is going to leave you—you've taken care of her for years and years. And I think everyone is going to need some time to figure it all out. Everyone." He knelt down in front of Abby and took her cold hands in his own.

"Abby. Look at me."

She raised her head. He could see that she was blinking back tears and it surprised him. Abby never cried. She jerked her hands away and swiped quickly at her eyes.

"All right, then. I'm going to go check on EJ." She left the room and Brad stood up, stretching, then went in search of blankets to make a couple extra bedrolls.

Alison caught up with Juliet just before she got to the barn. They went inside, out of the wind, and Alison handed the coat to the girl. Wordlessly, Juliet accepted it, but merely hugged it to her chest. She was crying and shaking from the cold, but seemed incapable of doing anything at the moment but standing there.

Alison gently helped her put the coat on and guided Juliet over to a stack of hay bales. She sat down next to her, this girl she truly believed was her daughter, and wondered what to say. But Juliet broke the silence first.

"Dad said you left us."

Alison swallowed her anger, barely. "I left to take the Chicago job. He was supposed to finish up the packing and bring you to Chicago with him."

Juliet rallied a bit. "So, if you're my mother, maybe you could tell me a few things. Like, what was my dad's name?"

"His name is. . . was Rob. Short for Robert."

"And my birthday?"

"August sixteenth," said Alison. She fumbled in her coat pocket and pulled out a battered leather wallet. "Here."

Juliet took the faded photo from Alison's hand. Slowly, she unfolded it. It was a picture of a younger version of Alison, holding a small child on her lap. The little girl was smiling and looking up at Alison. Two identical smiles.

Juliet began to sob, and this time she allowed Alison to put her arms around her. They sat there for a long time, saying nothing. At last, Juliet became quiet. She looked up at Alison.

"Mom?"

Alison closed her eyes and hoped fervently that she wasn't imagining all of this. She'd never thought she would hear that again. All those years lost. . . damn Rob anyway.

"Yes?"

"Nothing," said Jules. "I just wanted to say it."

"Come on," said Alison. "Let's go back to the house before we freeze out here. We can talk some more tomorrow, okay?"

"Sure," said Juliet. "Mom." She giggled.

Chapter Fifteen

The next morning dawned bright and cold, but the snow had stopped. Abby was finishing up in the kitchen when Brad walked in and sat down. "What's the next step, Abby?"

"I've thought about it all morning," Abby replied. "It's time to see what's happening out there. With your and Alison's more recent intel, and a couple extra adults now, I think we need to do some exploring."

"Well, we can tell you what's going on in St. Louis. What about elsewhere?"

"I don't know, Brad. We've managed pretty well around here so far. What do you mean, go somewhere? Another state? Out west where Ted was headed?" Abby looked thoughtful for a moment. "I just don't know—have you heard anything about other places? Surely there are other survivors. . . somewhere."

"Sit down a minute. There's something I didn't mention last night." Brad looked nervous.

Abby sat down. "Tell me."

"I saw your reaction when I talked about Colonel Hoefer. It's not just the same name, Abby. It's Pops." He waited, watching her.

She laughed. "Don't be silly, Brad. Pops is dead, his heart, right before the bombs hit. Impossible."

"I was 'dead' too, remember?"

Abby stopped laughing. "But, Brad, the old infirmary was completely collapsed. He couldn't have survived that; no one could have. Besides, Pops would never. . . ." She frowned. Were there any clues, any indication that Pops had been. . . no, none. It was absurd. "I don't believe it."

"Think for a minute, Ab. Did you see the building, or were you running up the hill? Could you even see the front, since you'd gone out the back?"

"But Noah saw it, when he woke up!"

"You told me that Noah was unconscious for nearly a day. Abby, I'm telling you, they're one and the same. Colonel Clarence Hoefer. He even gave me the code word to reach him. It was 'Pops'."

"No. I still don't believe it, Brad. I mean, I've known Pops since I was little! He never said or did anything, at all, that will convince me to believe that's the same guy." Abby shook her head. This was ridiculous.

Brad looked her in the eyes and quietly said, "Abby, he sent me to kill you. And Juliet."

That stopped her. Briefly. "It's not that I don't believe you, Brad, but... maybe you were confused, you know, because of the drugs?" Abby's head was spinning. She thought of all the times Pops had come through for them all, and now she was expected to believe he had been faking it? Or even worse, sabotaging their safety.

"All right, Ab. I give up. Guess you'll just have to see for yourself. You sure can be stubborn." He shook his head. "Change of subject. What are we going to do next?"

"Oh. That." Abby scrambled to change directions. "I think you and I should go into the city. Alison can stay here with the girls. I still have that cache at Babler, so we can travel light."

"Um, no you don't," Brad said. "We kind of blew it up a month or so ago." He looked rather abashed and, after glaring at him, Abby got up and went into the living room. He followed.

"Brad and I are going into the city," she said. "We'll be leaving tonight. Jules, you and EJ will stay here with Alison."

"We are?" asked Brad. "So you just decided? Typical." He rolled his eyes. "Never could get her to slow down," he muttered.

"Fine by me," said Alison. "I'd like to spend some time with Juliet. Jules, I mean." She smiled at her daughter. "And EJ too, of course."

The little girl was tugging at Abby's arm. "Yes, honey, I'm sure that 'Aunt' Alison can take you out in the snow while we're gone. Looks like you're stuck with us now," she told Alison, winking.

The day was filled with lessons for the girls and packing for Brad and Abby. They planned to drive to Babler, store the bulk of their supplies and leave the truck, and work their way into the city the following night. Towers were back up, but their long-range radios only worked for a distance of about twenty miles. One of their goals was to acquire some newer equipment, as well as replacement items and additional supplies.

At dusk, Abby hugged the girls and even Alison. Brad told them all goodbye very formally, making EJ giggle, as well as Jules. Then he broke the tension further by scooping EJ up and over his shoulder and lugging Jules under his arm while he danced around the kitchen. Amid squeals and laughter, Abby and Brad finally walked out the door.

As they drove north and east on Highway T, Abby could see the old power plant looming in the distance. The road twisted and turned, but there were few vehicles on the sides or in the road itself. Most of the people around here had gotten out while they still could, or had since vanished. Once through St. Albans, Abby turned left onto Ossenfort Road. This took them to the west side of Babler Park.

They continued north until Abby abruptly swung the truck off the road, jarring them both, and crashed through a grove of saplings. She braked in a small clearing and killed the engine.

"What the heck was that?" demanded Brad, rubbing his head where it had made contact with the roof of the cab.

"Trust me," said Abby. "It would have taken a lot longer and we'd be more likely to get stuck if I'd gone slowly. Now come on, help me clean up that mess we made."

"We? Tell me, do you go off-road on a regular basis?"

"Why yes, I do. Especially lately. I mean, in the last ten years or so. I have to keep in practice, after all!" Abby jumped out and landed lightly on her feet.

They spent the rest of the night going over maps and drawings, lining out the best route to take and where to go once inside the city limits. Brad warned her that construction had been an ongoing part of Colonel Hoefer's plan for several years and that part of that plan included a massive fence. He doubted it was completed; at least, as of a month ago. Wherever they went in, it would have to be through a breach in the wall itself, or in an unfinished area. He had two best guesses. They'd try for the nearest one first.

As dawn approached, Abby took the first watch. She'd wake Brad in four hours but, in the meantime, she was going to find a better place to stash their supplies. The park was heavily wooded, in this section at least, so she could explore with only the usual precautions, as long as she didn't wander too far.

Half a mile to the east, she began to smell the devastation. She climbed onto a rock outcropping and lay down, pulling out her field glasses. Focusing in on where she had once hidden her cache, the ravine and the stand of evergreens near the small cave opening, she gasped aloud.

The few trees that had remained were black and twisted; some were uprooted entirely and lay in a tangle. Boulders were scattered, and those, she knew, hadn't been moved by human hands. The entire cave had collapsed on itself. The silence was profound.

Brad and Alison and their squad had, under the auspices of the government, destroyed a large swath of the once-beautiful state park.

Abby froze. Choppers.

She hurriedly wiggled backwards, off the rocks, dropping to the hard ground. Unmoving.

The ominous black Cobras, two of them, hovered for a moment and then veered off abruptly to the east.

Abby let out her breath and stretched her cramped muscles. Then she retraced her steps back to the truck, thinking furiously as she walked. They could only be here for one reason. Her.

.

Chapter Sixteen

Abby hurriedly woke up Brad and told him about the choppers. He insisted that she get some sleep before they moved on, and besides, it wouldn't be dark for hours yet. It was too risky to travel until then. She slept fitfully for several hours, then spent some time cleaning her guns and sharpening her knife while Brad took a nap.

As the sun dropped lower, they pulled back out onto the blacktop, traveling as fast as they dared without lights. Abby wanted to put some distance between herself and the park, and she knew of a place that might just work. It was closer in to the city, yes, but had been abandoned decades ago after a family feud.

It took them nearly an hour to cover the five-mile distance, stopping to clear brush and branches off the road at least half a dozen times. Finally, they descended a steep, curvy road into the floodplain. They strained their eyes through the darkness, trying to make out any buildings that might still be standing. Fortunately, the road was now flat and straight and was lined with nothing but long-unused fields on either side.

Abby stopped the truck. "Okay, we're here. We'll unload, then stow the truck over that way, in that stand of trees." She pointed about half a mile away.

"Where's 'here'?" asked Brad.

"An old farm. I worked here one summer. It's on the river, although you can't access it anymore from here. Well, not easily. There used to be a house here, a pretty good-sized one, but just the basement is left. And the outbuildings are all falling down; at least, what's left of them."

"So we have a choice of sleeping quarters in a falling-down death-trap, or in an open basement?" Brad wasn't too happy, but he supposed it was better than sleeping in the truck.

"Hey, whichever, it'll keep the wind off us. Or, I suppose we could climb down in a grain bin—that would be toasty when the sun hits it."

Brad looked up at the giant metal bin next to which they were parked. "Um, no thanks."

"Fine. Smokehouse it is, then," said Abby, leading the way through a cast-iron gate still attached to its posts. The fence, however, was long gone. A faded red cistern poked up from the weeds beyond the gate. Abby pushed open the door to a small, narrow building. A flock of bats streamed out, startling them.

There were no windows, and the paint was peeling and cracked. The entire building leaned to the right, leaving them to wonder how stable it actually was and how long it would last. Long enough, anyway, Abby said aloud. "We won't be here long, after all, and we can always dig for our stuff if it falls down before we get back."

"I'm not worried about that," said Brad. "I just don't want it falling down on my head while I'm asleep. At least the bats left." He shuddered.

"Oh," said Abby airily, "I'm sure they kept down the mice and rat population. For heaven's sake, stop being such a girl!" Brad was not amused.

They built a small fire and made coffee and warmed up some food; Abby lit a smoke and leaned back against her bedroll. "So. Where do we go from here?"

Brad pulled out a map. "All right, this is where we are, and we need to go. . . here." He pointed toward the first of two small circles. "We'll try this spot, right near the old university. The wall runs roughly along Skinker Avenue. If that doesn't work, we'll go further south where it runs along the River Des Peres."

Abby nodded. "Okay, chief. Your call. Lead on." She stood up and put on her pack and slung the Mossberg over her shoulder. Brad finished putting out the fire and they started into the city.

The walk was an easy one, physically. It was just twelve miles and, while they couldn't safely hike down the middle of the road, the area was a virtual ghost town. No functioning traffic or streetlights; everything was in the shadows. There were no choppers in the air. The night was quiet and cold.

It was two o'clock in the morning when they arrived at the university campus, on the west side. Brad and Abby made their way past Francis Field, along the south side of the campus, then crept along the rose brick walls of Steinberg Hall. It appeared, in the darkness, to be mostly intact. The wall was just beyond, along the boundaries of Forest Park. And it had been completed.

Guard towers dotted the very top; searchlights scanned the area. The occasional bark of a dog could be heard. And there were men patrolling just outside, armed.

Silently, the pair made their way back toward the center of campus. Avoiding the craters in the turf, they squeezed under a stable-looking pile of rubble. They rested for a few minutes, shared a water bottle. Abby shrugged. Brad nodded. They crawled out and started for the second point of entry, the canal.

Shots rang out.

Both of them dropped and rolled, coming to rest about ten feet apart, sidearms out and ready to fire. At first, they saw nothing. Sirens screeched, beams of light swung closer and closer, and they scrambled into the shrubbery. Peering out, Abby could see a dark figure running down the street. More shots.

The figure fell to the ground.

The lights went out. The sirens ceased.

They waited.

Brad touched Abby's shoulder and indicated that they should go. They crawled out of the bushes and began walking south, skirting the body which still lay on the pavement, and moved quickly, putting distance behind them with every stride. Neither spoke until they entered the small suburb of Maplewood.

"Someone tried to leave," said Abby. "If there was one, there are surely more of them, people who just want out."

"Yes," said Brad. "But they're the ones who wanted to be there in the first place; not so sure we can count on them in a crisis. Those of us who stayed out, who are living away from all this. . . this craziness, we're the ones who are going to be able to stop it."

"Stop it? Stop what? Are you crazy? We can't fight them—you saw how it ended the last time. I just want to know what they're up to, what they're planning. So we can stay safe." Abby had stopped. "Brad, what are you thinking?"

"Come here." Brad pulled her over to a large headstone; they were in the middle of Resurrection Cemetery, halfway to their destination. They sat down, backs against the cold granite.

"Look, Ab, do you want to keep running and hiding the rest of your life?"

"I've managed pretty well so far!" she retorted. "Besides, I can't shoot them all. I don't have enough ammo." She sighed.

Brad grinned, in spite of the circumstances. "I intend to make sure you have plenty of chances at that, Abby. And think about this: what about the girls? Is this what you want for them?"

"No. But I don't see any choice. It's either that, or they grow up without a mother and have to fend for themselves."

"There are three of us, Abby, three adults, and the two girls. And there are more. We just have to find them. Come on, you like to make lists—here's the number one thing to put on it. Just keep it a mental list, okay? Just in case."

"Ha. I'll keep it mental, all right. I've been dealing with you for a long time, after all; it would make anyone mental!"

"Always a smart-aleck." Brad gave her a quick hug. "Now let's move."

Continuing south, through Affton, Abby remembered the wild flight from the city with Emmy, all those years ago. It didn't look much different now, except for the vines and saplings and weeds that had taken over the destruction. The overpass at Highway 55 was demolished, just as the one they'd stopped at back then. She and Brad kept going, until they reached the tall fence around the old Port Authority.

Abby pulled out her field glasses and switched on the infrared. It appeared as though the wall stopped just before the canal converged with the Mississippi. As she panned to her right, and zoomed in, she could see why.

There was a new barracks just across the River Des Peres. She handed the glasses to Brad.

"Hmmm," he said. "Could be problematic."

Abby rolled her eyes. "Could be? Right." She sat down and waited for Brad to finish his thought.

"Got it. See the railroad bridge? They only use the tracks anymore to move troops—only bigwigs use the choppers. No freight, because each city is supposed to be self-sufficient. There's virtually no communication between citizens from city to city, unless it's underground." He stopped and looked confused.

Abby looked at him in concern. "Um, Brad? You sounded. . . weird."

"I know. I felt weird too. Huh. Must have been something they programmed into me at some point."

"Do you think it's accurate? Or just something you're supposed to say?" Abby tried not to show how worried she felt.

"Yes. It's the right information. I know it." He rubbed his forehead. "Not sure how, but I do.

"All right, so we'll go down to the end of the wall. No towers here, no lights, and once we get to the end, we'll climb up the trestle and work our way across the river. Piece of cake."

"Okay. Sure. Piece of cake," Abby repeated, securing the field glasses in their case. "Right behind you and all that."

They crept close to the wall, quietly, listening. The night was still. The darkness pressed down on them as they slowly worked their way to the last bricks. First Brad, then Abby, dashed the last few feet across an open space and swung up into the timbers below the railroad bridge. In spite of being in good physical shape, they were both breathing hard when they dropped to solid ground on the far side of the tracks, opposite the barracks.

"We're in," whispered Brad, as they rested in a culvert. "We've got about eight miles to go, give or take, to the Federal Building. I'm going in alone, Abby. No arguments."

Abby bit her tongue. That was not happening. This, however, was not the time to discuss it. Or argue, if Brad preferred. They had to move out of the vicinity of those barracks.

Crawling out of the culvert, Brad behind her, Abby got her bearings quickly and began walking north, keeping to the shadows. They ducked behind old ruins, freight cars, and security fences, following the train tracks past abandoned warehouses and grain elevators.

Then they saw lights, up ahead and to their right. Between the tracks and the river stood a bustling building, people milling around even in the middle of the night. Trucks ground their gears and revved their engines. Searchlights on the roof periodically swept the area and Brad and Abby ducked quickly behind a shed.

"Supply rationing," said Brad. "They have to do it at night or there'd be riots. Town captains, non-military, bring groups down at certain times to replenish their areas. Damn. I forgot about this."

"Come on," Abby said. "We'll just move off the riverfront and cut through."

"More people out there, Abby. We need to lay low. Give me a minute to think." Brad watched the activity through a crack in the siding.

"No," said Abby. "We can't wait. It's not hard, I've done it before. Come on." She tugged at his arm and he reluctantly followed her. She led the way, across the old highway and onto Cahokia Street, then north on Marine to Broadway.

Brad pointed to the east and Abby turned, cutting through abandoned yards and past dark, silent homes. They emerged from the residential sprawl directly behind the old shoe factory. It hadn't been referred to that in years, however, and was now—or had been, before—called the Park. A massive labyrinth of buildings, offices, warehouses, and studios, the Park was—or had been, before—a conglomeration of businesses who wanted the cachet of an address on Cherokee Street.

They circled the huge complex until they found a spot that would likely be far from prying eyes, and ears, if anyone at all wandered into the area. Best they could tell, no one lived in this section of town. The sky was growing lighter by the minute, and they needed to take cover. Abby jimmied a lock, Brad shoved the door open, and they were inside. Too tired to explore any further, they went into what appeared to be a small office, windowless, and closed the door.

Chapter Seventeen

When Abby awoke, Brad was gone. Dammit, she'd told him last night, in no uncertain terms, that they needed to stick together. She remembered all too well what had happened last time, to Janey, and there was no Frank around here either to bail them out. Since he'd kept the details to himself, and she knew only that he was going into the main headquarters, the Federal Building, she was better off staying right here. Or close to right here.

She looked at her watch. Five o'clock. Only mildly surprised that she'd slept all day, Abby decided to do some exploring. She geared up and cautiously opened the door. Silence greeted her. She walked the dusty halls, pausing to look into open rooms, and finally emerged into the twilight.

Staying close to the building, she sidled around the corners and made her way to the street. To her right was a small wooded area. She waited and watched, decided that, truly, she was alone here, and dashed across. Abby felt a lot better once she was in the trees; the city, regardless of lack of population, was still too confining.

As the last rays of light broke through the clouds, she reached the DeMenil Mansion. Or what was left of it.

The four stately columns lay burned and blackened in craggy heaps on the front lawn. The ancient oaks were toppled. The enormous twin brick chimneys were simply. . . gone. Shadows played among the ruins, some dark and foreboding, others fleeting as the sun touched them.

Colonel Barton hadn't played any favorites when he'd determined that the best way to stop the rebellion was with his bombs and his choppers. Abby shuddered, again remembering her escape from the city. . . with Emmy. Her city, in spite of its often-claustrophobic effect. Gone at the whim of a madman. Or, more likely, a man who followed the relentless orders of his superiors, those in charge of the new government, those who wished to obliterate all independent thought, all freedoms.

Abby made her way carefully through the chaos to the back of the mansion, to where the cellar doors stood askew as if giant hands had ripped them from their hinges. She shined her flashlight down the stairs.

Satisfied that the scurrying sounds were merely rodents, Abby slowly descended, keeping close to the inside wall. At the bottom, she peered into the deep darkness that her light could barely penetrate.

For decades, probably much longer, rumors had swirled around the area; they spoke of caves and caverns and passages, far below the city of St. Louis, where breweries had once flourished and even slaves had huddled for sanctuary as they fled Missouri. Abby had heard, too, from the handful of old Indians in the area, that there were connections from here clear to Chicago. If, she supposed, one wished to go to Chicago; not her. Things were probably much worse up there.

Slowly, Abby began to make her way through the towering piles and stacks of old junk. Some of it, she noticed, appeared to once have been priceless antiques but were now merely more obstacles in her way. Much of the first floor of the mansion had fallen through, compounding the issue.

And then she saw a door, nearly hidden behind a large, tilted armoire and assorted small tables.

Setting down her flashlight, Abby moved the smaller pieces carefully, although she wondered why she was bothering. Surely they were beyond hope by now and besides, who would ever come down here to retrieve anything? Or have a use for it?

The armoire, however, was hopelessly wedged into its spot.

Abby sat down for a moment to rest, contemplating a new strategy. Suddenly, the hair on the back of her neck prickled and she rubbed her arms, trying to warm herself. She held her breath, listening. Nothing. Muscles tense, she grabbed her light and shined it around, watching and waiting.

Still nothing.

She set the light on the floor at her feet and stood, giving the armoire another chance to budge so she could pry open that door. Straining with her arms and back, pushing hard with her legs, Abby gave one more mighty shove.

The armoire fell to the floor, splintering into pieces with a loud crash. She reached for the old-fashioned padlock on the door. Within a minute, she'd picked the lock and pulled open the creaky door.

Abby stepped through, shining her light down the long, dank passageway. It seemed to go in a straight line, at least as far as the light would reach. She began to move slowly along, until the floor started to descend; she stopped. Contemplating whether or not to continue, she guessed that she'd gone perhaps 300 yards through the tunnel. She was likely directly below the highway at this point, maybe a little past it.

Ten o'clock. She had plenty of time. She wasn't expecting Brad to be back until morning. She could easily keep going for a while but planned to turn around in the next hour, especially if she came across any tunnels that might branch off from the main one.

Just as she was about to start back, Abby stumbled and lost her balance. She landed in a crouch, reaching out to the stone wall to steady herself. It was damp. She rose to her feet and realized that the problem wasn't her carelessness, but that the floor had simply dropped, sharply, and the tunnel was angling downward. Somewhere, she could hear water dripping.

Curiosity got the better of her and she kept walking, slowly, carefully. The floor was wet now, but had leveled off somewhat. The sound of water became more pronounced and Abby felt as though the very air was pressing down on her.

Another hour had passed when she realized the floor was beginning to rise. Then she came to another opening, on her left; a secondary passage stretched as far as she could see in the dimming glow of her flashlight. A few steps more, and she was confronted with stairs cut into the stone, rising high and steep. The inner part was worn, as though many feet at traveled this way once upon a time.

Abby checked her watch. She couldn't turn back now.

She climbed up the stairs. And stopped abruptly. There was a landing, yes, a small one, about five feet square. And an iron ladder going up the wall in front of her. She put one foot on the bottom rung. Then the other foot. She pulled herself up, all the way to the top.

There was nothing there, except a sort of trap door with heavy iron hinges. Rusted, they looked as though they'd hadn't been used any time in the last century. Or longer. She pushed on it. Nothing. She pushed again, and thought she felt a slight give in the old wood. Still it wouldn't budge.

Well, Abby thought. That was it. Nothing here; she obviously couldn't go any farther. Long past time to go back, anyway. If Brad went back to where he'd left her and she was missing, well. . . he'd be furious, to say the least. She climbed back down the ladder and began to retrace her steps.

Robin Tidwell

Chapter Eighteen

Alison and Jules were getting to know each other all over again, and it wasn't an easy thing. Jules was a teenager, with all that entailed, and Alison had gotten quite used to taking care of only herself. Fortunately, Jules was self-sufficient and mature, capable of handling any emergency or situation in which she found herself and, sometimes, even appeared to be more adult than her mother.

The day after Abby and Brad had set out, Jules was planning another foray into town. She'd already sat down with EJ and done her lessons, helping the younger girl, and was sharpening her knife when Alison sat down beside her.

"I don't think you should be leaving in the middle of the night like this, Jules."

Jules ignored her mother and continued with her task until she was finished. She picked up her Glock to clean and oil it, and Alison reached out to touch her arm. Quick as a flash, the knife was back in Jules' hand. Alison jumped back, shocked, and stared at her daughter.

"Sorry," Jules mumbled.

"Really? Sorry? You're a teenage girl, you should be. . . ." Alison trailed off, at a momentary loss.

"Really?" Jules mimicked her. "I should be doing what? Dating? Whom? Going out at night? Well, I am doing that, I guess." She looked a little contrite when she saw Alison's face.

"You're right. I don't know what I'm thinking, or what I'm doing. I just. . . I just thought it would be different, having a daughter. When you were born, no one expected the world to change so drastically. I thought I'd be dressing you up and seeing you off on your first date and taking you to get a driver license. All of that."

Alison looked almost as though she was going to cry. Jules couldn't stand that, not when anyone cried, especially when she herself did, and so she said, hastily, "It's okay. . . Mom. I can drive, even without a license. Abby taught me when I was eleven."

"Eleven?"

"Well," said Jules, "I was already pretty tall, tall enough to reach the gas anyway and still see where I was going. And we just did it around the camp. Abby thought I should know, just in case.

"Besides, even though in your day someone had to be like sixteen or something, back before then, kids drove all the time out on ranches and stuff. Sometimes into town, too."

Alison smiled. A little. "At least you're learning history."

"I like history. And writing. But not math. Ick." Jules went back to cleaning her gun.

"When did you learn to shoot?" asked Alison, after watching for a minute.

"I was four," Juliet said.

"What?" shouted Alison. "What the hell was Abby thinking?" She was furious. Her baby—shooting a gun?

Quietly, Jules set down the Glock and turned toward her mother. "Yes. Four years old. Your government was bombing the crap out of everything. We were hiding. We were scared. We were always afraid of something.

"And Abby took care of me. She taught me everything I needed to know. You weren't there."

Alison had tears in her eyes. No, she hadn't been there for Juliet. But she hadn't known, she hadn't been able to find her in time. Maybe this wasn't the time either. Maybe it was too late.

"I'm so sorry, Juliet. You're right, I don't know, I didn't know. But it wasn't my fault, it wasn't anyone's fault. It just happened. To us, I mean.

"And yes, it was my government. Then. It's not now. Never again." There was nothing else for Alison to say at this point, nothing she could do.

"Good," said Jules. She strapped on her knife and laced up her boots. Picking up her Glock, she bundled up and left the house, pausing to say good-bye to EJ.

Jules skirted the lake and tromped through the trees, making rather more noise than usual. She was just so angry, at everyone! Not to mention confused, and happy, and sad, and. . . just everything, all rolled up into one mess inside her head. She kicked a rock near the road and it skittered off across the gravel. She really wanted to punch something. Or shoot something.

She vaguely remembered when her mom had left. There had been a lot of boxes stacked around the house, and her parents were yelling. She wasn't sure if they were yelling at her or not, but she'd grabbed her stuffed duck, Gladys, just in case she was in trouble. And then her mom was gone.

Juliet had cried for her over the next couple of days, even though her dad explained that she'd see her soon. She didn't know what "soon" meant and anyway, she wanted her mom right now! And then the boxes were gone and her dad had put her in the car and they left. They were in the car for a long time before they stopped, and then they had a new house. It wasn't as big as the one they'd left, but she still had Gladys.

She waited and waited for her mom, and after a while she stopped asking about her. Then her dad told her that her mom had left them and wasn't coming back. She cried a long time after that. And she never mentioned her mom again. That's why Millie had thought that other woman was Juliet's mother. But she wasn't, and besides, she was mean except when Dad was around.

Jules tried never to think about her mother. Once in a while, like that last time when Abby had heard her crying, she missed her a lot and wished she'd come back. But she never really thought it would happen. And now. . . now she didn't know what to think.

She tried desperately to put everything in perspective: her mom had left to take a job; they were supposed to go to Chicago later. Her dad took her somewhere else. And Abby found her. That about summed it up. She supposed that if anyone were to blame, it was her dad. Funny, she never thought about him much, or really missed him at all. Huh.

Then she heard a twig snap. She froze.

After a moment, she realized it was just a small animal. Probably. She kept walking and was nearing the church in town when she heard another noise. Snap.

Dropping to a crouch, she pulled out her knife and scanned the immediate area. Movement in the brush, to her right.

"Don't move, little girl, I've got you covered. Just put down that knife, nice and slow."

Involuntarily non-compliant, Jules nearly jumped out of her skin at the sound of a voice that she'd never before heard. In fact, there'd been no sign of anyone for years and years and this man had just appeared out of nowhere? Taking a deep breath, she set down the knife.

A huge bear of a man squeezed between two saplings and warily approached her. "Do you have any more weapons on you?"

Still stunned, Jules shook her head. She kept her wits enough to avoid disclosing the fact that her Glock was in her coat pocket.

"All right, then. Set yourself down here for a spell and let's get acquainted. No point in losing our manners. What's your name?"

"Juliet. And what's yours?" Jules had recovered enough to begin to regain some of her composure.

"Well, you can call me Walt. Since that's my name and all. Now tell me, what's a little thing like you doing out here by yourself? You are by yourself, ain't you?"

Jules nodded.

"Uh-huh. So you want me to believe that you've just been packing around the area, all these years since you were a little thing all by your lonesome? Ever since the government went to hell in a handbasket?"

"Yes," said Jules.

"I see you're going to stick to one-word answers and such, and I don't blame you a bit. Well, then, if you're so inclined, you might be interested in joining up with me and my kids. You don't appear to be a threat, so I guess it's just best if you come on back with me. We'll take care of you and feed you and all that." This seemed to be quite a speech for Walt, as he almost looked embarrassed to have spoken at such length.

Jules wasn't afraid of him, but still. . . running into a complete stranger, in the woods? One who invited her back to his place? She'd read enough books to know that things like this didn't usually end well.

"Tell you what," said Jules, rising to her feet and pulling out the Glock in one smooth motion, "I'll follow you back to. . . your place. To meet your 'kids.' Let's go, Walt."

Walt didn't look angry. On the contrary, he let out a deep, booming laugh. "Well, I'll be!" But before he could ask Juliet if she knew how to use a gun, he heard the distinctive click. "All right then, little girl, come on. Follow me!"

Forty-five minutes later, Walt, with Jules a few steps behind, Glock still at the ready, reached a small clearing. A dirt plot to one side of a small log structure suggested a spot for a garden. A light wisp of smoke showed up against the dark sky. Walt gave a low whistle.

The cabin door opened and a small girl, maybe ten years old, appeared in the rectangle of light holding a heavy shotgun. A boy of about the same age walked out from around the corner with a pistol held in shaking hands.

"It's okay, kids," called out Walt. "I brought home some company tonight!"

"I've got her covered, Walt!" A voice came from somewhere in the darkness. Jules was beginning to think she'd gotten into far more than she could handle.

"Put them guns away, kids, it's okay. This here is Jules, I found her out wandering around close to town. Go on, now. Do what I say." Walt spun around and snatched Jules' gun out of her hand before she could blink. He clicked the safety on and handed it back to her. "Gotta be careful with that, little girl."

The two kids Jules could see had put their weapons away and the third one, the voice, jumped down from a large oak tree directly to her left. Her legs were shaking and she wanted to laugh. Or cry. Still, this could be a setup. . . but she didn't really believe that. She was astounded that these people had been living here, so close to them, and she'd had no clue.

"Come on in," said Walt. "We'll tell our story, if you'll tell yours."

Chapter Nineteen

Brad slipped through the door just as the sun rose. Abby was waiting, pacing, wondering just how close he was going to cut it. She was prepared to run, if necessary, but would rather not be ambushed if she could help it. She was holding the business end of the .357 at the door.

"Sheesh, Ab, put that thing away. Can't afford to have you take any more years off my life." He sat down and pulled off his boots. "Relax, we're safe here. Got the intel we need, and I'll tell you all about it in a minute. Give a guy a chance to unwind, would you?

"Hey, where'd you go, anyway?" He was looking at her damp jeans and boots. Damn.

"Oh, nowhere in particular," Abby said. "Go on, you first."

Brad raised an eyebrow questioningly, but Abby remained quiet. "Fine," he said. "So, I went downtown. And it was weird. I saw no one at all. No people. I mean, sure, they could have been asleep, but still—at seven o'clock in the evening? No lights on, anywhere, until I got into the military district.

"I still had most of my uniform, even if I was missing ID, so I kind of just blended into a barracks where I didn't know anyone. I mean, well, I didn't think I knew anyone. Turns out that I kind of did, but he was just infantry, so he hadn't heard about how things went down a few weeks ago. Lucky for me.

"So we're hanging out, grabbed some dinner, and I'm kind of pumping him for information; then an officer walked in. We all jumped up, saluted, yada yada, and then he came down the line. He stopped right in front of me and stared for a minute. Made me damn uncomfortable and all I could think of was that you'd be sitting here waiting and waiting.

"Anyway, I took off not too long after that, made some excuse about an assignment."

"Nope," Abby told him. "I wouldn't have been sitting here waiting, I can tell you that much. I'd have come to bust your sorry ass out of there. But go on—what did you find out?"

"First off, Pops is still here. And he's still looking for you. Apparently, I was just the one to use to find you. . . and Juliet. Sheesh, Ab, what'd you do to piss him off?"

Abby shrugged. "Beats me. But I still think you're wrong. Pops wouldn't. . . he just wouldn't, okay? Can we drop that part now? What else?"

"Abby, there is no 'what else', not really. He wants you dead. Or something." Brad took her hands in his. "I'm serious. Listen to me, Abby. He's not stopping. He's got patrols out everywhere. He knows you weren't at the camp when we came, but he doesn't know where you are now. I don't think you're safe anywhere in the area."

Abby stared at him. "But. . . why?"

"So you believe me now? Just like that?"

Her head was spinning. She did. She didn't. Pops? No. No way. But. . . .

"What about EJ?"

"I don't think he knows about her," said Brad. "My orders were take out you and Juliet; no one else ever came up. I'm thinking it has something to do with resistance—and not just your managing to stay alive all this time, I'm talking about resistance to VADER. You, me, Juliet, and the others. They're still trying to figure it all out, what went wrong. And, I'm guessing, find a way to make it work better the next time."

"But you said there was hardly anyone here. Why would they want to kill off more?"

"Just the wrong ones, Abby. People like us. People who don't want their form of government. That's what it comes down to. They want to rule, not lead. Their own little kingdom."

Abby was silent for a long time.

"Then we need to leave. Go somewhere they can't find us. Ever."

Brad cleared his throat. "Or we could fight them."

Abby laughed. "Right. All three of us. And two kids."

"It's a thought."

"Yeah. A crazy one. Go to sleep, Brad." She rolled over into her blankets and was soon asleep herself.

An hour later, she was awake again, staring at the ceiling.

Leave. Stay. Fight. The words kept repeating themselves in her head. Leave, and go where? Stay? Where they were now? Go back to the camp? She didn't know. Nowhere seemed safe, not around here, and so far they had no idea what was happening in other parts of the country. Except Chicago. And the only reason to go there, into the lion's den, would be to fight.

And she had the girls to think about. It was no kind of life, running and hiding and barely getting by—but the alternative was worse. Death. Maybe. She was just so tired, tired of it all.

She finally fell back into a restless, dream-filled sleep.

Jules made the hike back to the house, lost in thought. Mr. Whitman, for that was indeed Walt's name, had been a survivalist long before it became fashionable; or rather, long before it had become a necessity. Living alone, having little contact with his neighbors, it had been some time before he knew all that happened. He kept on, as he had said, because there wasn't anything else for him to do. Then, one day while he was out hunting, he'd heard a sound in the bushes.

Just like how Abby had found her.

But Walt found a little boy, David, with his small bow and arrow aimed directly at Walt's head. Walt talked him out of the tree stand he'd been sleeping in and took him home. Two months later, he came across a cabin much like his own. Inside, there were two small children, Elizabeth and Johnny; their parents were hanging from the barn rafters. Dead.

Walt brought them home.

He had a habit of coming into the town just once or twice a year, to scavenge, just as Jules had been doing. This time, however, he found Jules. Or she found him. Either way, thought Jules, it was an interesting turn of events. She wondered what Abby was going to say. And Allison.

She took the porch steps in a leap and opened the door.

"We have neighbors," she announced.

Brad and Abby arrived home that evening. Before they barely had gotten inside the door, EJ was bombarding them with Jules' news. By the time they had dinner, and EJ was getting ready for bed, she was all talked out. Thankfully, because Abby was exhausted from all the chatter. Sometimes it was a lot easier to be around adults, even if you were dodging Colonel Hoefer's men.

They had a lot to discuss, obviously, not the least of which was whether or not they should stay where they were now or leave for. . . somewhere else. Jules went first, since her information was the least unsettling and involved no real decision-making. After all, it was, as EJ had said, "news."

"So, this Walt has been living out there, with these kids, for ten years?" asked Abby. She found this a little hard to believe for some reason. Maybe she was suspicious of anyone who'd survived and avoided the patrols.

"Well," Jules said, "you lived with us."

The girl had a point. "True," said Abby. "And there are how many of them?"

"Four. Walt, and the three kids, Elizabeth, Johnny, and David." Jules blushed.

Alison and Abby exchanged looks. Brad spoke up. "So tell us about this David, Jules." Abby poked him and he at least wiped the smirk off his face.

"Nothing to tell," said Jules, airily. "I'm going to bed. Let me know what you all decide." And she rolled over, pulling the blankets over her head.

The adults managed to make it into the kitchen before smothering their laughter.

"Totally not like Jules to tell us to decide anything," said Abby. "Alison, your daughter likes to make the plans, or at least insert her opinion into everything. I'm thinking there's a little more to this David than we thought." She laughed again.

"She gets it from you, Abby, but that's just my thought. I certainly never try to call the shots."

Brad choked on his coffee. "Right. Okay."

When he'd recovered, he continued, "So will our plans include Walt and his gang?" He looked at Abby and Alison. "What? We all know you two are going to figure this out. Mostly. I'm just along for the ride."

"I suppose," said Abby, "that's up to Walt. But we need to make some decisions first." She turned to Alison. "Brad thinks we should fight."

"Hmmm," said Alison thoughtfully.

"You, too?" asked Abby. "How? With what? And for heaven's sake, why?" She bit her lip. "I'm tired of hiding, yes, but hiding or running or whatever you want to call it is practically the same thing. I'm a wreck. I don't want to do this anymore, dammit!"

Brad put his arm around her. "Ab, it's the only way to stop it. Yeah, you're tired of it. We all are, although you've taken the brunt of it all these years. Well, it's not just you anymore, you've got us now. And maybe Walt. Jules is practically all grown up, there's that too.

"If we don't fight, if we keep running, they're going to find us. Or find you. And Jules. And EJ, yeah, they'll find her too, Abby. Look at me." He turned her head gently and looked her in the eye. "No choice. Not if you want it to stop."

"Brad's right," said Alison. "Although I'll be the first to admit that I want to sink those bastards. They cost me a lot already. But, Abby, think about it. Maybe we can stop hiding. Or," she added, "maybe we'll all end up dead. But it's better than sitting around waiting, and I intend to take more than a few with me."

Brad glared at her.

"What? You both know it's true."

"I'll fight," said Jules from the doorway. She went to stand beside her mother. "And so will David. We, er, talked a little bit last night." She blushed.

Abby looked up and smiled sadly. "I knew you'd be listening. All right. We'll fight. But only," she said directly to Brad, "because I want to. Not because you said so."

Chapter Twenty

They spent the following day sorting and making lists of what to pack and what to leave there, stored as securely as possible. They opted to have two caches, one in the barn and one in the attic of the house. Alison and Jules set out late in the day to begin moving the items that were stockpiled in town. Jules won the driving argument by stating sensibly that she knew where they were going. Alison gritted her teeth and hung on, although she was pleasantly surprised that Jules indeed knew what she was doing.

They reached the church first and quickly loaded nearly everything that Jules had stored there. It was nearly full dark when they finished at the train station and moved across the street to the old restaurant and inn.

Jules went straight to the rear of the building, to the walk-in cooler in the kitchen. Alison paused to squint at the antique bar and its backdrop of shattered mirrors. A quick check revealed that nothing remained except a few dirt-crusted glasses and some old syrup canisters, rusted and molding. Alison sighed. Figured.

She caught up with Jules just in time to see her daughter lugging a heavy case of something through the lobby.

"Oh, there you are. Mom, could you grab the other one back there?"

Alison stared at Jules. "So you drink, too?"

Jules laughed. "No, Mom. Duh. This is for Abby. She doesn't drink much, but yeah. . . there's more stuff, in the back room. I figured since we're leaving, may as well take whatever we have room for. Guess whoever left it forgot about it or something."

Alison didn't answer, she just got to work. Checking out the storeroom.

"Yes!" she nearly shouted, forgetting for a nanosecond that she was supposed to be quiet and quick. She grabbed two bottles of tequila and stuck them in her coat pockets before picking up the last case of beer.

When they got back to the house, they left most of the stuff in the barn except for a few bundles. They found Abby patiently trying to explain to EJ why she simply could not take all of her books. She looked to Alison for assistance, who blithely said, "Nope, sorry, can't help you there. I seem to have skipped the reasoning with six-year-olds section."

Jules took over the task as Abby left the room in exasperation. She slumped into a chair, but brightened considerably when she saw the newly arrived supplies. "Cheers," she told Alison, raising a can. "Help yourself."

"No thanks," said Alison. She lifted her bottle. "But 'cheers' anyway! Hey, where's Brad?"

"Oh, he went to meet Walt." Abby shrugged and took another drink, missing the look in Alison's eyes.

"Do you think that was smart? I mean, maybe Jules should have introduced them or something. If he's some kind of survivalist guy, he might shoot first and ask questions later."

"Nope. You're right. He should have waited. But I haven't heard any shots, and he's been gone a while."

Alison looked marginally relieved. She glanced out the window. "I think he's back. Someone's coming. Two someones."

Abby jumped to her feet and had her gun out seconds before she heard Brad whistle. She opened the door and Brad came in, along with a young man almost as tall as he. They shook off some newly fallen snow and removed their coat before Brad introduced David.

"Nice to meet you, Miss Abby, Miss Alison," said David. "Mr. Brad told me all about you both."

Hearing voices, EJ and Jules burst through the door, but Jules backed out quickly when she saw David. She returned a moment later at a more decorous pace. "Oh, hello, David." She was blushing as she held out her hand.

Alison and Abby exchanged winks over their heads, which went unseen by the teenagers, thankfully. Brad was grinning openly at them.

"Uh, hello, Juliet," David said, formally, taking her hand briefly.

"Well, good," said Brad, "Now that we have all that out of the way, let's get this all lined out. David wants to come with us. Walt isn't so sure, but he's thinking about it. He really needs David to help out here, but he knows he can't hold him back forever. And then there are the two littler ones, Elizabeth and Johnny."

Abby was thinking. She knew Jules was interested in David and, really, she couldn't see David being anything but an asset.

Walt, too. But two little kids? How old were they, anyway? And she didn't really care if they had any skills, she just couldn't put a couple kids in the line of fire, so to speak. Or literally.

The room was silent. They were waiting for her to say something.

Then they heard the choppers.

Jules doused the fire; Alison blew out the lantern. Brad and Abby grabbed the rifles by the door, and EJ ran for the ammo box. David had rushed to the living room behind Jules, peering out a tiny spot where the blanket didn't quite cover the glass when she gestured quickly and whispered. Alison joined him..

There was nothing they could do, really. Just wait and watch. And hope the choppers weren't armed. Or aiming. They hovered for a good thirty minutes, circled, and flew back to the east.

"How in hell," said Abby, through clenched teeth. "How?"

They gathered in the living room. "All right. We're going. Everyone. Jules, take David back to Walt's. He can get what he needs and pack up. See if Walt and the kids are coming with us. Get back here as quickly as you can." Abby was thinking as she spoke, fast and furiously.

"Brad, take EJ out to the barn and start loading up the trucks. Alison and I will finish up here." She gave EJ a quick hug as the little girl went out the door, then she turned to Alison.

The former captain seemed to be frozen in her chair. She roused briefly when Abby shoved the tequila bottle into her hands, shuddered, and took a long drink. Wiping her mouth, she croaked, "God, I hate those things." Looking more like her usual self, Alison finally stood up. "Tell me what to do."

They made short work of rolling up the blankets and bedding, and packing the girls' books and personal items. It was growing colder, but at least the snow had stopped. They lugged everything out to the barn so Brad could finish loading. EJ was standing precariously on top of one of the cabs, directing him to open spots to stow smaller packages. Abby wasn't worried; the kid was as sure-footed as a goat.

They went back inside to warm up a bit, stirring up the fire just enough to thaw their freezing hands. At last, Jules and David were back, along with Walt and the younger kids. They didn't have a lot of gear, mostly blankets, weapons, and ammo. The kids were dressed in so many layers they looked like beach balls with arms and legs.

Introductions were made hastily, and Brad directed them to the barn. Abby and Walt would take one truck, with David and EJ. He and Alison and Steph, Johnny, and Jules would drive the other one. The last of the gear was stowed and they were all aboard when Brad thought to ask, "Um, Ab, where are we going, anyway?"

"We're going to camp."

Brad was stumped. "But. . . Pops already wiped it out!"

"Yeah. Maybe. Here's the thing, though: I don't know what he took out, and neither do you. I still have some things down there, and I know of a few places that he's probably forgotten about. Seven hundred acres there, Brad. And besides, he knows we aren't there. Get it?"

And he did. Since Pops hadn't found him, or Abby and Jules, he was more likely to keep hunting—anyplace but where he'd already looked.

Simple. Brilliant. They headed south.

Abby and Alison left the others at the trucks, now hidden at the base of Sunnytop on the lake side of the hill. They'd hiked up to the top just as the earliest of the sun's rays reached the peak. Abby quickly scaled a tall tree and pulled out her field glasses.

Scanning from left to right, she could see that the cave where she'd lived all those years was more than likely completed demolished. The entire side of the hill was burned and black. Directly across the valley, the top of Pioneer appeared to be untouched; but the next valley over, as well as Purple Mountain and the site they'd stayed at once upon a time, were gone. She swung back for just a second to look at where the old infirmary had once stood. . . .

Disheartened, Abby lowered herself to the ground.

"Let's start bringing everything up," she told Alison. "Go on down and let Brad know. I'll meet you back here in, oh, an hour or so."

Abby walked along the ridge, alone, Mossberg over her shoulder. For a brief moment, she almost felt her old self again, her younger self, back when things were a lot simpler. And safer. She moved down off the hill and crossed a gravel road, overgrown and with deep ruts, then began ascending again until she came to Site 4. They'd never used it, but had emptied out the cabinets where the extra canvas had been stored.

She unlocked a nearly new padlock and surveyed her cache. Besides the AT4, her legacy from Janey, there were a collection of weapons that would make any soldier proud. And all the accompanying ammo. She had one more stash, mostly additional ammo, but had no idea if it was still intact. She grabbed what she could carry and locked up the rest.

A short time later, she walked along the top of Purple, looking down through the twisted, dead trunks of hundreds of trees below her. She paused at the old graves from long ago; it had been quite some time since she'd hiked over this way from the cave. But she remembered them all, every day.

Abby descended into a small, hidden valley on the north side of the hill. There was the spring to which she and Juliet had gone to play hooky once or twice. That's where they'd set up camp. She surveyed the area, mentally marking out the site, and stashed her pack and everything she'd gathered at Site 4. Then she began the walk back to meet up with the others.

As she approached the spot where she'd last seen Alison, Jules came running to her. "EJ's disappeared!" Her heart in her throat, Abby raced ahead, Jules trying to keep up.

Brad and Walt were deep in discussion, and Abby could hear the others calling for EJ as loudly as they dared. "What happened?" she demanded. "Where is she?" She was breathing hard, but not from exertion; her face was pale and her hands shook.

Brad put his arm around her. "We brought the last of the supplies up, and EJ was here. Then she wasn't. That's all we know. No one took her, Abby; there's no one here but us." He walked her over to a fallen log and made her sit down.

Abby tried to calm her mind. . . to think. If EJ wasn't answering, she had wandered very far indeed. But that didn't sound like her; the little girl knew how to follow directions, she knew how important that was and had known practically since birth. So she was unable to answer. Or. . . she was answering, but couldn't be heard.

"Cave," said Abby. "There's a cave up here, somewhere. I never looked, never had the time somehow, but I recall Pops telling us once about several of them, up here on Sunnytop."

"Well," said Walt slowly. "that's an idea, now. Would she go in a cave, by herself?" The others had made their way back by now, and little Elizabeth clung closely to Walt, her eyes huge. Her brother stood beside her, holding her hand.

"No," said Abby. "Unless she fell in. There are no rock formations up here, so if there's a cave the entrance has to be at ground level. Where was the last spot you saw her?"

"Over there," said Elizabeth, pointing. "We were just walking around, not far, and when I turned around she was gone."

Abby took a deep breath. "Okay, then, we'll start there. Everyone spread out a bit, and I'll call for her; the rest of you, listen for EJ to answer." She staggered when she stood up, her legs still shaking. Alison reached out to steady her but Abby put out her hand. "No. I'm fine. I just need to. . . to get a grip on things." After a moment, she was as fine as she was going to be until EJ was found, and she began to call her daughter's name.

Walt heard the answering cry just before Abby did, some fifteen minutes later. She dropped to her knees and began shoving aside leaves and sticks, calling EJ. Then she slipped, and nearly went head-first into the widening gap. Walt grabbed her arm to stop her fall.

"EJ! Can you hear me?"

"Mommy?" Her voice sounded tiny.

"EJ, are you okay? Are you hurt? Tell me what you can see down there."

"I'm okay, Mom. I landed on my feet. Mostly." Everyone smiled in relief. "But I can't see much, it's dark you know." Brad chuckled and even Abby smiled this time.

"Can you walk closer to my voice? Can you see any light up here?" Either that cave was awfully deep, or EJ had wandered off a bit. Abby wasn't sure which it was, but as long as EJ was found they'd get her out.

Then, about 20 feet below, Abby saw the little face turned up toward hers. She almost cried in relief. "EJ, is this where you fell in?" The opening, even cleared of debris was really small—almost too small for EJ to have fallen through and certainly too small for any of the adults to get through.

"No. I walked a little bit, until I couldn't see very well."

"Brad, hand me your light."

David knew immediately what Abby was doing. He intercepted the light and tied it securely to a loop of rope, then handed it to Abby so she could lower it down the hole. She smiled at him gratefully.

"All right, EJ, take this light and start walking to where you fell in. Don't untie it, and if the rope stops, you stop too, okay?"

"Okay, Mom. I got this." Abby almost laughed.

"And EJ, when you get there, or when the rope stops, shout as loudly as you can."

"Okay, Mom. Sheesh." This time, Abby did laugh, but it was a nervous one.

Robin Tidwell

Chapter Twenty-One

BOOM!

The choppers circled, the bombs fell. Colonel Hoefer had started the new year with a bang, literally as well as figuratively. He was determined that this would be his year, his triumph, his reward. In fact, he'd even gone along on this mission as an observer. Apparently, he was the only one capable of doing the job and he wanted to be right there, on the edge of the action. Not in it, of course. That would be too dangerous for someone like himself.

From the air, the tiny town of Labadie appeared to be ringed with thick, black smoke. The colonel's chopper set down on Front Street, in the vacant lot next to the old train station. He strode confidently down the street to the restaurant and inn, where he intended to set up his headquarters. The men would be bivouacked in the train station, apart from him and his officers. They were expendable, after all, merely mercenaries. The staff were all career men, and not one would hesitate to use any of the others as a stepping-stone to greater things.

Major Wilson spread out a map of the area on some tables hastily shoved together. The northern part of St. Louis County had several large, red Xs marked on it, as did a large chunk of Jefferson County. Babler Park was similarly identified. The officers huddled around the table, discussing the parameters of this mission in hushed tones, while Colonel Hoefer gazed out the window. He was imagining a scene in, perhaps, the French Revolution, some painting or other that he'd seen once; pity he had no sword.

He finally deigned to grace the others with his presence and he studied the map thoughtfully. Abby perhaps was here, locally; she had been there, of that he was certain. He was also convinced that she hadn't gone north, nor had they found any trace of her there, and he knew that Brad had carried out the bombing of Babler and had destroyed Abby's supplies in that location. Most of the park, in fact, had been wiped out. It would be decades before it regained any resemblance to what it had been once.

So. She hadn't gone north or south. She wasn't in the city, in fact, he'd tracked her out here. So here she must be—because he was seldom wrong. Occasionally, of course, he failed to deliver what his superiors requested, but that was hardly his fault. Someone always came along to interfere with his plans, like Brad. . . or that Alison.

Step one: search this area of Franklin County. Perhaps a bit further, into wine country. Plenty of places to hide there. A few small towns were still fairly intact, scattered here and there off side roads away from the larger tourist spots. And farms, too, of course. They had their work cut out for them. The best they could hope for was that Abby would make a mistake and run. But of course, Colonel Hoefer had a plan for that, too.

"Men," he addressed the group around the table. "Inform your squad leaders that every building in town must be searched; pay special attention to anything that appears out of the ordinary, such as trap doors, heavy furniture, and so forth.

"These fugitives are resourceful and dangerous. They must be terminated without delay; however, prior to allowing that, they must be brought here, to me. I have many questions which must be answered."

The captains scrambled to leave the room and assemble their men. Major Wilson joined the colonel by the large front window.

"I'm curious," said the Major, "Why these two in particular?"

"I knew them once," said Pops. "A long time ago, before they turned against us."

Twenty miles away, Abby and her group were finished with the camp set-up. EJ had been pulled out of the underground cave at the same spot into which she'd fallen earlier in the day, a fluke which should have at least resulted in severe injury but had left her merely bruised. Abby was grateful enough that she listened to EJ's nonstop monologue about the incident without showing the least of her frequent impatience.

Finally, though, even she grew weary of her daughter's repetition and solved the issue with sitting her down to eat dinner. Alison had put together a passable stew, considering the immediate lack of provisions, and the group gathered around the small fire.

The three youngsters were huddled together, whispering, and Jules and David both claimed they were sitting so close because of the cold wind. The adults weren't fooled. Even Walt looked amused.

"Well," he said. "That was some trip, folks. Have to say, I'm looking forward to stretching out to sleep tonight; that truck was a bit cramped. But before I do, I'd like to know what the next step is in this plan of yours?"

Abby looked up. Everyone was watching her.

"Well, initially we had to get away. So, um, we did that. And now. . . ." She looked at Brad. "A little help here?"

"What, me? I thought you had this." He looked startled. "Well, um, yeah. We fight them."

"Huh," said Walt. "Do you have a plan? Or something?"

"Hey," said Abby, looking at Brad again. "This was your plan, remember? I was all for hiding out, but no, you said we had to fight them. And then I agreed. So now what?"

Alison spoke up. "We have to fight on their terms. . . um, beat them at their own game. You know what I mean." She stopped. "Basically," she added, "we need to line out their agenda, and ours, and plan the opposition for recruitment and training. And then we'll be ready to infiltrate, either overtly or covertly."

Brad looked at Abby.

"I think she has the plan, Walt," he said. "Go on, Alison. Where do we start?"

"Oh," she answered, "I don't want to step out of line." She looked down demurely.

"Bull," laughed Abby. "You do too! Go ahead, spill it. We can always out-vote you if it stinks. Or withhold tequila." She winked at Brad.

Alison laughed too. "Yeah, you got me there. And don't mess with my tequila! But seriously—what do we have now? Walt, me, you, Brad, Jules, and David. That's six of us."

"Five," corrected Abby. "Someone has to stay with the kids."

"Hey, we're not kids!" said Elizabeth, indignantly. "I'm almost a teenager and Johnny here, he's a great shot. We can help, too."

"Yes, dear," said Abby, "But I'm not in the habit of sending nine-year-olds off to fight. I'm not real thrilled with teenagers doing it either."

"I'm not nine," Elizabeth assured her, "I'm twelve. I'll be thirteen in just a few months."

Abby looked questioningly at Walt. He nodded.

"Either way," said Abby firmly, "you're not going anywhere."

"Where was I?" asked Alison. "Oh. So, five of us go into the city. We find a spot to hunker down. David and Jules will really stand out, because of their ages; there just aren't many teenagers in the cities these days. So they'll have to stay put." Alison eyed her daughter. "Will you two need a chaperone? Because we really can't take you if you do, we can't spare anyone to babysit once we get downtown."

"Um, no," mumbled Jules, blushing.

"No, ma'am," spoke up David. "I want to fight, not. . . ." He turned beet red.

Alison grinned. "Takes care of that," she said.

"Yep," said Abby. "She didn't even see that one coming."

It was Walt's turn. "I reckon I'll stay here with the kids. Johnny won't talk to no one but me anyway, and Elizabeth and EJ will be a big help. We'll hold down the fort here, so to speak."

"Johnny doesn't like to talk," added Elizabeth. "Not since our folks. . . died." She put her arm around her little brother. Johnny smiled sadly, but still didn't speak.

"But, Mom, can't I go with you and Jules?" EJ had suddenly realized that the conversation was serious and she pulled her nose out of her book. She'd only ever been around Abby and Jules, and then Brad and Alison had shown up, and now there were more people. It was a lot for a six-year-old to take in all at once.

But Abby knew that EJ was pretty darn resilient and, while she wasn't thrilled with leaving her again, it was what had to be done. "No, EJ, you'll stay here with Mr. Whitman.

"All right, it's settled. But we'll be here a few days yet, getting ready to leave and finalizing our plans. And we need to go over some things with Walt and the kids."

"All the buildings are clear, sir."

Major Wilson nodded. "Dismissed." He walked over to Colonel Hoefer who was, once again, gazing out the window, lost in thought.

"Colonel, all the squads have reported. There is no one in town. Shall we begin searching the immediate area? Colonel?"

"Yes?" said Pops, turning towards the other officer.

"I said, sir, shall we begin the next phase?"

"Of course, Major. Must I point out everything, be responsible for every single detail? Yes, yes, search everything. Pay special attention to that church down the street, and the trucking company warehouse. Then we'll move out farther. They must be here.

"In fact, to be sure of it, once each building is cleared, I want it detonated. Every one of them."

"Yes, sir." Major Wilson took his leave, giving his superior a penetrating look which, fortunately, was lost on the colonel.

Pops went back to his window-gazing. Incompetents! He knew she was here. She had to be, because if they couldn't find her, that meant she had truly gone underground and combing the entire countryside was not an option. If only they'd send him more troops and equipment, he could flush her out. And the girl, Juliet. That would slow her down.

He frowned. That girl wasn't so little anyone, was she? Perhaps she should be the one to whom he should turn his attention. She must be, what? Fifteen? Sixteen? He'd best give this more thought. Perhaps he needed another plan.

Robin Tidwell

Chapter Twenty-Two

Abby and Alison shared a tent. EJ wanted to stay with her new friend Elizabeth. Jules was their designated babysitter, a position that didn't go over quite as well as hoped. David and Johnny bunked with Brad and Walt, and Johnny was thrilled to be included with them.

Alison poured a shot for each of them before they turned in, and Abby made a face as hers went down. Sure, it would help her sleep, but she'd almost rather drink some cold medicine. It tasted about the same. Still, it was warming, so she didn't complain. Much.

"You know what they say," said Alison. "Cut off the head, and the snake dies; that's our goal. The colonel."

Abby was silent.

"The Federal Building is where all the offices are housed. I'm pretty sure Brad and I can get in there. Our operation was top-secret and hardly anyone knew me anyway, since I'd just gotten here before we were sent out.

"So, if we move on Colonel Hoefer, and he's, er, out of commission, then there'll be some confusion and a break in communication. That's how they set it up—one big cheese, lots of little cheeses.

"What do you think?"

"First," said Abby, "what am I supposed to be doing while you're off gallivanting to assassinate this guy? I know the kids will be serving as lookouts and running messages, we've covered that, but what did you have in mind for me? Assuming, of course, I'm okay with killing the colonel."

Alison frowned. "Of course we have to take him out. That's the first step. What's the problem?"

"Let me tell you about Colonel Hoefer." And Abby did. She told Alison how she'd first met Pops, and how he'd been down here with them for all that time, struggling right along with the whole group. About Millie, and how he'd been with her, and how he'd taught Jules some of her lessons.

"Wow," said Alison. "all that, he turned out to be a real bastard? No wonder you have mixed feelings about this. But I can assure, if Brad hasn't already, that this is not the same guy you knew, or thought you knew. I appreciate the time he had with my daughter, but it kind of makes my skin crawl, you know?"

Abby did know. It made hers crawl too. "all right, assuming we take him out. Or you and Brad do it, or whoever and however. What do you want me to do?"

"Blow up stuff, of course," smirked Alison. "Brad said you like that kind of thing."

"Well, yeah. Who doesn't?" Abby smiled wickedly. "Speaking of, I heard something about you too, and I have a present for you. Call it a late Christmas gift." She reached under her bedroll for a long object, wrapped in oilskin, and handed it to Alison.

Alison looked puzzled for a moment until she opened the package. It was the AT4.

"Merry Christmas," said Abby. "Brad said you liked big guns. I have ammo for it too, of course. It was a legacy from. . . from a dear friend. We went through quite a lot together and well, I want you to have it."

"I should be giving you a gift, Abby. You raised my daughter all these years, kept her alive and well." Alison was about to cry.

"Naw, that's okay," said Abby. "Find me some C4 and we're even!"

In three days' time, they were ready to leave. Brad and Abby had gone over everything with Walt, including escape plans if it came to that, as well as a rendezvous point. Abby had taken him to her caches, scattered around the area, and he'd pronounced them nicely done. She took this as high praise, as more of Walt's background became known.

His family was from Arkansas and had lived off the land even into more modern times. He'd only gone to school through the sixth grade, but had worked on ranches in the area all his life when he wasn't helping out on the family plot. They never had much, he'd said, not even indoor plumbing until he was nearly grown; that's when he'd built his own cabin near his folks. His brothers and sisters had all left town as soon as they were able, but he stayed. He hunted, he fished, he had a nice little garden. Hardly ever had need of cash money, and had never owned a car.

Walt planned to teach the kids left in his care all he could, just in case someday he wasn't around. Johnny was already, at age eight, a fair hand with trapping and fishing, and Elizabeth was an excellent shot. He figured she and EJ would get along just fine. "And maybe that little EJ can teach me a thing or two," he said. "about book-learning and stuff."

Abby smiled and impulsively hugged him. "I'm sure you all will do just fine."

The five of them were cramped in the truck, but Abby remarked dryly that Jules and David didn't seem to mind. She was worried about Jules, and she knew that Alison was too. Jules had never known anyone her own age and, while David was nice and very polite, she was afraid that Jules might get in over her head. Of course, she was being way overprotective and knew she needed to stay out of it. Now that Alison was here, it was her place, really, to do or say anything. Still, she kept her eye on them.

The truck bounced over ruts and tossed the occupants around the double cab while they drove cross-country, without lights as usual. Brad was behind the wheel and Abby couldn't resist giving him some pointers along with her precise directions. Of course, Alison chimed in frequently too.

"I'm starting to think you two are ganging up on me!"

"Duh," said Abby, noticing from her vantage point in the back that Brad's hand had snaked over to cover Alison's for a brief moment. Hmmm. Interesting development.

Hours later, Abby roused Jules and David, who had dozed off, as they had reached their destination: the former military installation and cemetery just south of the city limits. Brad drove around to the river side of the huge compound, to the old trading post building. There, they swiftly unloaded their supplies and Brad took the truck into the trees near the railroad tracks, easily within sprinting distance, but near a planned escape route.

The old wooden doors creaked as Abby led the way down into the cellar. It was damp and cool, especially in the winter, but had the advantage of being windowless with thick walls. There was only one way out, which could be good or bad; easily more defensible, yet it could become a death trap under the wrong circumstances.

They arranged their bedding and supplies, weapons stacked in the corner, and sat down to finalize their plans. They were just over a mile from the city limits; from there, it was another seven miles to the old brewery and an additional three miles to downtown. The bulk of their supplies would remain here, but they'd pack in enough to manage for a day or two. Radios were to be used only for emergencies or clarification if a possible complication occurred.

David and Jules were given maps of the city to study, memorize, and burn. Alison sat down with them to cover the details and explain their roles, as well as give them pointers on how to behave and to blend in—neither had been in the city, ever, let alone under this new government.

Abby and Brad moved across the room.

"Here's the plan," he told her. "We're starting at the hospital. David, Alison, and I." He raised his hand to stop her objections. "I know what we said, but he won't be in any more danger than he will later when he's running messages and serving as a lookout. We have to pick up something for you. Alison knows where they keep the explosives."

Abby gave him a look. "Yeah, but she says it's policy, in every city. Stored where no one would think to look. Except us. Anyway, he'll run it back to the brewery. Then you can take it from there."

"I don't like it, but I guess that's the way it goes. He knows what he's carrying, right?" She wanted to be sure that the kids knew exactly what they were getting into.

Brad shrugged. "Says he does. Now, after that, Alison and I are going into the Federal Building to find. . . to find the colonel. What?" He saw the look on Abby's face.

"Nothing. I guess. I just find it easier to call him that than. . . than 'Pops'." Abby mostly believed what Pops had become, but not entirely. She still didn't understand why he was after her, personally.

"Yeah. I get that."

"So my targets are still at Olive, Lucas, and Broadway?" Abby had memorized the map coordinates, but was nearly obsessive about checking details. This had to draw as many troops as possible, and certainly nowhere near where the kids would be or where their escape route was located.

"Just make sure that they go off consecutively. We want to cause enough confusion to be able to slip inside and get the bastard."

"Got it," said Abby. "I'll leave as soon as David gets back. Just remember, it'll take me a good hour or so to get to the first target."

"Right," said Brad. "We're giving you two and half altogether, before we go in closer. Just to be safe."

Within minutes, they were ready to move.

Single file, they moved along the tree line as far as the Port Authority. The thin line of cover along the edge of the Mississippi didn't provide much protection against visibility, but no one was around. When they reached the railroad bridge, Abby was still bringing up the rear. She felt her heart leap into her throat as Jules swung up onto the beams, but the girl was like a monkey. Abby let out a sigh of relief. Must have been from all that tree-climbing when she was little.

All five of them crossed the canal without incident, and all five of them barely breathed as they maneuvered around the barracks. Just a few miles to go. Suddenly, off to their right, a small boat appeared on the river. Brad froze and the others followed suit. He pointed. Three men, in a jon boat. The trolling motor was nearly silent. They waited, unmoving, until the boat disappeared around a slight bend.

Brad led them another mile before he stopped again. "Think about this," he whispered. "Three men, no uniforms. Out way past curfew. We can't be the only ones."

"Right," Alison retorted. "Or they're just murderers, or rapists, or soldiers supplementing their pay."

They kept going.

Finally, the old brewery. They followed Brad around the buildings and through the complex to the same door Abby had jimmied open a few weeks ago. Once inside the office, Jules and David sat down and wrapped up in blankets, shivering. They were both in great shape, physically speaking, but the cloak-and-dagger methods had taken a toll. Both, however, claimed that they "just needed a minute" and both appeared eager to continue. The adults went over the plans one last time.

Abby gave Alison a hug and turned to Brad. "Don't get yourself killed, okay? Again?"

"Right back at ya," he responded. "well, except for the 'again' part." Then he grabbed her and swung her around, just like she was one of the kids, and gave her a big kiss on the cheek. "And that," he added, "is for never letting me get away with a damn thing." He blew a kiss towards Jules and went out the door with David and Alison.

And now, they waited.

Robin Tidwell

Chapter Twenty-Three

The trio of rebels walked carefully along Cherokee Street until they crossed Jefferson. Alison nearly laughed when she saw David look both ways; he caught her look and rolled his eyes. "Hey," he whispered, "the city can be a dangerous place."

"Well, yes," said Alison, "but not from traffic!" Brad turned around to shush them both.

They kept walking, cutting through Tower Grove South and past the park, keeping in the shadows, alert for any soldiers. . . or survivors. They were halfway to the old St. Mary's Hospital.

A voice stopped them dead in their tracks: "Who's out there?"

Alison looked at Brad. She grabbed David by the arm and they all ran, stopping only when they reached the crumbling ruins of the Hampton overpass. David was pale and shaky, and Alison struggled for breath. Brad had his gun out, peering into the darkness.

"I'm starting to think this wasn't such a bright idea, Brad. Do we really want to send David back, alone?"

Brad looked at the teenager. He seemed to be recovering quickly. "No choice," he said. "David, you're okay with it, right?"

"Yes, sir. I can do it. I just know to be more careful."

"Thatta boy! All right, let's get this finished." They started off again, cutting through dark, deserted neighborhoods. At last, they reached the back side of the hospital.

"Damn," said Brad. "Look!" He pointed toward the old convent. Soldiers were everywhere. Since religion had been banned, they'd turned the compound into a barracks. This was not going according to plan.

Well, not Brad's plan. Alison, however, was prepared. She opened her pack and pulled out her old captain's coat and cap. Slinging the pack over her shoulder, she told them, "Stay here. I'm going in. And don't argue!" She slipped away into the darkness.

"Damn," said Brad, again.

It was nearly an hour before Alison returned. "There," she said. "Mission accomplished." She carefully set down the heavy pack. "And I got some caps and," she flourished a small, rectangular object, "remotes."

"Good job," said Brad. "But, next time, can we discuss it before you take off on your own?" He wasn't entirely happy.

"Sure," said Alison. "Whatever you want. And by that, I mean just 'whatever'. So there." She stuck out her tongue in his general direction and turned to David. "Okay, kid, this weighs a ton. Well, thirty pounds or so. It won't hurt you unless there's one hell of a detonation; you can drop it, shoot it, light it on fire, nothing but a big stink and some fumes to clear out your lungs. Or, you know, dissolve them eventually.

"Get this back to Abby as fast as you can, but don't get caught. Or shot. And take a different route than the way we came. Whoever hollered at us is probably long gone, but you never know."

"Yes, ma'am," said David. "And good luck to you two!" He slipped off into the darkness.

Brad and Alison went south near McCausland to avoid Forest Park; it had been used as a detention center the last few months. Then they turned east and followed the railroad tracks, keeping to the deep ditch along the side. They took cover behind a falling-down office building at Clark and Jefferson.

"What's the plan, boss?" asked Alison.

"Plan?" said Brad, grinning. "Am I supposed to have a plan? I thought you had the plans. You know, like running into a hospital to grab some C4."

Alison punched him on the arm. "Get serious!"

"Ow," said Brad, rubbing his arm. "Good thing that's not my shooting arm! The plan is to wait. What time is it?"

"Three-thirty."

"Wake me in an hour." Brad stretched out and closed his eyes.

David burst through the door as though the hounds of hell were upon him, waking Jules and sending Abby into a crouch, knife in one hand and .357 in the other.

"What the hell?" she said.

"Um, sorry, ma'am, but. . . there was someone. . . a ways back. I just wanted to. . . get here." David was breathing hard.

"All right, sit down. Breathe. And as soon as you can, tell me what happened." Abby opened the pack David had set on the table and began checking the contents. Jules handed the boy a water bottle.

He gulped it down, then spoke. "We were in Clifton Heights, near the east side, and we heard someone holler,

'Who's there?'. So we took off running. No one shot at us or anything," he added, when Jules looked alarmed. "Anyway, Brad and Alison told me to take a different way back, so I did. I went all the way down to Chippewa this time.

"But right around, um, Jefferson, I heard someone again. Same thing. So I took off and ran the whole way back."

That made Abby's decision. They were short of time, and someone was out there.

"Gear up," she told the kids. "Jules, hand me your pack." She explained the new plan as she placed blocks of the explosive in Jules' pack.

"I'm not leaving you two here. David, you're going to the Broadway location; Jules, you get Lucas Street." She pulled out her map and showed them. "Got it? Good. Now, you take the C4 and you pack it in a crevice. You can be firm with it, it won't blow up. I promise." She smiled grimly. "Any building in your area will do—we aren't out to cause destruction, just a lot of noise. Oh, and pick an empty one, please. And don't get caught. That's number one.

"While you're packing it in, shove two of these detonators in there. Make sure the plastic is completely covering them. Then get your butts back to the meeting spot, here." She showed them the circle on the map. "Once we're all back there, I'll fire it off with the remote.

"If anything goes wrong, hightail it back here and wait for the rest of us. Let's move."

They slipped out the door and moved north, single file and spaced apart. Each had a sidearm out, safety off. The sky far to the east was beginning to become lighter, but dawn was still a good hour away. When they passed the DeMenil Mansion, Abby pointed and held up two fingers. Jules nodded. David looked bewildered for a moment, then he understood. This was a secondary safe spot. In case he'd been followed on the way back to the brewery.

At the two-mile mark, they split up. Abby went west to cut through the SLU campus, while Jules and David continued along the river. Jules would leave him near the Eads Bridge and move down Lucas Street.

Abby broke into a relaxed run, knowing she had the farthest to go and time was running out. She checked her watch. Five-thirty. Brad and Alison would be moving into the Federal Building now. She turned up Compton and kept going.

When Jules and David reached the bridge, they stopped. "Let me go to Lucas, Jules, it's farther and it'll be easier for you to get back to the rendezvous from here." He took her hands in his.

Jules smiled at him, but shook her head. "No, David, no change in the plan unless absolutely necessary. Go do your job, and I'll do mine." Impulsively, she stood on tiptoe and kissed his cheek. Then she disappeared into the darkness.

Brad awoke with a start. Alison put her hand on his arm, and he sat up, fully awake. It was time to go.

The sidled around the corner of the building and stayed close to the walls until the street changed both direction and name. Then they both slipped back into their military personas, coming around to Market Street, walking purposefully and in full view.

They approached the entrance, and the soldier on duty saluted; they paid him no attention and continued to stride through the double-glass doors and across the lobby. Silently, they took the elevator to the fourth floor.

They both jumped when the ding signaled their arrival and looked at each other sheepishly. They stepped out and almost immediately into the requisite janitorial closet.

They waited.

Abby reached the parking garage. She crept around the side of the structure that faced Olive Street and worked quickly to set her charge. She'd used the stuff before; it didn't take long to pack in the ten pounds or so. She made sure the detonators were covered, then went back the way she'd come.

It was just past six o'clock and the first rays of sun were reaching toward the gap on the river where the Arch once stood.

Jules hurried along to an old market on Lucas Avenue. She pulled out the C4 and unwrapped it. Weird. It was like clay, but very smooth. She shrugged. Do the job, she told herself. It was more difficult to pack in the window frame than she'd thought, and she briefly considered another spot but, in the end, all it had to do was make a big bang and not bring down anything. She stuffed the detonators inside and closed up her bag.

Now, to get back. For a second, she had to get her bearings. The sky was beginning to lighten. She turned and went back down Lucas to Tucker, then cut across several blocks. She met David at an abandoned Metrolink station and they walked the rest of the way together, hurrying to beat the ever-approaching daylight.

Abby was waiting impatiently. She knew Brad and Alison had been inside the building for a long time and, the longer they stayed, the better the chance of them being caught. Execution, no doubt, would soon follow. And no benefit of trial or even accusation; their mere presence would warrant an immediate death sentence.

Finally, the kids arrived. The pale glow to the east was brighter. Abby picked up the first remote.

BOOM!

And the second.

BOOM!

The third.

BOOM!

Within minutes, sirens penetrated the early morning stillness. Abby pulled out her field glasses and watched as soldiers poured out of the barracks on Market Street, moving toward the explosion on Olive. David whistled from his vantage point, and Jules passed the signal along to Abby. More troops were moving east. Another contingent left the Federal Building itself and ran to the north.

Abby checked the time. Nearly seven o-clock. Time to go back to the brewery. The rest was up to Alison and Brad. Take out Pops. Abby still couldn't wrap her brain around that whole scenario, but now wasn't the time for contemplation. They had to get under cover. There was a diversion, yes, but regular citizens were surely awake by now and would be coming to check out all the commotion.

David and Jules trailed Abby by several yards as they moved south to Lafayette Park. There, they paused to catch their breath and look back at the chaos. They could see plumes of smoke rising many blocks in the distance but, mercifully, the noise of the sirens was muffled.

They began moving again. East to Soulard, then due south along the riverfront through the warehouse district. They'd heard a few people out and about, footsteps and muted voices, but managed to avoid them. David was about to cross the open space when Abby jerked him backwards.

She pointed.

Several men stood outside the brewery, near the entrance they'd been using. Abby wracked her brain, but could think of nothing left behind that would indicate they, or anyone, had been there recently. Except for the dust on the floor. They'd been in such a hurry that she'd completely forgotten that.

She tried to remember if she'd told Brad about the tunnel. Too late now. She motioned for the kids to follow her, and they retraced their steps, back to Arsenal Street. If those men had field glasses, and if they happened to be looking at the right moment, they might be seen. But there was no other choice.

Chapter Twenty-Four

By the time they heard the uproar in the hallway, as dozens of troops rushed past their hiding place, Brad and Alison had had more than enough of the close quarters. The air was heavy and thick and smelled of bleach. They burst out the door as silence reigned, and made their way quickly down the hall toward the colonel's office.

Straightening her collar, Alison knocked briskly while Brad stood against the wall to the right of the door. They were banking on the fact that, while Pops would send everyone else out into the line of fire, he himself would stay behind to monitor the situation via radio.

"Enter!"

Alison took a deep breath and swung open the door, striding through as she did, and in three quick steps was face to face with the man behind the desk.

"So," said the colonel. "You're alive." He scrutinized his subordinate through narrowed eyes. "And you came back here, why exactly?"

"We came for you, Pops," said Brad, as he entered the room.

The old man paled. "You! I knew you'd be back, I knew those idiots would screw up!" His face contorted with rage.

"Someone always screws up and I end up paying for it. Well, not this time." He fumbled under his desk, but Alison already had him covered.

"Captain! Arrest this man immediately." Pops had regained his equilibrium and reverted to his commanding role.

Alison looked around, bewildered. "What? Me? Are you some kind of whacknut? I came here with him, and we want some answers. What's your deal, anyway?" Her sidearm never wavered, aimed directly at his forehead.

"Now, come on," said Pops, transforming his expression yet again, this time into that of a jovial old man. "Surely we can be reasonable. Brad, obviously your programming is not complete and we must readmit you to tweak things a bit. As long as we can agree, of course, that this. . . this harridan is removed from my presence. Better yet, terminate her, and we'll get down to business."

"Harridan?" shrieked Alison. "You old goat. . . you pompous ass. . . you—you dirtbag! You are the problem, not Brad, not me! What the hell do you want with Abby, that's what we want to know! And you better start talking, now!" She brandished the gun. Brad looked rather amused.

"That's none of your business," Pops said. He looked nervously at the file cabinet in the corner. "Brad? Take her out, please. I'm getting a headache."

Brad lounged against the wall, deceptively relaxed. His gun was in his hand. "Now, Pops. You know I'm not gonna do that. Just spill, already. Clue us in on the big secret here."

"No," said Pops. "In about ten seconds, a squad will be coming through that door. Then you'll both be history. And soon enough, Abby and that brat Jules."

BAM.

Alison held the smoking gun. Pops slumped in his chair.

"Sorry," she told Brad. "But I'd had about enough of his crap. Now, help me get this file cabinet open, please. That's what he was worried about."

"No need," said Brad, full of admiration for a woman who could blow away the enemy one minute, and say "please" the next. "It's right here." He picked up a stack of folders from the desk, thumbing through them.

"Crap." Alison had moved swiftly to the window. "They're all coming back."

Brad looked up, and quickly stuck the folders in his pack. "Let's go."

They ran down the hall to the stairwell door. Opening it, they could hear footsteps ascending.

"Fire escape?" Brad asked.

Alison shrugged. "Why not? Fire escape, closet, what's one more cliché?"

"Great," said Brad, grabbing her arm and turning to run. Then he stopped. And kissed her.

He laughed at her shock. "Hey, you said one more cliché!"

She blushed, and they ran to the window at the end of the hall.

***

Abby flattened herself against the cold brick wall of the DeMenil Mansion as a group of people slowly meandered past. Jules and David were deep in the shrubbery, ten paces behind her, silent and still. When the street cleared, she chirped once, twice, and the two teenagers crept along the wall to join her. The three of them slipped around the back and opened the heavy cellar doors. David closed them slowly as they maneuvered down the dark stairs. At the base, Abby finally turned on her light.

Jules handed round granola bars and water. That was all they had, at the moment. It would have to do. They should have been back at the military installation by now, but were waiting for Brad and Alison. And they all knew the protocol: there was just one hour to wait. If they hadn't returned by then, Abby was to take the kids back to the truck, and back to the camp. No stops. No heroics.

She told the kids to get some rest, but David insisted that he was fine to watch. Jules told him not to be such a guy, that she'd had more sleep than he, and that she would stay awake. Exasperated, Abby told them both to stand watch if they wanted, she was going to sleep. And she did.

She could hear Jules and David whispering for a nanosecond before she was out cold.

***

Brad and Alison ran down Tucker until they reached the railroad tracks. They followed those again, along the ditch, until they came to Broadway. The area was deserted, so they slowed their pace and appeared to casual observers as though they were out on an assignment. The uniforms they still wore convinced any citizens to give them a wide berth.

Alison checked the time. They were late. They had just over thirty minutes to get to the brewery or the others would head south without them, assuming that something had gone wrong. Of course, they could likely catch up to them before they left the area, but Brad had briefly mentioned the contents of those files and said he was reluctant to leave unfinished business.

As they came into Lyon Park, Brad smelled smoke. Alison pointed toward the brewery. There was a column of wispy smoke, rising high from the center of the compound. They both knew that Abby wouldn't be lighting any fires in broad daylight; nor would she have any reason to do so.

"Now what?" asked Alison, as they huddled under some bushes.

"Let me think," said Brad. Then, after a moment, "Start with taking off these uniforms." He pulled off his coat and hat and stuffed them in the shrubbery. Alison followed suit.

"They aren't military; soldiers have no reason to be in this area. So that means they're civilians."

"Not that it matters," said Alison, "Either way, we could be in serious trouble."

"Here's the big question: did they arrive before Abby and the kids, or after? In other words. . . ." But he didn't have to finish the sentence. Alison knew. And she was scared out of her mind. Not for herself. For her daughter.

"The tunnel," said Brad suddenly. "Abby said there's a cave, a tunnel, below this area. She was checking it out the last time we were here. Over there!" He pointed to the other side of the overpass.

They moved cautiously across the open space and under the elevated highway. They were directly behind the overgrown rear yard of the DeMenil House. Alison pulled out her knife and they both hacked a path through the vines and scrub. Brad saw the cellar door first. He gave a low whistle. Nothing.

He motioned for Alison to wait, and he slunk forward, ducking behind a garden statue that was missing its head. He reached the wooden doors and leaned over, spying a wide crack. He whistled again, a little louder.

An answering chirp came back from the depths of the cellar. He pried open the door and came face to face with Jules' Glock.

"Oh. Hi, Brad!"

Robin Tidwell

Chapter Twenty-Five

The five fugitives huddled in the dank basement and considered their options. They could emerge after dark, and travel west and then south. Or possibly, the group they'd seen would disband by then, or sooner. They could, Brad suggested, waltz over there and introduce themselves.

Alison and Abby both shot down that idea.

The kids were mostly quiet, knowing they had neither the skill nor the knowledge to contribute to the discussion. They sat together, Jules' head resting on David's shoulder. Cute, thought Alison. Then she asked, "What about this cave or tunnel that Brad mentioned?"

"There's a door back there," Abby gestured, "that opens into a tunnel. The guy that built this place had a whole network of caves to work with—he even built some rooms down here, so they say. I'm pretty sure that the tunnel, though, goes all the way under the river. I went all the way to the end, and there were steps up to a wooden hatch of some kind.

"I couldn't get it opened, though, so it's likely a dead end. But there was one other tunnel that branched off to the left."

"Hmm," Brad mused. "maybe with all of us, we could shove it open—but then we'd be across the river. Wrong side. What about the other tunnel?"

"I don't know," said Abby. "I didn't have time to check it out."

"Come on, David," said Brad. "Lets us menfolk go exploring."

"I'm coming too!" said Jules. "I need something to do." She looked at Abby, then at her mother.

"Really?" said Alison drily. "Playing with C4 wasn't enough adventure for one day?" She turned to Abby. "I don't know where she gets it."

"Uh huh. Right."

The door to the tunnel opened easily this time, and Brad took the lead with David bringing up the rear. They walked in silence, marveling at the construction, shining their lights along the walls. They came to the secondary tunnel and turned left.

"Too bad it doesn't point south," said Brad. "That could be handy." They went only a short distance before the tunnel opened into a larger space. A room. There were still old-fashioned electric lights hanging from the low ceiling, but the room itself was empty.

"Can we go back to the main tunnel and go to the hatch Abby mentioned?" asked Jules.

"Sure," said Brad. "At this point, we have nothing but time."

As they walked beneath the Mississippi, Jules was a little creeped out by the dripping water and the feeling of closeness. David thought it was cool, and said so several times, much to her annoyance. They climbed the steps at the end and shined their lights to the ceiling, and the door.

"You two stay put," said Brad. "Let me climb up and see if I can open it." After a few minutes of shoving his shoulder against the door, he called down for David to come and give him a hand. Jules kept her light trained on the ceiling, about ten feet up.

Suddenly, light flooded the small landing where she stood, and David told her to climb up. She did so gratefully, glad to be out of the darkness. The three of them stood on the Illinois side of the river, gazing back at St. Louis.

Jules stretched out on the ground. The sun was wonderful, in spite of the chilly air temperature. She got to be outside in the daylight so seldom lately. David and Brad wandered around a bit, still staying within sight of Jules.

They went downriver and studied the current. Fairly swift, and few sandbars were visible; too dangerous to cross without a boat of some sort. "Ever read Mark Twain?" Brad asked David.

"Sure," said David. "Are you thinking of building a raft?" He looked eager to begin.

"No," Brad laughed. "But there's an idea! I was just remembering his stories about the river, and Huck Finn."

"Bet they had a blast," said David. Brad realized that these kids would never have the memories that he did: playing in the woods, taking float trips, camping. They lived all that, on a serious note, and there was little time to play—or safety in any situation.

"Come on, let's go back," Brad said, clapping David on the back. "Jules is probably asleep."

And she was. Reluctantly, she followed David down the ladder while Brad replaced the old wooden hatch. On the way back, Jules led, but stopped so short that David ran into her. "Look," she said. "Another door."

On their left, but since they were traveling in reverse, this one pointed south. It was barely visible, set into the stone itself instead of being a shallow recess. That's why they'd missed it, and Abby had too. And this one appeared to be locked.

The tiny padlock was obviously designed to keep people out of whatever was behind the door, but was not for heavy security. Brad easily broke the lock, and they pushed open the door. Another tunnel, but this one curved to the right. Jules took the lead again; but as they walked, they seemed to be going back to the main room where Abby and Alison waited.

Then the tunnel took a sharp turn to the left and opened into a room, not as large as the first, and there was a door on the far side. "I feel like Alice in Wonderland," muttered Brad.

"Who?" said Jules. Brad sighed. They just didn't get it.

"Oh," said David. "I know! The girl who fell down a hole and kept finding doors and things. And that cat. . . ."

"Exactly," said Brad. "Although I hope we don't find the Cheshire cat. Or the queen."

"Off with her head!" said David, laughing at Jules' look. "Don't you read?"

"Yes," said Jules loftily. "I read. I read history and politics, not about cats and doors."

"Literature," said David, not offended in the least. "It's literature. A classic."

"Whatever."

They got the second door open and went through into yet another tunnel. Brad checked his watch. They'd been gone two hours. Time to turn back soon. But when he told the kids, they begged to go just a little farther. He couldn't resist. He was rather enjoying this. They kept going.

Alison and Abby had been talking one moment, and the next, they were sound asleep. In the last twelve hours or so, they'd driven up to the city and jogged around a good portion of the downtown area, had very little to eat or drink, blown up a few buildings, and they were exhausted.

But Alison did tell Abby about the encounter with Pops.

"I know you think he was a good guy, Abby, and maybe he was. Once. A long time ago. I think there was something wrong with him; I mean, really wrong. He was going back and forth between being all commander and king-of-the-hill and alternating with some really weird delusions.

"I'm just saying, yeah, I'm sorry I had to shoot him. But I'd probably do it again." She yawned.

"I understand," said Abby. "Mostly. I think. Except right now I'm too sleepy to think much."

Abby awoke to voices. Coming from the top of the cellar steps. She clapped her hand over Alison's mouth, which of course brought Alison to full awareness. She frowned, and Abby removed her hand. She pointed upward.

Quietly, the two of them gathered the packs and moved towards the tunnel door. Once inside, Abby reached around the doorframe and grabbed a table leg, pulling a few pieces of old furniture down against the door. She yanked it shut against the resulting crash. Listening for just a moment, she turned and followed Alison down the tunnel when she heard louder voices crashing down the cellar stairs.

They reached the door to the left that Abby had discovered her first time down there. They ducked into the recess and she grabbed her radio. It crackled to life.

"Brad, where are you? What?" The reception was terrible. She looked at Alison. "I think he said something about 'keep going'."

"Go where? This just takes us to a room, a cave, right?"

"Yeah. Hang on. What, Brad? Okay, got it! Alison, come on, this way!"

They stepped into the main tunnel and crept along, Abby feeling the wall to her right. There it was! She pushed open the door and Alison closed it behind them. "Come on," Abby said, "they should be up ahead of us!" They practically ran down the passageway, hampered slightly by the extra packs.

The tunnel opened into a room, and Alison was the first to see the next door. They burst through, dropped the packs, and pulled the door closed. "Brad?" Abby called.

"Right here," he answered, coming around the bend. "What's going on, anyway?"

"Someone's coming," she said. "They were outside the cellar doors, talking, and I'm sure they came down after we went into the tunnel. I pulled some stuff over in front of the door, but I don't know if they'll see it or not."

"Got it. Come on, we better hurry."

"Where are the kids?" asked Alison.

"Up ahead. You won't believe what we found!"

They passed several open archways along the sides of the tunnel, but didn't even pause; still, it took them a good half-hour. The tunnel ended at a set of steps and they quickly climbed. At the top was a ladder, just like the one across the river, and Abby could see daylight at the top.

And to her immense surprise, the railroad trestle about 200 yards ahead.

"I hate to belabor the point," said Alison, "but again, where is Jules? And David?"

Brad pointed.

What appeared to be two little monkeys were swinging across the bridge, almost to the end. Alison resisted the urge to wave, assuming they could see her.

"Let's go," said Brad. "We're almost back to the truck." And in thirty minutes, they were.

Robin Tidwell

Chapter Twenty-Six

Abby thought they should put some distance between themselves and the city, so they drove as far as Arnold before stopping. Alison built a small fire and Jules heated some cans of stew. They ate ravenously. Recovered as much as possible, and energy at least temporarily restored, they piled back into the truck and traveled cross-country back to the camp.

Abby had missed EJ terribly; she'd tried not to think of her while she was gone, knowing that if things had turned out differently, she might never see her daughter again. Alison, at least, had Jules with her, although that certainly wasn't without its complications. And danger.

They pulled through the gates before midnight. Brad had radioed ahead to let Walt know they were coming and the younger ones were waiting impatiently. Walt was sitting by the fire, smoking his pipe, and he smiled at their arrival.

EJ ran to her mother and wouldn't let go for quite some time, insisting on snuggling with Abby all night. Elizabeth and Johnny listened intently to the adults' conversation, but soon went to bed, under protest. Jules and David soon followed, to their respective tents, and then Brad gave them all a full report.

"Well, I reckon that colonel character had what was coming to him," said Walt. "Shame, but that's the way it is. So what did he want with Abby and young Jules?"

"I'm afraid," said Brad, pulling out the stack of folders from his pack, "that they weren't the only ones. There are half a dozen dossiers here. And they all have one thing in common: they all survived VADER."

"From what I understood," added Alison, "they're looking for a cure, or an antidote. Most of those who survived the initial virus were supposed to survive; but there are some, like us, who were somehow immune."

Abby nodded, remembering Susan and Mike who had been held in the hospital for testing. She'd never learned what happened to Mike, but she had seen Susan, briefly. She supposed she was long dead by now; she'd looked close to it at the time.

"So, basically, those who were immune but targeted initially are the ones that the colonel was after. But he seemed to have a special hatred for Abby, at least, and probably. . . probably Jules too." Alison looked stricken, realizing how close she could have come to executing her own child.

"There's nothing in my file," said Abby, going through the papers.

"Try this one," said Brad, handing her a red folder marked with her name. He watched her closely, unsure of the reaction she might have.

Abby read the paper on top. Then she read it again. Her head snapped up, eyes blazing. "That's ridiculous!"

"Abby," said Brad helplessly. He wanted to reach out to her, but he knew from experience that it was best to leave her alone, let her rant and rave for a bit.

"There is no way. None. End of story." She stalked off with EJ, intending to tuck her daughter into bed and stay there herself as well. She'd had a long day, a long 24 hours, and this was just the limit.

Brad sighed.

"What is it?" asked Alison. Brad remained silent.

"I'm guessing it's something she don't want us to know," said Walt. "Maybe she'll tell us tomorrow. Or never. At any rate, I'm going to bed. These old bones are tuckered out. Those kids near wore me out the last day or so." He got up and went to his tent.

Alison and Brad stayed by the fire, talking in low tones. Somehow, they ended up moving closer together. Alison shivered, and Brad put his arm around her. "Cold?"

"A little," she said. It was quite some time before she spoke again. "What was the deal with that kiss, anyway?"

"Uh, well, you know. Heat of the moment, and all that." Brad turned red. He wasn't entirely sure where Alison was going with this.

"You could do it again."

It was a long time before they left the fire.

***

When Alison came into their tent, EJ was sound asleep but Abby was still fuming, staring up at the roof.

"Do you want to talk about it?" asked Alison, tentatively. Abby didn't answer. "Well, okay then. Guess I'll go to sleep." Alison got ready for bed, still hearing nothing from Abby's side of the tent except EJ's faint wheezing. She hurriedly changed her socks and pulled on a clean t-shirt, scooting deep into the sleeping bag and covering her cold nose. She turned on her side and yawned.

Just as she was dozing off, Abby finally spoke. "Do you ever think about your life, and wonder how it all happened, and if those times you thought maybe something was wrong with you, well, it really was?"

"Huh?" Alison raised up on her elbow. "Could you say that again?"

"I'm not sure," said Abby. "It didn't make a lot of sense, did it? I could use a drink."

"Me too, but it's too cold even for me to get up and grab a bottle."

After a moment of silence, Abby said, "I was seven when my parents died. Car accident. I wasn't with them. Did you ever wonder if you were adopted?"

"Sure, I think most kids do, at some point. Especially if their older brothers or sisters try to convince them." Alison made a face, remembering her big brother. He hadn't been among the survivors.

"Well," said Abby. "I guess I really was adopted."

"Oh my God," said Alison. "Is that what was in the file? And you just found out?"

"Yes. I don't remember my dad very well, but he was always nice. We'd go on bike rides sometimes, or to the carnival. And he always liked to stop for ice cream. My mom, that was a different story. It didn't matter what I did, it was never right. She didn't beat me or yell at me. Much. I could just tell she didn't really. . . like me, I guess. Maybe wished I wasn't around."

"Wow. That's a lot for a little kid to deal with. Like Jules, thinking I didn't want her. Oh my God." Alison tried to take it all in, not the least of which was how her own daughter might be feeling. She got herself back on the subject, trying to stay in the moment, for Abby. "Did it say anything else? About your birth parents, I mean."

"Yes. It named my father. My real father, I guess. Alison. . . ." Abby turned toward the woman who had rapidly become a sister to her. "Alison, it said. . . it said he was my father." And

Abby, who never cried, burst into tears, trying nevertheless to keep from waking EJ.

"Holy crap," said Alison. "Pops? The colonel? He was your dad?" Abby nodded, miserable.

Holy crap, thought Alison. I shot Abby's dad. Blew his brains out. But he needed killing, if anyone ever did. But. . . oh, my God. And he was after her, hated her so much. Why? She didn't want to ask anything else, afraid of the answer, but she did anyway.

"Was there anything. . . anything else that would have explained. . . ." She couldn't even form the words. "Wow. I just. . . Abby, I don't know what to say."

Abby had stopped crying. She tried to get a grip on her emotions. She took a deep breath. "There's nothing to say, Alison. Really. I'll get past this, I'll. . . damn!" She was losing it again. No. Stop. It probably wasn't even true, it probably. . . of course, it was true. Why else would it be in her file? In case she happened to see it? To screw with her? No, he had never thought she would find it—why would he? He was in charge, in control, he was calling the shots. All those years she'd known him, he had to have known that if she'd had a clue she would have said something.

"Really," she told Alison. "I'm okay. I'll deal with it, one way or another. Might take a day. Or two." She tried to smile. It didn't quite work. She reached over and turned out the light. "Goodnight."

Alison lay there for a long time, sleep eluding her.

By morning, things seemed almost normal. Abby got up and washed her face, braided her hair, put water on for coffee. She helped EJ get dressed and settled her down by the fire with her lesson books. Elizabeth and Johnny sat down with EJ and Abby handed them their breakfast. Alison finally dragged herself out to the fire and poured some coffee.

"Morning!" Abby said brightly.

Alison stared at her. "You slept? That makes one of us."

Brad and Walt joined the group at the fire. "Wow," said Brad, "nothing like washing up in a cold spring when the air temperature's what? Low 30s? Brrr."

"You're crazy," Abby told him. "Truly nuts."

"Thanks a lot. Walt here, he recommended it. Says he does it every day."

"So you're both certifiable. No offense, Walt."

"None taken," he grinned. "You should try it sometime."

"Ugh, no thanks!" Abby grinned back. "I hate the cold."

"Would you all knock it off," demanded Alison. "I'm tired and this coffee's not doing it for me, and what are we going to do next? And where are Jules and David?" She looked around.

"I'm on it," said Brad. He strode over to the tent where David was still sleeping and disappeared inside. A second later, David came bursting through the flap, barefoot and wild-haired, looking desperate for escape. Brad stepped outside and finished the water bottle he held. "Doesn't pay to sleep in, son!"

Abby tossed him another bottle. "You seem to have run out," she said, nodding in the direction of the tent where Jules had been staying with the younger kids. Immediately after, a screech came from that same direction, followed by a muffled, "Dammit!"

Abby shrugged and looked at Alison. "Your daughter."

"You raised her," Alison shot back.

"Touché." They clinked their coffee mugs in a toast to teenagers.

"So," said Walt. "I'm guessing you all need to go back up to the city, huh?"

Abby looked away. That was the last place she wanted to go. She was tired. They'd gone to St. Louis, Pops. . . her father. . . was gone. The entire place should be in a state of confusion, and she guessed it would take a few days, at least, to replace that psychotic son of a bitch. Now would be the time to strike, to organize.

But no, she didn't want to go back.

She surprised even herself when she answered Walt. "Yes. We have to."

EJ looked up. "But, Mom. . . ."

"I'm sorry, EJ. Uncle Brad and I and Alison will be leaving this afternoon."

The entire group was silent, then they all began to talk at once.

"I reckon I can take care of the kids."

"Mom, Abby, can David and I go this time?"

"When do I get to go? I'm old enough!"

"Damn." This last from Alison, who really just wanted to take a day off.

Brad stepped in. "One at a time! First, Abby's right. Walt, appreciate that, that'd be great. Jules, I'll answer you: no. David?"

"Um, what Jules said," he mumbled, turning red.

"Ah, I see," said Brad with a smirk. "Same answer: no. And Elizabeth, I'm sorry, not this time. That goes for Johnny, too." He smiled at the little boy, who smiled back but never spoke.

"Does that cover everyone? Oh, and Alison? Suck it up, cupcake." He ducked as her empty mug flew through the air, perilously close to his head.

Abby jumped to her feet. She'd seen EJ slip off alone to the tent, and she followed, calling over her shoulder, "Figure it out, Brad. I'll see you at lunch."

EJ was sitting on Abby's bedroll, holding tight to her blankie. It was the same one that Abby had used to bring her back to the cave the day she was born, out in the woods. She ducked her head, sobbing, when Abby walked in.

Abby sat down next to the little girl and wrapped her arms around her. They sat there for a long time, until EJ stopped crying. She looked up at her mother. "Why do you have to leave again? You just got back."

"Oh, EJ. I don't want to leave, but I have to go back. We have to finish what we started. I won't be gone long, and Mr. Whitman will take good care of you."

"I know, Mom, and I like to play with Elizabeth. And Johnny. Even if he doesn't talk. I can talk enough for both of us." EJ was completely serious, but Abby smiled anyway. "I just miss you. First it was just us, in the cave, then we left, and Uncle Brad and Aunt Alison showed up. And then everyone else, and we came back home. But we're not really home, that's over there, and not here."

"Sweetheart, you know I love you, and I just want to fix things so you don't have to live in a cave, or in the dark all the time. I have to go, and that's that. But I don't want you to be sad. I'll come back, and things will get better. Now, what would you like to do this morning? I'm all yours until lunchtime."

"Really?" said EJ, her little face lighting up.

"Yes, really!" Abby tugged on the little blonde braid, just like her own. "Come on, let's go do something fun!"

Chapter Twenty-Seven

"We have to strike while we can," said Brad. "I'm proposing that you, me, and Alison go back up to the city and try to make contact with that group we saw at the brewery. They aren't military, I'm sure, which means they're on our side. Probably.

"So here's the deal: tonight, we leave. Go back to Jefferson Barracks and sneak into the city. I'll go in and meet these people. Alone."

Abby nodded. "Works for me."

"No," said Alison. "You shouldn't go alone. I don't like it."

Brad shook his head. "Have to. That leaves the two of you, if anything goes wrong, to get back here. I don't want to take a chance on just one person having to make any decisions and maybe avoid some trouble."

Clearly, Alison wasn't happy, but she could see his point. Sort of. "I suppose you think you're invincible? What if I went in? If they turn out to be military, I could make some headway; and I'm probably better at negotiations than you."

Brad smirked. "I saw you 'negotiating' not long ago. No, you're not going in. And that's final."

Alison stomped off to pack, tossing her hair and making a rude hand gesture in Brad's direction. Abby tried to stifle a laugh at the look on his face.

They drove the usual route up to St. Louis, Abby, Brad, and Alison. They set off around midnight to go into the city itself, skirting around the east side of the old brewery to descend into the cellar of the DeMenil Mansion. While the intruders had gone as far as the cellar, they appeared not to have found the doorway into the network of tunnels and caves.

Brad, despite Alison's continued objections, left them to go in search of the same people they'd been trying to avoid on the last trip, just days ago. Abby and Alison set about making repairs to the cellar doors and camouflaging their presence. They moved some extra supplies inside the tunnel, far enough past the entrance that they wouldn't be immediately seen, in case escape became necessary.

Then they waited.

The best course of action, Brad had decided, was to be open and upfront about his intentions. He walked boldly down Cherokee Street, plainly visible in the moonlight. Within minutes, he was surrounded by well-armed men who weren't exactly putting out a welcome mat. He was summarily parted from his weapons, his hands were bound, and he was marched to the old brewery to be left in a small closet barely large enough to turn around in, let alone sit down.

Then he waited.

Finally, with wrench, the closet door flew open. Four heavily armed men escorted him down the hallway to an office furnished with a table and two chairs, and left him alone. Again, he waited. And then, a slight figure, dressed in black leather, entered the room. A lantern was set on the table and illuminated.

Her name, she told him, was Stefanie.

"And that," she said. "is all you need to know right now."

Brad was a bit bemused. He wasn't quite sure if she was someone sent to interrogate him, prior to him being thrown to the dogs, so to speak, or if she was someone of importance in this organization. For they were organized; he could see it when they'd first approached him, confident and efficient as they took him prisoner.

"Now," she continued, "who are you?"

Brad gave her his name, assuming his best course of action was to be completely honest but, at the same time, answer only her specific questions and volunteer nothing. Especially the nearby presence of Abby and Alison. That could wait, possibly indefinitely.

"What are your politics?" Stefanie demanded.

Brad hesitated. Politics? Had it come to that? What exactly did she mean?

"You can't answer that?" She removed a radio from her belt, prepared to call in the troops.

Brad took a deep breath. "Of course I can answer the question. I am against the government, as it currently stands, and believe that anyone who so wishes can live as he chooses, albeit without infringing on others' rights.

"Is that enough of an answer?"

"Yes. It is. Next question: where are you from? How did you find us?"

"Well," said Brad, "I believe it's you, or your men, who found me. Literally. I was just walking down the street." He was starting to relax a bit, thinking that, if it came down to it, he could easily overpower this Stefanie and make a break for the window behind her.

"Don't be a smart-ass," she snapped. "And what idiot would walk alone down the street in a city engaged in warfare? Of course we took you prisoner. Again, where are you from?"

"Recently? Or originally?" He held up a hand; or rather, both his hands, since they were still bound together. "Never mind. Originally, I'm from right here in the city. Recently, I'm from south of here. Madison County."

Stefanie raised an eyebrow. "Really? Nearly all of that county's population was killed off by VADER. Still," she mused. "I suppose it's possible that some small handful survived; this long, however, is unlikely.

"Try again, cowboy. Where are you 'recently' from?"

"Don't I get to ask any questions? Why should I give up all my information, when you've given nothing but your name? And I can see you have a few thugs working for you, of course."

"Hmm. Testy, are we? The reason you get to answer while I do the asking is because you are the one who is the prisoner. But I will humor you, briefly. Mostly because I don't believe you are a threat to us; more like some bumbling yokel who accidentally discovered us.

"I have told you my name. It is Stefanie. I am the head of this organization. I have one hundred soldiers under me, here, in the city; there are many others scattered around the area, several groups. We have been fighting the government since shortly before VADER appeared. We are well-armed and well-connected.

"I tell you this mostly so you know that escape or reprisal is futile, and so that you may be more amenable to answering my questions. I would hate to use this."

Brad realized, suddenly, that Stefanie had been tapping an object against her leg as she spoke, as if for emphasis. It was a taser. Interesting. He'd been shot, stabbed, left for dead, but a taser still wasn't an object with which he really wanted to tangle.

"So," he cleared his throat. "So, you've been fighting the government for what, ten, twelve years?"

"Twenty," she said. "Twenty years. Like my father before me. Until Colonel Barton executed him. This new colonel, Hoefer, he was after us constantly since he came into power here. At least, until his recent assassination."

Brad saw his chance. "Shot between the eyes, was he?"

Stefanie's own eyes narrowed. "How do you know this? The official story is that he died of a heart attack. One of our people was there. He saw two figures escape immediately after he heard the gunshot. He confirmed the colonel's death, and fled, to bring us the news. That was two days ago."

"I know, because I was there. We went out a window and down the fire escape. He was shot with a .45."

Stefanie was silent for a moment. "This is the truth. This is what our man said. But you did not shoot him?"

"No, my partner did. He kind of, er, made her mad."

"I think I would like this partner of yours. So, how many people do you have?"

Brad was fairly sure he could trust Stefanie. She did have that taser and, by her telling, a hundred men to beat him into submission or kill him or, at the very least, prevent his escape. He had to take the chance, at any rate. Counting quickly, he said, "There are nine of us."

"And you came here alone? Or with your partner?"

"Yes. With my partner."

"Tell me about your group."

Brad was thinking rapidly. He was nearly convinced, but didn't want to endanger the others unnecessarily. He decided to continue hedging his answers, much like the count he'd given Stefanie. "Five women, four men."

"I see. So, tell me, Major Blake, how much longer do you hope to remain alive?"

What the devil? Brad was well and truly flummoxed. How did she know? What else did she know?

Stefanie laughed at him. "Oh, we know much about you, Major Blake. We know you were part of the resistance, and were then recruited by the government. Against your will as well as your knowledge, that is true. We probably know more about you than you do, yourself. We have had a dossier on you for years, and as soon as you were brought here, our team began comparing the files.

"However, we had believed you to be dead. The government had reported that, and we had no reason to verify or to seek to find out differently. Now it is a different story, as they say. You are alive, and appear to have come to your senses."

Brad stepped back as she approached with a large knife in her hand. She simply cut his bonds, and turned away. "Please. Sit." She lifted her radio and barked a command, and the door opened. Two men entered with water bottles and sandwiches, then retreated.

"Now," said Stefanie. "We will share a meal, and talk, and then I will meet the rest of your people. We have much to plan."

Another man entered the room, and set down Brad's weapons. He held out his hand and smiled a welcome. "I am Carmine, Stefanie's husband. Very nice to meet you, at last."

Chapter Twenty-Eight

Alison was the first to hear the radio chirp to life and she nudged Abby. They heard a series of clicks, incomprehensible and unknowable to anyone but Brad. They both sighed in relief. He was in, and he was safe. Considering the length of time he'd been gone, with no communication, they had just been discussing their options.

Given the present uncertainty, they decided to catnap in shifts; Abby took the first watch, trusting in her own patience more so than her friend's characteristic lack of such. She sat at the base of the cellar stairs, Mossberg across her lap, and fought against the rising tide of thought that permeated her mind.

As she had told Alison, her mother indeed treated her as though she were an inconvenience, a burden. As such, Abby tried desperately to win the woman's approval but always seemed to fall short. She had few memories of her mother that included anything like happiness or any of those traditional mother-daughter moments of which she'd heard, but never experienced.

Perhaps, if her mother had lived longer. . . but perhaps not. And her father. Abby remembered him as being often torn between his wife and his daughter, sympathetic but firm, usually siding with his wife whenever possible in order to keep the peace. But sometimes, rarely, he and Abby would have their own adventures together. She liked him best during these times, but they always ended far too soon.

She supposed her adoption shouldn't have come as such a shock. There had been signs, she was sure, but mostly just a feeling of not belonging, not being wanted. Which was odd. Most people adopted a child because they wanted one. She guessed she'd never know the reasons. It was far too late for it to matter and, besides, they were all gone. All dead. Even Pops.

Abby wondered when Pops had discovered that she was his daughter. Surely not that first time she'd met him, when she was seven. Did he know during those years they were all living at the camp? Did anyone else know? No, any one of them would have mentioned it. But did Pops know? And even so, why would that make him hate her so much, to want her dead?

And another question: who was her mother? Her real mother? She knew that was a futile query; there was certainly no one left to tell her, to give her the answers. No one at all.

She rubbed her eyes. This was giving her a headache. She decided, then and there, that she would stop thinking about it. That's all. Just stop. She could do nothing to change the past, and certainly nothing to change the facts, and that's all there was to it. End of story. Time to move on.

And time to sleep. She woke Alison to take the next watch and fell into restless dreams. She awoke with a jerk when she heard Brad's distinctive whistle outside.

Carmine had come along with Brad, and introductions were made all around. No one said a word about the tunnel door;

that was going to remain among the three of them. They packed up and walked across the street to the brewery.

The command center was larger than the office in which Brad had first met Stefanie. When all had gathered, and the discussions began, Abby hung back. She lounged against the wall, alert, but appeared to be disinterested. She wanted to be sure of what they were getting involved in, and she preferred to observe before committing.

Carmine introduced a number of lieutenants, explaining that each was responsible for a company of twenty-five soldiers. Abby quickly calculated: based on the current occupancy of the room, at least 125 men and women were fighting on their side. She hoped fervently that it was the right side because their choices were limited. Either they'd join up, or remain neutral. There'd be no resistance to a force this size.

Stefanie arrived and explained that she'd just been meeting with a messenger. She had had the latest news from the Federal Building and wanted to confirm it before greeting them all.

"So," she began. "Colonel Hoefer is dead. Many of the government soldiers are leaving, afraid they will not be paid on time, or even at all. Rumors are flying that St. Louis will soon be abandoned. Chicago has assured the troops that things will remain the same, but for some reason they are not convinced." She smiled grimly. "Possibly, that has something to do with Jose and his team." She nodded in the direction of one of the lieutenants, and Jose acknowledged the accolade.

"Jose is responsible for misinformation," Carmine whispered to Brad.

"We have decided to aim for the top, the chief if you will. We have discovered, through our connections, that a new commander will be sent here within two days. Her name is General Kathleen Scott."

Alison blinked. Thus far, she had been listening but not paying particularly close attention. At this announcement, her mind wandered back to her own days in Chicago.

She'd been at loose ends when she first moved up there from Austin. She worked a lot of hours, came home to an empty apartment, and only met people in the course of her job. She had little in common with most of them, so focused on her duties. When her search for Juliet had come up empty, repeatedly, and she had given up, she turned even more fixedly to work.

Soon she was in line for a promotion, and that's when she met Kat.

The two had become friendly, if not close, and shared an occasional drink. After a short time, Alison began to know some of Kat's friends and soon she had an active social life: parties, restaurants, weekend trips. As government officials, they had access to the best of everything. While most citizens were trying to merely exist, those in certain positions were living the good life.

Alison met a lot of Kat's friends. Two of them were really into backpacking and camping, and she spent many long weekends far from Chicago, tromping around in the woods. Eric and his girlfriend, Marta, had even given her a key to their camper and told her to go down there any time she wished.

That's how she discovered their hidden cache.

In spite of her friendship with Kat, Alison had ignored her repeated hints to go along some weekend. Sometimes Alison just needed to get away, alone. She was looking for, of all things, a bottle of tequila one night when she noticed a loose floorboard. She found a hammer in the toolbox and set about nailing the board back down, when she realized she'd have to remove and reseat the whole thing.

There was a space underneath that board, filled with ammo boxes. Full ones. She hastily fixed the board, nailing it securely back into place, and resumed her tequila search. Successful at last, she poured a drink and sat down to think about this new development.

Sure, Eric had occasionally talked about a government collapse, but since Alison had been off duty during her forays to the campground, she'd paid little attention. She'd thought it was just talk. And certainly, several times when she was about to throw something away, like dryer lint or a square of foil, Marta would stop her and store the trash in a bag or box. Once or twice, she'd interrupted a conversation between the two of them, but it was so quickly smoothed over that she wondered if she'd imagined it.

She shrugged off the entire incident and went back to the city the next day. It wasn't long after that Kat began to unexpectedly show up in her office, hovering, and a few times, Alison suspected, tried to lead the conversation around to Eric and Marta. Never was the word "traitor" mentioned, but Alison wondered at Kat's intense interest in the couple.

Several weeks later, Eric had vanished. When Alison tried to call Marta, she couldn't get through. She never saw her again. Kat, however, asked that Alison accompany her one day to the holding area. Kat left her alone, and within minutes, Eric was shoved through the door. He was bound and shackled and had obviously been badly beaten. As he stumbled against her, he whispered something.

Hiding her shock, Alison followed his hasty message and stood tall, hands on her hips. "What the hell have you done,

Eric?" She continued to berate and question him for the next fifteen minutes, angrily insisting that he tell the truth, until Kat returned. She called the guards to remove Eric, and walked with Alison back to her office.

"I can't tell you how pleased I am that you are not aligned with that. . . that piece of garbage," Kat purred. "You must understand, I had to be sure, given how much time you've spent with them lately. But, you have passed the test that my superiors and I had devised. I would, however, if I were you, be very careful in the future."

Alison began to shake as soon as the door closed behind Kat. She'd heard things, of course, that they did to prisoners. But Eric was one of their own. Wasn't he? And truthfully, most of the horror stories she'd heard had to do with the others, the survivors. Things they did to prisoners. Not the government. Why, the government was there to take care of everyone, make sure they had food and clothing and a place to live. And medical care. All that people needed. Oh, everyone had a job. The government made sure of that. No one was paid, but then again, money wasn't necessary anymore.

So how could a good government like this one do something like that to Eric? Unless he and Marta were right about. . . what? The entire incident got Alison to think long and hard, and to reevaluate her own position. And, as Kat had. . . warned her, she was going to be very careful indeed.

It wasn't long after that she was transferred to St. Louis.

And now, Alison realized, Kat had obviously been promoted. And she was coming here.

Chapter Twenty-Nine

"What?" said Alison. She came out of her reverie with a start.

"I said, let's get moving!" Brad pulled her to her feet.

"Where are we going?"

"Weren't you listening to anything? Sheesh. We're going to Carmine and Stefanie's house, the five of us, to finalize our plan." Brad frowned.

"We have a plan?" asked Alison. "Um, yeah. Okay." She turned the wrong way down the hall.

"What's wrong with you anyway? Come on, we need to catch up. I have no idea where this place is and you're back here in dreamland." He pulled her the right direction, and they caught up with Abby, who gave her a strange look but said nothing.

Alison shook herself. Get it together, girl.

They walked south to Chippewa Street, then cut through Dutchtown and turned east, stopping in St. Matthew's Cemetery. Carmine spoke quietly on his radio, then gestured for the others to follow him. Single file, slowly, with Stefanie bringing up the rear, they crossed Gravois Road and moved cautiously up a narrow residential street. The houses here were small brick, flat-topped buildings with deep front porches. And they were mostly intact, but empty as far as anyone could tell.

Carmine climbed the steps of one and the others followed him inside. "The bathroom is here," he pointed, "if you'd like to wash up. There are clean clothes in the bedroom closets, ladies to the right, men to the left. Please, take your time. Stefanie and I must speak with our men first, then we will eat."

"Go ahead," Abby told Alison. "I can wait." She grinned when Brad pushed past her, insisting to Alison that there was room enough for both of them. She guessed they wanted a little alone time.

Abby wandered into the living room, pausing to warm her hands at the tiny fire burning cheerfully in the brick fireplace. It wasn't large enough to attract much attention, she supposed and, after all, those who lived here in the city were supposed to be here, and surely knew about hiding when necessary. She admired the woodwork in the old-style house, particularly the columns between the living and dining rooms. In spite of the windows being covered with blackout cloth, there was a certain charm about the place.

The kitchen was small too, with an island in the center and coal-black cabinets. A back door led to a tiny landing and steep stairs, which ended in a long, narrow fenced yard. She looked out, but saw no other people, no movement whatsoever. She went back inside to the living room and sat down on the sofa, wondering what was taking Alison and Brad so long; then she decided she really didn't want to know.

She awoke a short time later when Alison nudged her arm and told her that her bath was ready. Bath? All she'd planned was a quick washing and a change of clothes. She allowed herself to be led into the bathroom, and she about fell over when she saw what was waiting: a full bathtub. An old-fashioned clawfoot tub. With hot water. No wonder they'd been in there long enough for her to take a nap!

Twenty minutes later, Abby was finished and dressed in clean clothes. She would have stayed much longer, all day probably, but she knew the others were waiting. She joined them in the kitchen, where Stefanie directed them through a door to the basement. A long table took up most of the room, and Carmine was seated at the head. Several men and women were there as well, and Stefanie told them to sit down, and eat. They would talk during lunch.

Glasses of wine were poured, and plates were passed. Abby hadn't seen this much food in years, and she knew she'd better take it easy. She was used to jerky and granola bars and canned stuff, not—was that toasted ravioli? Holy smoke. She looked questioningly at Stefanie, who laughed at her expression.

"Yes, Abby, it's real. Please, eat. We have plenty. Carmine's sister is our cook. We don't always eat this well, but we manage, especially when we have guests." She dinged her spoon against her wine glass. "Everyone! We must talk about this new general, and how best to continue our plan. And of course, what will happen after we are successful!"

Conversation turned toward the new commander, and whether or not she should be dealt with en route, or after she had arrived. Alison suddenly spoke.

"I know Kat. I mean, General Scott. I used to work with her."

Dead silence.

All heads turned toward Alison and she blushed, but continued. "We were colleagues. Friends. For a short time. And then. . . . Friends of mine, and I thought hers, were taken in for questioning. Well, one was. And he was beaten, badly. The other one, his wife. She disappeared."

"And what happened after that?" asked Stefanie, ice in her words.

Alison swallowed, hard. "Kat took me to a room, alone. And they brought Eric. I. . . I had to pretend that I wasn't shocked at what they'd done, and Eric. . . he whispered to me what to do and say. So I did. I saved myself. I think. At least at the time.

"And then I was sent here."

"I see," said Stefanie, exchanging looks with Carmine. He appeared tense, although Stefanie had relaxed a bit and her hand was no longer on her sidearm. "And did you know that Eric and Marta were part of the rebellion?"

"What?" said Alison. "No! I mean, I suspected something the last time I was at their camper, alone, and found. . . something. But I never knew anything! They never said. . . ." She trailed off miserably.

Then she looked at Stefanie. "You said Marta's name. Not me. I didn't. . . you knew them?" Tears welled up in her eyes. "I'm very sorry," she said. "They were my friends."

"Please," said Carmine. "Tell us more. Marta was my niece. We have had no contact for several months, and now I know why."

"Do not blame yourself, Alison," said Stefanie. "You did what you had to do, just as Eric and Marta. They knew the risks, we all know the risks.

Alison felt her hand being squeezed under the table, and she smiled at Abby. Brad put his arm around her, as she told them about her friendship with Eric and Marta and their little camper out in the country. When she was done, Carmine excused himself after stopping to whisper something to his wife.

When they were finished eating, Stefanie led them through a door in the south wall of the basement. A short tunnel connected the house next door; it was small and cramped, and even Abby had to duck her head a bit. It opened into a large room, the walls covered with maps, and in one corner stood an old-fashioned chalkboard.

"Before we begin," said Stefanie, "I wish to explain to you how we live here, how we exist. This is where we plan our strategy, the war room, if you will. Upstairs, the floorplan is much like the house in which we entered, except it is furnished as a barracks of sorts for our soldiers. The house on the north side is where Angela prepares our meals and tends her garden. Angela is Marta's mother. Carmine has gone to speak with her.

"I can see that you all are surprised by the way we live. The authorities do not bother us, much. We must still be careful, but we have many soldiers on the inside who help protect us. However, the government believes that only Carmine and I live here, and we have been able to pay their bribes to keep our electricity and water running. Very few can manage this, outside the downtown area where all is provided.

"The government pays its soldiers well, and our men and women who have infiltrated the enemy simply help provide for our very large. . . family." She smiled at them. "Do you have any questions, except perhaps the obvious: are we like the Mafia families of the old days? I will answer that one. In many ways, yes."

Abby was intrigued. She thought of Jules' love of history and knew she'd love to meet Stefanie. That, in turn, brought up images of EJ, so she hastily redirected her thoughts. "Let's talk about this plan a little more. I know we had said to er, take out the new commander just as she arrives, but I'm wondering if perhaps we couldn't get more intel first. I know that Alison can't go anywhere near the woman, she'd be recognized right away, but someone else could do that. We have enough information about her, and I'm sure we could get more." She looked at Alison, who nodded.

"Of course. I could tell you about the Chicago command, and some of Kat's history. And her weaknesses. She does have them, in spite of what her superiors may think."

Brad agreed, saying, "Yes. I think Abby's right. If we simply shoot her, we learn nothing and they send someone else. This is our best chance to find out what's going on. . . maybe in other places too. But who's going to go on the inside?" He looked at Abby, knowing her answer.

Abby ignored him and looked directly at Stefanie. "We are. Stefanie and I."

"No!" shouted one of the lieutenants; Abby thought his name was Mario. "It is too dangerous for women."

Stefanie laughed at him as the room erupted in comments and shouts. "My brother," she explained to Abby. She clapped her hands loudly, once, twice. The room became quiet.

"Abby is correct. We will find out as much as we can, and she and I will go in and deal with this general. Now, let us make the final plans."

Mario sulked in the corner, while the rest of them discussed deployment of which companies to what locations, and the best time to strike. Brad volunteered to lead a group back to the hospital to obtain more explosives, but Carmine, who had returned, graciously declined his offer. "Come with me," he said, taking Brad back through the tunnels to Angela's house.

They were gone for an hour, and on their return Brad sidled up to Abby and said, "Um, we can blow up an awful lot of stuff with that cache he's got—wait'll you see it!"

Abby smiled at him and nudged him back. "That's your job this time, tough guy. I'm going to be busy. Check this out." She showed him the configuration they'd come up with, red lines on the map where their soldiers would travel to key points. "And here," she added, "Is where you and Carmine will be waiting, ready to rescue us."

"Yeah, right. Like you've ever needed rescuing."

"Your girlfriend might," said Abby, pointing.

Brad glanced over at Alison, who was waiting to brief them on the general and killing time chatting with Mario. At least he appeared to be coming out of his funk, but he looked totally enraptured by Alison. Brad decided he better put a stop to that, and he took two quick strides over to them, putting his arm around Alison while he jumped into the conversation. Abby smirked at him and he waved her off, grinning.

Turning her attention back to the map, Abby studied it carefully. Their own soldiers would be undercover, of course, and she wanted to be sure that she knew who was whom and when and when not to shoot. From the house here in South City, the first group would move east back to the brewery and pick up additional men; then they'd go into the city, roughly by way of Highway 55. The second group would travel along the Kingshighway line, far into the north part of the city before cutting east to the old Fairground Park. And finally, the third and last contingent would move northeast, to a site near the Federal Building.

Abby was to accompany the first wave, and Stefanie would be with the second group. The two of them would meet near the Musial statue at the old stadium. Or what was left of it.

A fourth cadre of men were to be deployed the Forest Park area, on the east side near the guard tower. Their job was to, as Brad put it, blow up stuff. This would cause what mercenaries who remained there to investigate the series of explosions, allowing the rebels to obtain control of the tower and the gate. This was their planned escape route.

Alison took the floor. "I'm not sure how much I can tell you about Kat, I mean, about General Scott, but I'll tell you what I know. I met her some time ago, in Chicago, and we worked together but we weren't actually close. She was a hard person to get to know, very close-mouthed about her personal life, very business-like most of the time. She'd loosen up once in a while, if we were out at a club or somewhere.

"She didn't like to go outside the city, even though there aren't any rebels anywhere near Chicago. I guess we. . . they got rid of them all," Alison added ruefully. "She had a desk job, and that was it. If she knows anything about firearms, anything practical, I never saw any signs of it. Some of us would talk at work sometimes about handguns or target practice, but she never was around or showed any interest.

"Kat's very ambitious. I guess we can see that now."

Stefanie handed her a sheet of paper. "Is this she?"

Alison shivered a bit. "Yes. That's Kat."

"All right," said Stefanie. She looked at her watch. "It is now nearly nine o'clock in the evening. Group Two will leave at four o'clock, Group One at five, and the last one at six, along with Mario's men. Angela will have breakfast for everyone before we leave. Now, boys upstairs and to bed! Ladies, you will please come with me."

Stefanie led Alison and Abby back to Angela's house. They climbed the stairs and met a pleasant woman, slightly older than they, with graying hair fastened in a low bun, much like

Stefanie wore. "Angela has a wonderful garden out back," she told them. She hugged the older woman, her sister-in-law, and bade her goodnight, then showed Abby and Alison the room they would share.

It was a small bedroom, nearly identical to the one next door at Stefanie and Carmine's house. Abby collapsed gratefully onto the bed, still clothed, knowing she had to get up to leave with the group at five o'clock. Alison, however, wanted to talk. Abby sighed and rolled onto her side, propping up her head. "So talk. Ten minutes, that's all you get," she warned, rubbing her eyes.

"Tell me about Brad," said Alison. "I know you've know each other for a long time, and he's talked about you of course. But he's not very forthcoming about himself and even then, it's more like he's telling me what he did and where he lived."

"Well, um, like what?" asked Abby, perplexed. To her, people just were. . . people. They had their own quirks, their own personalities, and you just got to know them. She couldn't remember the last time she'd had a conversation like this anyway, there'd been an unusual shortage of girlfriends over the last ten years.

"Oh, I don't know," said Alison, "stuff like. . . his family, I guess. Was he ever married? Or have kids?"

Abby thought back to that first winter at the camp. "Yes," she said shortly. "Her name was Zoe and she and the baby died. At the camp.

"Now can we go to sleep?"

"I'm sorry," whispered Alison, tears falling.

Abby took her hand and squeezed. "It's okay. You didn't know."

Chapter Thirty

The sun was barely peeking through the low cloud cover when Brad and Alison, with Carmine, huddled beneath the ruined overpass at Highway 44 and Hampton Avenue. There were six others, all equally chilled and tense. Carmine kept studying the sky.

Finally, he turned to the others and said, "Let's go."

Once they reached Highway 40, Carmine took two men and broke off from the group; they were going around the park, to the far side near the old history museum, and they'd be the first to set off the charges. A lot of charges. The intent was to draw the interest of as many as possible from the guard tower and barracks near the city/county line and the newly built wall.

Carmine saluted Brad, bowed to Alison, and disappeared into the brush with the others.

The next group, two of them, moved east to the Muny Theater. They, too, would fire a series of explosions to draw more soldiers from the wall. They were scheduled to begin half an hour after Carmine's charges blew, and that was just ninety minutes from now.

The timing of it all had to be precise. Abby was moving north by now, nearing the Arch grounds where the new helipad had recently been installed, and Stefanie, with her men, should be close by as well. They couldn't wait long, once they were in place, for fear of discovery. But much depended on the timely arrival of General Scott.

Alison, Brad, and the other two men were to approach the guard tower and barracks and remain hidden for the time being. There was plenty of tree cover as they moved along the ditches on either side of Government Drive. They came within roughly a thousand feet of the barracks before ducking into a supply shed to wait, silently.

Abby had had reservations about Mario until they set off that morning. The young man, nineteen years old and, she realized, not much older than David—or Jules, was calm and confident when he was on a mission. He reminded her, in some ways, of Emmy: a bit scattered and fixated on small things, until you put a gun in his hand and pointed him towards an enemy. She was rather impressed.

The soldiers had a certain respect for him as well, and not due solely to the fact that he was Stefanie's kid brother. They met up with the others at the brewery just before six o'clock. Mario divided the roughly one hundred men into five companies, in order to maneuver through the city more quickly. He kept Abby close by, telling her that he'd promised his sister to watch over her. Abby was touched. She doubted she'd need as much "watching over" as some of these guys here, but it was a nice gesture.

The five companies traveled different side streets, moving north to the Arch. Mario's group, with Abby, went slowly up the roundabout path of Ninth Street, making the final dash along Seventh and under the highway. Most of them faded away, into the shadows, moving east; Mario and two others escorted Abby to the stadium gate, where Stefanie was waiting, then they, too, went to join the others.

The Musial statue appeared intact, but the flowers and greenery surrounding the base were long dead. Stefanie dug down into the frozen soil and began to tug on a black trash bag; Abby helped her lift it out and they lugged across the plaza area to the stadium entrance. Inside were two overly large government-issued military uniforms.

They dressed quickly, pulling the bulky clothing over their own, snapping the straps of the black helmets and lowering the mirrored visors. Abby shuddered. It was creepy, being dressed like the enemy. At least now they could walk about openly, without being stopped or questioned. And ordinary citizens would give them a wide berth.

They walked east on Clark to Fourth Street, dodged deep craters on the grounds of the old Millennium Hotel, and crossed Memorial Drive just as the snow began to fall. The air was heavy and damp and, in spite of the sun having risen a good two hours ago, the day itself was about as gloomy as one could expect.

The heliport was at the end of Market Street, in the once-green space at the base of the Arch. All that was left after Barton's mad bombing of the city were the two legs, one rising a mere thirty feet, the other, not quite twice as high. Both were blackened and burned, and the twin ramps descending into the museum beneath were filled with rubble, and impassable.

Stefanie and Abby moved into place, some distance away from the rest of the troops milling about. Stefanie surreptitiously pulled out her radio and whispered into it. Abby checked her watch. Almost time.

Stefanie nodded and gestured. Abby raised her hand in acknowledgment. They heard the sounds of a chopper begin its descent and they both looked up. The general was on her way. Nine o'clock. Exactly on time.

BOOM!

An explosion several blocks away, coming from the massive parking garage, now useless, that Stefanie and Abby had passed minutes ago, hit and rippled through the gathered crowd. Many clapped hands over their ears, some dropped to the ground. The women were prepared, however, and moved in from different directions toward the general. She had exited the chopper and was striding towards them, bodyguards surrounding her.

"What the devil is going on here?" she demanded, above the faint sounds of screaming. "I had heard this was rather a rough place, but seriously? What a welcome!" She looked around. "You, and you, come with us. I certainly need additional protection and you two appear well-armed." Abby and Stefanie were, of course, very well-armed, but certainly not with regulation weaponry. Both, however, complied, seizing this unexpected opportunity.

The plan had been to take out the general almost as soon as she'd left the chopper, but the general's reaction to Mario's explosion—for it was indeed he who had set the charges—had slightly complicated the matter. Under the circumstances, they joined the general's entourage.

The mercenary troops on the Arch grounds had disbursed to the parking garage to contain the scene, but Stefanie wasn't worried about Mario. He and his men were long gone and taking up positions all along Market Street, waiting for her signal.

BOOM!

They were walking past Kiener Plaza when smoke billowed up to the north. That would be the rebel troops at Fairground Park. Neither Abby nor Stefanie so much as flinched, but the general didn't notice as she ducked behind them and the rest of her guard. Abby sniffed. Didn't take much to be a general these days.

A sergeant, from the looks of his insignia, spoke rapidly into his radio, then addressed the general. "Ma'am, we seem to have issues in the northern sector. Since our men have found no perpetrators at the garage, they are now deploying in the direction of the explosion. We had best move a bit faster, ma'am, to get you under cover."

"Have we a shortage of troops here in St. Louis?" asked the general. "Is this a new development? Because I was not informed of this." She looked irritated, as well as uncomfortable and slightly fearful. "Your job, Sergeant, is to protect me. I expect no more shenanigans will interrupt my arrival."

"Er, yes, ma'am. Yes, General." The sergeant was bewildered. Seemed to him that a commander should be a little more. . . commanding. Or something.

They continued up Market Street, the sergeant ordering his men to have their weapons at the ready. Abby and Stefanie complied, naturally.

General Scott continued to speak, asking questions and pointing at the falling-down buildings, some of which actually appeared to house civilians. She asked, too, about the barracks and numbers of troops and the weaponry. The sergeant was not at all confident in his answers, explaining that things had been somewhat disrupted by the assassination of Colonel Hoefer three days ago. The general was not impressed.

"You!" she said, poking Abby in the arm and startling her so much that she nearly discharged her weapon. "Perhaps you can fill me on this benighted town?"

Abby thought quickly.

"Yes, ma'am," she said crisply. "There are approximately two thousand troops stationed here, some of whom have, as the sergeant implied, defected. But those were worthless, cowardly scum, ma'am, begging the general's pardon." There, she thought. A reasonable soldierly imitation. She hoped. And a little misinformation, actually, as the count of active troops at this moment was closer to five hundred. She hoped.

"Very good," said General Scott. "See, Sergeant, leave it to a woman to be accurate." The sergeant in question merely gave a Abby a strange look and metaphorically scratched his head.

They were approaching the World War II Memorial when the sky to the west over Forest Park lit up.

***

Alison was stiff and cramped from sitting in the shed with three other people. Well, just one now, Brad, because the two men who had accompanied them had gone to the far side of the barracks. She held her new toy, an M107 sniper rifle. Really couldn't wait to use this baby, especially against the right people for once. Brad tapped her on the shoulder. It was time.

They went outside and crept along the ground; slow going with a nearly thirty-pound rifle, but they didn't have to go far, just within a mile of the tower. Alison set up the M107 and got into position. Brad stayed behind her to avoid blowback, ready with the additional ammo. He checked his watch, then touched her leg. She scooted around a bit, getting comfortable, channeling the weapon in her mind.

BOOM!

That was the site next to the history museum.

BOOM!

That was the second explosion, near the Muny.

She could see her targets through the sight, just two guards on the top of the wall. There would be two others on the far side, but they weren't her concern. BAM! The kickback knocked her on her side and she quickly let go of the weapon to avoid an accidental discharge. She righted herself, re-sighted the M107, and took aim again, prepared for those who would surely follow her first two casualties.

Carmine and his men arrived, slightly out of breath. He sent one of them up the nearest tree with a pair of field glasses, and the reports came rapidly.

"A detachment has left the guardhouse."

"A large group is heading towards the museum."

"Many more are coming this way!"

They all froze. They could hear the sounds of many boots pounding down Government Drive. Soon, the sound faded and everyone breathed deeply.

"Guards are coming out of the tower and spreading around the perimeter."

That could only mean that these men were all that were left; otherwise, they would have stayed inside, hidden and protected.

"Alison," asked Carmine, "How many do you see?"

Alison peered through the sight. "Twenty, I think. No, twenty-four. Two dozen."

"All right. You're up."

She took careful aim, prepared for the backlash, and fired.

BAM! BAM! BAM!

She paused for an instant to reload and, within several minutes, the guards were either down and breathing their last, or had disappeared. In at least one case, maybe more, disappeared almost entirely. Fifty calibers was nothing to expect to recover from, and Alison was good at her job.

Carmine waited, listening. Shots fired from the other side of the barracks and tower had stopped. "Come," he said. "We go in now."

Alison wiggled away from the M107 and got to her feet, a little shaky from the sheer effort of firing that monster. She followed Brad and Carmine and the others as they raced to the structure, hoping just a little that she'd get to use regular weapons today, too.

The group that had gone to North St. Louis had worked their way down to Market Street, half of them going into position around the Federal Building and the others continuing on to the barracks and the tower. Abby and Stefanie, accompanying the general, had reached the corner opposite their destination when runners began to arrive with news.

General Scott waved them off and directed them to speak with the sergeant leading her detail. "These two," she indicated, "are coming with me. Surely they can direct me to my new office."

"But, General Scott, ma'am. . . there is a crisis!" said the sergeant, helplessly. What the hell had Chicago sent them this time? First a maniac, then a sociopath. This one was as bad as both, or worse: she seemed completely clueless. She'd arrived less than two hours ago, amid explosions across the city, and only wanted to see her office?

"Deal with it, Sergeant. By whatever means necessary." And she ascended the steps, flanked by Abby and Stefanie who did their best to appear accommodating. "Show me my office," the general commanded.

Fortunately, Stefanie knew the layout of the building and she led the way. Abby trailed behind, taking in the locations of any exits, watching for interference. They took the elevator up to the top floor, listening to the general "You may call me Kathleen in private" babble about her position and her inside track and even a few choice phrases for the deplorable conditions which had competed with her arrival. Abby mentally shook her head, and she could tell that Stefanie, too, was astounded at the general's attitude.

Abby stopped in shock as they entered the office. This is where her father. . . where Alison had. . . . She quickly got a grip when she saw Stefanie looking at her, raising her brow questioningly. She tightened her expression and continued inside. Kathleen waved them towards two chairs and proceeded to seat herself behind the large desk.

She jumped up almost immediately and screamed, pointing to the wall. It was covered in blood and. . . something else. Abby knew what else. She felt a little sick, given her relationship with the former owner of those pieces of. . . whatever they were. She didn't want to know. Really. But she did.

Stefanie took charge, taking Kathleen by the arm and leading her outside to the hallway. She motioned for Abby and, together, they half-dragged the sobbing woman through another door and made her sit down. Stefanie slammed the door behind them and drew her gun. This would be child's play.

"Kathleen!" she said, sharply. "Pay attention!"

The general looked up, face tear-streaked, makeup running.

"Is this any way for a general to behave?" She smirked. "Abby, give her some water. It's time to chat."

"I am the general," said Kathleen. "You are my subordinate. I won't follow your orders!"

"Ah, but you will," Stefanie told her, in a silky voice. She removed her helmet and tidied her hair, and shucked off the smelly uniform as well, while she continued, "you will tell us all we wish to know, and then we will kill you. Probably. It really depends on the information you give us.

"Abby, your turn. Make yourself comfortable, my friend, we may be here for a while." Stefanie held her gun pointed directly at the general's head.

Abby did as she was told, relieved to be able to access her knife and her sidearm more easily. She wondered exactly what Stefanie had in mind, but she was totally on board. Anyone who could be so calm and cool under fire, in charge of an entire army of several hundred men, was a good person with whom to be allied. Abby was ready for whatever played out.

"Kathleen. We know who you are. We know all about you. We know how you climb upon the backs of others to reach your goals. We also know how incompetent you actually are—even if we had not seen that ourselves, this very day.

"As we speak, our troops are decimating yours. Your city is becoming ours. We are taking back what was stolen from us. Give us answers, and you may live." Stefanie had pulled out her knife, a butterfly, sharp and thin and deadly.

The general stared at her captors. She was pale, but composed. The babbling had ceased, and her eyes narrowed as she spoke. "You can't win. We are too powerful. Listen."

And they heard choppers.

"You may escape," Kathleen continued. "You may not. But you will not win. Not now, not ever." She slipped a capsule out of a tiny pocket in her sleeve and, before either woman could make a move to stop her, she bit down on it, hard. "And," she gasped, "you will not. . . have the. . . satisfaction. . . of killing me!"

BOOM!

Apparently, the sergeant or someone else had called in the troops. It was time to leave the building.

BOOM!

BOOM!

Chapter Thirty-One

Abby and Stefanie raced down the stairs as the building shook; just as they made it onto the street, it began to crumble. Thick smoke filled the air, and people were running helter-skelter in every direction.

"This way!" called Stefanie, and Abby veered to her left, crossing Market Street and racing to the west. The worst, they knew, would be the downtown area. It was Colonel Barton all over again, and Abby flashed back briefly to her escape with Emmy, ten years ago. Only for a moment, though; she was too busy right now fighting for her life.

They ran as far as the old SLU campus, mostly piles of rubble since the last bombing, and took shelter on the west side of Marguerite Hall to catch their breath. Within minutes, they were up and moving, through the Central West End and into Forest Park. Here, Abby took the lead and they slipped noiselessly through the undergrowth until they reached the back of the art museum. They stopped here, slaking their thirst, returning their breathing to normal levels. Or as normal as possible.

BOOM!

Stefanie tried to call Carmine, or Mario, or anyone at all, on her radio; there was no response. She and Abby circled around to the south, and crept as close as possible to the barracks and tower. What they saw made their blood freeze.

Two choppers were hovering, releasing not bombs, but soldiers. More and more, a black rope snaking down to earth, filled with mercenaries and weaponry. The sounds of battle grew louder, deafening. Abby grabbed Stefanie's arm and they ran back to the maintenance shed they'd passed earlier. Just before they reached it, Stefanie tripped and crashed into the hard ground. She landed right next to the M107.

Quickly righting herself, she grabbed the bag of ammo and tossed it to Abby. "Get behind me," she said as she began to load the weapon. She got into position and took careful aim, firing and firing again at every shiny black helmet in her sights.

At last, she rolled away from the gun and got to her feet. "Ready?"

Abby nodded, and they worked their way closer and closer to the barracks. Stefanie's skills had bought them some time, but not much. The choppers had left, but Abby suspected they'd return. It was a rout. The best course of action at this point was to get their people out and away. Going west didn't look like much of an option, as they'd originally planned, so they'd gather whomever they could find and run for the south, back to the house or the brewery, or even through the wall at the railroad bridge if necessary.

Stefanie saw Carmine stagger through a breach in the walls and she ran to him, oblivious to anything else. Before the smoke obscured her vision, Abby saw the two of them stumble and fall. She rushed around the back where the fighting seemed less fierce, pulled out her gun and grabbed her knife, and forced her way inside. Clearing a path, and leaving a few bodies in her wake, she flew around the corner and ran smack into Alison.

"Ouch, dammit!"

"Zip it," Abby told her. "Where's Brad?"

"Haven't seen him for a while. Where have you been, anyway?"

"Playing escort for the general. Long story, I'll tell you later. Let's move!"

They moved cautiously down the hallway, having to clear only three of the enemy before reaching a bunker. The door was open, but it was dark inside. "I'll cover you," Abby told Alison. "Ready?"

Alison nodded. Abby let loose a stream of fire into the darkness and Alison darted past her, Abby on her heels. A voice spoke from inside.

"Dammit, now you two have to shoot at me? Sheesh, can't catch a break around here!"

"Brad?" asked Alison. "What the hell are you doing in there?"

"Oh, nothing much. Having a little rest. Which I could totally manage except my leg is killing me. Some jackass shot me. And not Abby," Brad added, teasingly. "Not this time, anyway."

"Oh for Pete's sake," said Abby, pulling him to his feet. "Alison, take him out the way we came in, go back to that shed, and wait for me. I'm going to look for the others.

"If I'm not there in half an hour, take Brad back to Stefanie and Carmine's. Don't argue, go!" Abby turned and ran down the hallway.

"You heard the boss," said Brad. "Give me a hand here, would you? No, the other side, since it looks like we'll have to shoot our way out of here." The pair began to awkwardly head for an exit, Brad leaning heavily on Alison.

Abby was frantically searching for Stefanie and Carmine. People were running and shouting and the trick seemed to be to shoot first and then ask questions. If the one you shot still lived, of course. Not many did. She fought her way outside, thankfully appearing on the side from which she'd seen the couple disappear.

There were many bodies. Most were dead, some within minutes of that final breath; the wounded had either escaped into the woods or holed up inside the barracks. The air was heavy from smoke and the stench was nearly unbearable. Abby whirled around, and very nearly shot Mario straight between the eyes as he grabbed her arm.

"Come!" he said. "Quickly. Carmine and my sister are heading into the woods. The rest of our people have escaped already. . . or they are dead. Come!"

They ran, into the woods and out the other side, down McCausland Avenue near the wall itself, as it stretched out before them. They caught up with the others just north of Arsenal Street. A dozen or so of the men had stopped to rest; some were tending injuries, mostly flesh wounds that they merely shrugged off.

Abby saw Stefanie and gasped. She was covered with blood.

"No, no, it is not mine. Carmine took the worst of it. This," she indicated her arm, clumsily bandaged, "is nothing."

And then Abby saw Carmine, lying on the ground. His head was bleeding, in spite of the bandana wrapped hastily over the wound. He labored for breath, pale and shaking.

"Come," said Stefanie. "We must go." Some of the men lifted Carmine and they began to walk the rest of the way to the house on Rosa. Abby and Mario brought up the rear, watching for any signs of pursuit.

When they reached the small neighborhood, they were stunned at the sight. But not surprised. Not really. The area was leveled. The smoke had dissipated, it had happened hours ago. Everything. All of it, gone. Carmine and Stefanie's house, gone. And Angela. Surely she had not made it out. No one could have, not this disaster.

No choice. They had to go on, to the old brewery. Stefanie sent two men to check the houses, to look for Angela. The rest of them continued on. . . and Abby hoped that Alison and Brad were safe.

It was just a few miles, but it took them over two hours. The men took turns carrying Carmine; he was fading fast. There was a collective sigh of relief as they approached the brewery. It was still standing, still appeared intact.

Alison was there, with Brad.

The men took Carmine inside, followed closely by Stefanie, and they set him gently down in the large conference room. His lips were blue and he was barely breathing. Stefanie took his hand, as tears streamed down her cheeks. Mario sat on his other side, back against the wall, knees pulled to his chest. Waiting.

Each of their soldiers paid their respects, touched his arm, saluted. Abby and Alison said their goodbyes too, and helped Brad over to sit with him until the end came.

And it did.

Stefanie kissed him, and pulled a blanket over his face. Mario began to sob. Their men remained stoic and unmoving, heads bowed, until Stefanie nodded at them. One of them poured drinks for everyone and they toasted Carmine, their chief.

Eventually, the soldiers filed out to prepare their quarters for the night. Stefanie sent Mario with them, but stopped Abby as she rose to follow Brad and Alison to the room next door.

"I will stay here tonight," Stefanie said. "With Carmine. But you, you and Alison and Brad must leave before the sun rises. You must get out of the city, and back to wherever you are going, before daylight.

"Abby, I want you to take Mario with you."

Abby wasn't sure what to say. "But, Stefanie, shouldn't he be here with you. . . now?" She glanced over at Carmine's body and bit her lip.

"No. He is my baby brother, and it is too dangerous here. He will want revenge, and he will be killed as well. Take him with you. Please." Stefanie put a hand on Abby's arm. "Please. I know he will be safe with you."

"And if he doesn't want to go?"

"He will go," Stefanie said, with the barest hint of a smile. "He will go, because I will tell him he must."

Chapter Thirty-Two

They left St. Louis that night and traveled back to the camp, arriving near dawn. The kids were all still sleeping, but Walt was waiting by the fire, coffee ready. Abby introduced him to Mario, who was practically asleep on his feet, and Brad showed the boy where he'd be staying. He left him in the tent to catch a quick nap and sat down at the fire with the others.

Walt relit his pipe and remained silent while the others told him about the situation in the city.

"Seems to me," he said slowly, "that now we have enough people to make a difference. But the government is always going to have more guns and bigger weapons."

"Even if we took the city," said Brad, "we'd never be able to hold it, not if they wanted it back badly enough."

"Well, now," Walt said, "do we want it? Do we need it? Seems to me we got everything we need right here, or even in other places. Long as they leave us alone."

"That's exactly it, Walt," said Abby. "For more than ten years they haven't been leaving me alone!" She got up, agitated, and began to pace around the fire.

"I came down here because of VADER. I stayed because of government interference and well, because they kept trying to kill me. And that was just on principle, because I survived, because we all had survived. And then it got personal.

"Well, that personal reason—he's gone. But I don't think the government itself is going to stop. Hell, they blew up their own city, and surely some of their people, just to stop us. And that was yesterday! If they were going to give up trying to exterminate us, because we don't fit their mold and won't follow their orders, then they'd do it now. Give up, I mean, and leave us alone."

"I think Abby nailed it," said Walt. "And that's why I propose a wait-and-see plan. Let's figure out a place to hide, if we need to run from here, and see what happens next. Maybe they'll come for us. Maybe not. Maybe they've used up enough of their resources getting nowhere fast."

EJ burst out of the tent and threw herself at Abby. "I thought I heard you talking out here!"

Abby smothered her daughter in kisses, relieved to be finished with the conversation. Elizabeth stumbled sleepily over to the fire, and Abby put her arms out to the little girl. The three of them snuggled into a blanket and both girls tried to talk over each other, telling Abby what they'd been doing the last few days.

Jules was the next to emerge. She half-heartedly waved at everyone and filled her coffee mug before she sat down next to Alison. "Tell me everything," she said.

Abby and Alison exchanged looks, and Alison shrugged. Jules was fifteen, after all, and had been up there with them the first time. Alison started with Kat, General Scott, and told her all about the battle at the tower.

"An M107? Cool!" Jules looked suitably impressed.

Alison was startled. "What do you know about the M107?"

"I read," said Jules, loftily. "Did you bring it back with you?"

Abby smirked. "She's your daughter, all right."

Alison started to tell her that it was lost to the enemy, but just then, Mario walked out to the fire. Jules' mouth dropped open and she stared at him. Her mother resisted the temptation to tell her she'd brought her a souvenir anyway. Jules turned beet red and shoved her coffee mug into her face.

David followed on Mario's heels and, throwing a challenging look at the newcomer, seated himself beside Jules. Alison tried to hide her smile but failed, which earned her a whispered, "Mom, cut it out!"

Little Johnny had slipped out nearly unnoticed during all the covert teenage drama and was sitting at Walt's feet, wrapped in his blanket. He smiled at everyone, but didn't speak.

"Well, kids, why don't you tell everyone what we've been up to while they were out gallivanting?" Walt tapped the ashes out of his pipe and poured another cup of coffee.

"Well," said Elizabeth, "Walt took us out shooting. EJ did better with the handgun, but I won the rifle contest. Of course," she added, "that's 'cause I'm older."

"And I taught them how to track," piped up EJ. "Just like you showed me, Mom!" Abby smiled and hugged her again. "Johnny moves a lot more quietly than I do, though," she said ruefully.

"How about you young ones go get dressed and we'll just show them what else we practiced. But after breakfast. I imagine everyone's getting pretty hungry." Walt built up the fire a tad and Johnny, who had already washed and dressed, unlike the girls, helped him with the cooking. Everyone else went into their respective tents, except Mario. He asked if he could help too, and Walt was never one to turn down assistance when it was offered.

Spring came at last, and the moderate temperatures were welcome. Rain fell, too, and the woods became green and full again. They shifted their campsite back farther, on the hillside above the spring, and worked diligently to widen the small opening of another cave that Elizabeth had found.

She had EJ had gone tracking one day, and discovered it tucked back at the side of a ravine on the north slope of Purple Mountain. The opening was barely large enough for the girls to squeeze through, but they managed. The cave opened into a wide space, but with a rather low ceiling. However, at the back, there was another opening in that ceiling that looked as though, long ago, someone had lashed a makeshift ladder in place.

Once the entrance was large enough, Brad and Walt set about fixing it up to use as a shelter. They taught the kids how to lash and even made some rough-looking furniture. Mario and David fashioned a store-room off to one side and began to move in extra supplies. EJ and Johnny and Elizabeth camouflaged both openings, and everyone was pleased with the final result.

Remembering their own days in school, Abby and Alison relaxed their educational standards over the summer and let the kids run wild. They'd developed a co-parenting arrangement of sorts but, with Alison and Brad having become "an item," as Walt had stated, he took on the role of Jules' father. "And a much better one than, Whatshisname," Alison confided to Abby.

Brad seemed to take it in stride, except when Jules would try to play him against some decision or other that her mother had made. The other kids still called him "Uncle Brad," and Johnny especially seemed to follow him around.

Johnny blossomed with all the attention and the people surrounding him. He knew he was safe at last, and slowly, slowly began to open up and to even speak occasionally. His sister was maturing as well, and seemed a lot less inclined to make pronouncements and try to lord it over the younger ones. EJ in particular was pleased with this; Jules had never been bossy with her, and Elizabeth sometimes annoyed her greatly.

Jules, however, was distracted. She and David had become close over the months since they'd first met. Two teenagers, both living separate and isolated lives, both on the verge of adulthood. It could have been a recipe for disaster. At the same time, both were reserved and remarkably mature for their ages, and neither wanted to disappoint their assorted parental figures.

Alison and Abby kept a close eye on them, finding creative ways to separate the two when they sensed that things might be progressing too far. At this stage, nothing good could come of any kind of relationship other than that as friends.

But when Mario had arrived, Jules was hit with a thunderclap.

She didn't neglect her duties, exactly, but rushed through them, often earning a sharp rebuke from her mother. She found excuses to hang out wherever Mario was working, and spent more time in her tent, presumably daydreaming.

Alison finally sat her down to have a chat.

"Mom! I know all that. And I'm not going to do anything. . . Mario doesn't seem the least bit interested in me, anyway." She tossed her braid over her shoulder and walked off in a huff.

"Well," said Alison. "That didn't go well."

Abby laughed. "You forgot that she was here with me when EJ was born. She knows what might happen, for sure. And I had to er, explain a few things back then."

"I missed a lot, didn't I?" Alison sighed.

"Cheer up!" Abby told her. "Maybe you can preside at the birth of your grandchild one of these days."

Alison smacked her on the arm and followed her daughter, in a huff.

Almost before they realized it, fall was arriving with a gorgeous display of color. The nights were crisp and clear, and soon they'd move into the cave.

And then a messenger arrived from St. Louis.

Chapter Thirty-Three

It was George, one of Stefanie's men. He told the anxious group that yes, things were still fairly calm in the city and no, the government had yet to send a replacement for General Scott. There had been no raids or bombing, but the mercenaries were running amok and the atmosphere was tense. Then he took Mario aside for a private conversation.

When they returned to the fire, Mario told them he'd be leaving in the morning with George, that Stefanie had become ill. She had insisted he remain there, but George's father, one of the lieutenants, had sent his son secretly to find them. He was worried.

Jules quietly withdrew to her tent, and David, noticing, rolled his eyes. He liked and respected Mario and he knew how Jules felt about him, but she didn't have to be a brat about it. He followed her while Mario continued to discuss his plans.

She was sitting morosely on her bed when he lifted the flap and ducked into the tent. "Hey, what's the matter with you anyway? He's just going up to St. Louis. His sister needs him."

Jules gave him a look. "I know, I know, okay? I just wish he didn't have to go."

"Yeah, well. Quit acting like you don't care and that you're the only one with feelings. It's about Mario, not you. Grow up already."

David stopped when he saw her face. It wasn't that of a spoiled child, but a sad young woman. He held out his hand. "Come on, let's go back outside. It'll be okay. Now try to smile, or something. You look pretty scary like this."

"Huh," said Jules, tossing her head. "Keep bugging me, I'll show you scary!"

They went back to the fire. The younger ones were sent off to bed while the adults caught up on the rest of the news from the city. They talked long into the night, but Jules managed to get a private moment with Mario.

She waited until he and George walked back to the cave, so Mario could show him the work they'd done. She silently followed them and was sitting on a large rock when they came back out. George saw her first, and he grinned and bowed in her direction, before calling over his shoulder, "I'll see you back at the fire, old man!"

Mario halted abruptly when he saw Jules. The cold air frosted their breath and it mingled together as he stood before her. He took her hands in his. He leaned towards her, and Jules closed her eyes.

He kissed both her cheeks, and said, "I will miss you." He squeezed her hands, and was gone.

Jules sat very still for a long time. Then she wiped away her tears and went back to the fire.

Mario and George left at first light.

The group moved into the cave the next morning, clearing the campsite of all their belongings, removing all traces of the firepit and all evidence of their presence. The project took the entire day, and everyone was exhausted and looking forward to sleep.

Days turned into weeks, then months, with no word from St. Louis. Winter came, then the new year. They began to speculate less and less about what might be happening and began to talk about perhaps moving elsewhere, finding other survivors. But without news, it was hard to know in which direction to travel or even where to go and what to do.

And then spring arrived. The days became longer, and they could all see how restless David was becoming. He finally sat down with Walt one day to talk about his future.

"What's on your mind, young David?"

David shrugged. "Everything, I guess."

"Well, spit it out, son. Although I guess we do have all day, pretty much." The old survivalist lit his pipe.

"I want to leave," said David, looking down.

"I figured as much. Because of Jules? That girl mopes around so much, I'm about ready to leave too."

"Naw, Jules and I. . . there's nothing between us. Really. I just want to go somewhere, see something else for a change. See what's out there."

Walt nodded. "I get that. You're young, rarin' to go. And I'm just teasin' you about Jules, son. You're what, nineteen?"

"Yes."

"Well, you don't need my permission, I guess. Where you think you might be heading?"

"I'd like to go west," said David. "I've been talking to Abby about when she was out there, Arizona and New Mexico and all that."

"That was a long time ago, David. Things have changed."

"Oh, I know that. But if I avoid the cities, if there are any still out there, then I'm not worried. I can take care of myself." David was confident and smart, and mature enough to know that there were still dangers—but ones he was willing to face.

"You can sure do that, son. I'll hate to see you go, but you have to do what you have to do. If it's calling you, then go ahead. When did you plan to leave? And, more important, when did you plan to tell everyone?"

"I'll tell them tonight," said David, his brown eyes shining with excitement. "And leave in a few days, as soon as I can map out a route and gather the supplies I'll need."

"Alrighty then," said Walt, standing up and giving David an unexpected hug. "I'll miss you, boy." And he turned abruptly and walked away, head bowed.

By dinnertime, though, Walt seemed to have recovered. He stood up for David when everyone protested his leaving, and he talked to Johnny and Elizabeth, too, who looked upon David as their big brother. Everyone settled down and began to talk excitedly about his upcoming adventure, making lists and giving suggestions.

Except Jules. She stomped off to her tent and refused to come out.

The next morning, she found David at the firepit before the others arrived.

"I'm sorry," she told him. "This time, I was being a spoiled brat."

"Yeah," he said, "you were. Are you over it now? 'Cause I really want to talk to you about something."

Jules looked a little apprehensive, but said, "Go ahead."

"I know you must think I'm nuts, going off by myself, but it's different for me. You've got Abby and your mom and Brad. And the others too," he added hastily. "But my folks have been gone a long time, and well, there's Walt and the kids, but. . . it's different."

Jules scooted over next to him. "I understand. I'd like to go too, but you know what they'd say to that!" She rolled her eyes dramatically. "Maybe, you know, when I'm like twenty or something."

David laughed. "Maybe. But I wouldn't count on it." Then he turned serious again. "Look, I won't be gone forever. I'll come back. And maybe I can find another place for all of us, a better place, without that damn city hanging over us all the time.

"Then again, maybe you like the city. Mario's there, after all."

"No," said Jules firmly. "I like it much better here, where I grew up. Other than those couple of days in St. Louis and a few months up in Labadie, I've always lived here. And anyway, I haven't heard a single word from Mario in forever!"

As though her very words had conjured up the young man himself, he came walking up the road toward them, waving and smiling.

"No. Way," said Jules, gaping. "No way!"

David smothered a grin as he stood up to greet Mario and Jules backed up quickly, hidden behind a tree, to rapidly fix her hair. She hoped no one noticed.

Unfortunately for her, not only did Alison appear from her tent at that precise moment, but David made sure to wave in her direction as he talked to Mario.

"What in the world is going on here?" Alison smiled at the sight of the young man from St. Louis. "Mario! We're so glad to have you back!"

Soon everyone came outside to the firepit and they all began talking at once. Mario held up his hand. "Please, I can't answer you all at the same time!"

Finally, they settled down, and coffee mugs were filled and passed around. Jules stayed close to the younger kids, sitting beside EJ, watching Mario for any signs of . . . what? She wasn't entirely sure what she was waiting for or hoping to see. Or hear. She still hadn't spoken directly to him and she felt like her face was on fire.

Mario began, "This is very difficult, but I first must tell you about my sister. She has passed away. It was not violent, as perhaps she would have wished, in the heat of battle, but from illness. There are no more medicines in the city, at least, none available to those such as us.

"When George came for me, last fall, Stefanie was very sick. Bronchitis, we believe, or pneumonia. It makes no difference. She went quickly, not long after I arrived.

"I am very sorry to have to tell you this."

Abby drew a sharp breath, and willed herself under control. No. Not Stefanie. . . . Alison had tears rolling down her cheeks. Everyone was very quiet for some time.

EJ broke the silence, tugging on Abby's arm. "Mom, is that the lady you told me about?"

Abby nodded, and hugged the little girl. "We're so sorry, Mario," she said, speaking for them all.

"Yes, thank you. But it was many months ago and I am past most of the sadness. I have been very busy since then, as I am now the head of our little family. Several of our lieutenants were also ill, and some did not recover. However, I bring more news as well. Some of which you will not want to hear, either."

Abby glanced at Walt and he took the hint. "Come on, kids, let's go rustle up some breakfast for everyone." He led the younger ones back to the cave to gather the cooking things and supplies.

Mario continued. "We have observed quite a lot of activity in the city, especially to the west and north. Thankfully, we have remained safe to the south. But in other places, it appears as though the government is packing up entirely and moving on to. . . we don't know where, yet. But they are definitely leaving.

"While good news, this does create some additional problems for us. It is likely that we will lose power and water which, while we can do without, does present some issues." He smiled. I suppose we could come down here and live off the land, but we are city people and, while I, for one, would certainly enjoy it, some of my men would rather remain on pavement." This time, he smiled directly at Jules, and even though she was seated, her knees felt wobbly. She ducked her head and busied herself with cleaning her knife.

"The third thing that I wish to pass along is that there have been more choppers seen in the area. They have been circling and hovering to the north of St. Louis, well outside the city. My men have been gathering intel on this new development, and the information is not good.

"They are using a special building, north past Black Jack, to house those to whom they refer as 'examples.' These include the very young as well as the older people that they have rounded up from out in the countryside. To the north and the west," he repeated.

"It is only a matter of time before they come to the south."

The adults took in this new information with varying reactions. Abby's first thought was to run, but damn, she was tired of that. She knew, though, that they couldn't fight back. Unless they had their own chopper. Or half a dozen.

Brad was ready to go into the city and fight. He was always ready to go somewhere, in fact, Abby and Alison both were surprised that he hadn't suggested going west with David. This would be right up his alley.

Alison first said what they were all thinking. "This is about the kids. And maybe someone Walt's age. So we need to protect them, get them out of here, and go. . . where?"

"Yes," said Abby, "But I'm curious. Mario, have your men said anything about the reason for this?"

Mario shook his head. "They do not know, but of course they are checking into everything, around the clock. I am due for a report soon; George knows the way, he should arrive here this afternoon."

Abby looked at the others. "VADER. It has to be VADER. They still haven't found a way to counteract it, and the older people are survivors. They have to hold the key."

"But the kids?" Brad asked. "Some of them, sure, but what about the younger ones, like EJ?"

"Re-education," spoke up Alison. "It was discussed, but never implemented. Until now."

Chapter Thirty-Four

"Like what they did to me," said Brad.

Abby was horrified. From the few things Brad had revealed, he'd been kept nearly comatose for many months, physically helpless, and pumped with a constant barrage of misinformation. The drugs alone were frightening to contemplate.

"David," said Abby. "You were planning to leave tomorrow, right?"

"Yes, ma'am."

"I'm sorry," she apologized, "but we're going to ask you to put your plans on hold. I know that none of us, really, can tell you what to do, but Walt and the kids have to go somewhere a lot safer than here. Temporarily, of course. After that, I see no reason why you can't still have your adventure."

"Whatever I need to do," said David. "I understand."

The kids were cooking breakfast, under Walt's direction, and Brad made sure everyone knew what was going on over the course of the next day or two. They all scattered after the meal was finished, some to pack, some to divide supplies, others to consult maps. And they waited for George.

He arrived late in the afternoon, just in time for supper. He pulled up a log and sat down with the others, looking to Mario for permission to speak. Mario nodded, and George told them what they'd discovered. And it was bad. Really bad.

The government was not only "re-educating" the children, but some, who were deemed intractable or too indoctrinated by parents or guardians, were systematically being eliminated. The rest were being held in the Black Jack facility until transport could be arranged, presumably to Chicago. The older folks were given no chance at all and were immediately executed.

They'd also heard that the round-ups to the west and north had been completed, and that the southern efforts would begin tomorrow, at first light.

Walt and David and the kids were ready to go, and Walt had showed them, on the map, exactly where he was headed. It was a tiny town, if one could call it a town, actually, about sixty miles to the southwest: Cook Station. Walt had gone down there many times as a child, hunting with his dad. He knew the area well, right near the Meramec River.

It was killing Abby to send EJ away, but she knew the little girl would be in good hands and, really, it was the safest option. The rest of them were planning to stay put at the camp, hunker down, and watch and wait.

Supper was rather subdued, no one talked much, they simply ate because they needed to. No one noticed as Mario and Jules slipped off into the trees.

"I missed you," he told her.

Jules was speechless as he took her hands in his. For a moment, she thought her heart had stopped beating. He leaned in closer, and they kissed. Her pulse skyrocketed, making up for the lost beat, and her stomach flip-flopped.

Mario led her to a nearby log and they sat down. She surreptitiously wiped her sweaty palms on her jeans as he put his arm around her. "We must talk. I want us to be together, but not now. You must stay here and be safe."

"But. . . ."

"Hush," he said, kissing her again. He helped her up and squeezed her hand briefly as they walked back to the firepit.

They said their goodbyes to Mario and George and the two men departed from the camp. Walt rounded up the kids and got them tucked in, but David stopped to talk to Jules as she was putting out the fire.

He tipped her chin up and looked at her closely. "What are you plotting?" he teased. "And what have you been up to?"

She jerked away from him, mumbled, "Nothing," and paid particular attention to extinguishing the last few embers.

"Uh-huh. I'll bet. Well, you may as well talk, because I'm not going anywhere until you do." David sat down and began to double-check his pack.

"Fine," said Jules. "Sit here all night if you want, but I'm going to bed!"

David stuck his foot out as she flounced off, head in the air. He caught her easily, before she hit the ground. "What's the matter, Jules? Did he try something?"

"No!" said Jules, trying to control her rising voice so she wouldn't disturb the others. "He—he kissed me, that's all."

"All right," said David. "But just a word of advice, Jules. Don't go after him. Don't try to go to St. Louis. Stay here and be safe."

"That's what he said. And I'm not planning on it, so relax."

"Right," said David with a grin. "'Impulsive' should have been your middle name. I mean it, don't do anything stupid, Jules."

"Of course not," she assured him, wondering how he could read her mind or if it was just a lucky guess. She knew she couldn't get away with it, anyway, her mother would be watching her like a hawk, and Abby and Brad too. Damn.

"And Jules?"

"Yes?"

"I'll come back, you know. As soon as I get Walt settled in." He smiled at her and she gave him a hug before they went to their respective tents. She blew him a kiss and disappeared inside. David looked resigned, but shrugged it off and he, too, went to bed.

Abby laid awake for a long time that night, EJ tucked securely under her arm, snuggling close. She couldn't quite believe that her daughter, her baby, had to go so far away. Back in the old days, an hour or so drive would have been nothing. Not now. They had a long hike ahead of them, several days probably, and there would be no communication.

EJ would be fine, she knew that. Really. It was just that. . . she'd only ever been apart from her for a couple days at a time, and EJ had never been in any real danger. Her daughter was smart and capable but still, she was only six. What had she been thinking? But no. . . it had to be like this.

At last she fell into a restless sleep.

Jules wandered around the next morning after everyone left, and desultorily started and stopped half a dozen chores before plopping down with a heavy sigh. Abby sat down next to her.

"Guess we're both at loose ends, huh?"

"Yeah. So, what are we going to do? Just sit and wait? And what are we waiting for anyway?" Jules was plucking blades of grass and throwing them back down. Over and over.

Alison joined them. "Brad and I were up late last night, talking. He thinks we should hang tight for the time being, wait and see what else Mario can find out. Then maybe do some exploring ourselves."

Abby frowned. "It'll be at least five days, closer to a week, before David gets back. We can't do anything until then."

"Of course," said Alison. "But we need to figure out something after that. I, for one, am not looking forward to hanging out with you two grumpy individuals for more than that week. Sheesh, lighten up!"

"Fine," said Abby and Jules at the same time.

Alison threw up her hands. "Oh, this is gonna be fun!"

Robin Tidwell

Chapter Thirty-Five

David was back in three days, not five. The minute they saw him come running up the road they knew something terrible had happened. Abby's heart was racing and she flew across the gravel.

"David!" she screamed.

He stopped abruptly, gasping for air, and reached behind his back for a large bundle. He gently lowered it to the ground and Abby tore open the blankets, crying hysterically. David sank to the ground, exhausted, as Jules arrived. Brad and Alison were right behind her.

It was EJ. She had a large, purple lump on her head, her face was white, and there was blood on the blankets. She was very still.

Abby's hands were shaking as she fought to free her daughter. The little girl made no sound at all and Abby leaned over her, listening. She was breathing, thank God. She scooped her up and half-ran, half-walked under EJ's weight, back to the fire. Alison went with her, and together they checked the damage.

A bullet wound in her shoulder. Looking pale herself, Abby carefully turned EJ on her side and saw that the projectile had passed clean through. But she was still bleeding. The women cleaned the wound and packed it with gauze, wrapping the shoulder tightly. Abby felt EJ's forehead; a slight fever. She sent Alison to get some wet cloths. Unless it went much higher, that was the course they would follow for now.

She was more concerned about the bump on the side of EJ's head, near her left temple. She didn't yet know how long EJ had been unconscious, but she wasn't going to leave her daughter to find out. She looked up and saw Jules and Brad helping David towards the campsite.

David could barely stand, but his breathing was returning to normal. They sat him on the ground, on a blanket that Alison had spread out for him. He refused to lie down and began to tell them what had happened, in between gulps of water.

"Slow down, son," said Brad. "We can wait until you're ready. Take it easy, you're okay now."

"Yes. I know that. But, the others. . . ." David took another drink. "Is EJ going to be okay?"

"I think so," said Abby, with a small smile. "David, I can't thank you enough for bringing her back. I really just. . . can't. . . ." Her voice broke and she touched David's hand as she began to cry again.

After a minute, it was over. "Dammit. I never cry." But she started and again and couldn't stop for many more minutes, until finally lapsing into a choking sob. "Thank you."

Then David began to tell them about the raid.

"After we left here that morning, we walked about twenty miles before we camped for the night. We made sure to stay under cover, and Walt found us a protected spot in grove of trees. We kept the fire small, the noise low, we did everything we were supposed to do.

"The next day, we started out again. We were somewhere around Potosi, I think, when the choppers came."

Abby tensed. Those damn choppers. Again.

"Walt was in the lead. Elizabeth and Johnny were right behind him, and EJ and I were bringing up the rear. We were behind the others a little way, not much, maybe fifty yards.

"They shot. . . they shot a net out of the chopper. They came down real low, and dropped it. They got the others, and then. . . .

"EJ ran. Not toward Walt, but she made a break for the trees, to our right. A shot was fired. I saw her go down. I rolled into the ditch and stayed down. I didn't move for, oh, half an hour? Maybe less. Seemed like a long time.

"The choppers left, and after a while I circled around to where EJ'd run and I found her. I tried to stop the bleeding, did stop most of it, I guess." David paused to drink some more water. "I patched her up as best I could and bundled her on my back. Been running ever since, on and off."

Abby laid her hand on EJ's forehead. Still too warm. But not hot. Still unconscious. It had been, what a day? Two days, nearly? There were still questions to be asked.

Brad and Alison exchanged glances. "David," she asked gently, "what happened to Walt and the children?"

David turned his head away. He took a deep breath.

"Walt's dead. They shot him. They took the kids in the chopper."

Alison gasped. Brad shook his head and his face was grim.

Jules had been silent throughout David's recital. She kept looking at EJ, clearly worried, trying to take in everything at once. She made David lie down and covered him with a blanket, then sat beside him as he fell into a deep sleep.

Abby nodded at Brad, and he and Alison moved away from the fire.

"We're going up there, aren't we?" asked Alison.

"Yes."

"And Abby's okay with this." This time it wasn't a question. "What about David and Jules?"

"David's in no shape to go anywhere, not for a few days at least," he told her.

"And Jules?" Alison was afraid she knew the answer.

"I think she should come," Brad said. "We could use the help, she knows what she's doing, and I'm thinking she'd really like to go, er, to St. Louis." He looked slightly abashed as Alison gave him a penetrating glare.

"Yeah. Okay. You say that like it's a vacation," she accused him.

"Come on, sure it'll be a little dangerous, but you know she thrives on that—like her mother."

"Does no good to try to sweet-talk me, Brad. Look at what happened to. . . look what happened! I don't want Jules to. . . to. . . ." Alison stopped. She couldn't even form the words.

Brad put his arm around her. "It'll be okay. Abby will stay here and take care of EJ, with David to help her or come find us if. . . you know. And Jules can come with us. Problem solved."

"Didn't think we had a 'problem,' but okay, whatever," Alison mumbled. She stomped off to clean her guns. She just wasn't quite sure right now at whom to aim.

Just before midnight, EJ awoke. "Mom? My head hurts."

Abby breathed a silent prayer of thanks, more worried than she had let on, and kissed EJ's little cheeks over and over. "Mom, stop. Ouch!" EJ grabbed at her shoulder. "What happened?"

"You got shot, EJ, now be still and let me check on you."

"I did? Cool!"

"Hush!" Abby checked the bandages, relieved that the bleeding was almost stopped. She put another cool cloth on EJ's bump and noticed that her forehead was finally of a normal temperature. She gave her a drink of water and helped her get more comfortable.

"Ouch," said EJ again. "I didn't think getting shot would hurt so much. And why does my head feel funny?"

"Apparently," said Abby, "you tripped and smacked it on a rock."

"Oh. Where's Elizabeth, and Johnny? Are they out playing somewhere?" EJ was about to fall back asleep.

"We'll talk in the morning, sweetheart." Abby kissed her again.

EJ bolted upright, heedless of the pain in her shoulder and her head. "Mommy! I remember now!" She began to sob softly. "The bad men took them, didn't they? And they shot Walt too, I saw it!"

"Oh, EJ. . . ." Abby's heart was breaking to know that her little girl had seen what happened. EJ cried herself to sleep, sobbing piteously, and all Abby could do was sit with her and hold her hand.

Abby stepped outside the tent to get some air and to stretch. Alison and Brad were ready to go, but Jules was rigging a crude shelter over the still-sleeping David. It was too risky to drive, even in the dark, and they had a good six or seven hour hike ahead of them. They wanted to get into the city before dawn. Abby waved them off down the road, and went back into her tent to try to catch some sleep.

EJ was much improved by morning, and ravenously hungry. Abby was surprised to see David up and awake, building the fire, tending to breakfast. She yawned and accepted the mug of coffee he offered. He smiled shyly and thanked her for letting him sleep.

Abby smiled back. "Are you kidding? You saved EJ's life—I'll never forget that, David, and I owe you a lot more than a good night's sleep."

"Mom, don't be getting all mushy and stuff!"

"EJ's awake?" asked David. "She's okay?" He looked anxiously toward the sound of the little voice.

"Yes," said Abby, "she's fine. Go on in and see her."

Abby could hear them talking, and in a few minutes David appeared, carrying EJ to the fire. The little girl sipped her watered-down coffee and smiled. Then grimaced in pain. "Ouch."

"Time to change your bandages, little one." Abby warmed some water and steeped a handful of flowers in it. She dipped a bandana into the water and wrung it out, cleaning EJ's wound and rewrapping it. "Here," she handed EJ another mug filled with tea. "Drink this, it will help, and it won't make you sleepy."

"I'm already sleepy," answered EJ, draining the mug. David scooped her up and took her back to bed.

He came back out and told Abby, "I'm kind of sleepy too. Do you mind if I take a quick nap?"

"Of course not. Here, you may as well have some of this. I imagine you're going to be pretty sore by the time you wake up."

David made a face when he tasted the tea. "What is this?"

Abby laughed. "Coriander tea. We've used this for years, ever since we ran out of Advil and Tylenol and all those others. EJ doesn't even notice the taste anymore."

"What did you put on her shoulder?"

"A marigold poultice. It's antibacterial and antifungal. Comes in handy a lot out here."

"Interesting," said David. "Where did you learn all this?"

"Mostly from reading," Abby told him. "That is, for the plants and things around here. But when I was out west I learned a lot about medicine from the older Indians and the medicine men."

"Well," David sighed. "Maybe someday I'll get out there myself and get to see everything, like you did." He yawned. "Goodnight, Abby."

She kept busy all day, striking the tents that weren't being used and moving everything back farther into the woods. When David and EJ awoke near lunchtime, she fixed them something to eat and stayed with EJ while David made several trips to the cave with all their gear. They took down the last two tents and put out the fire, finishing the move before the sun went down. Abby wasn't taking any chances that someone might spot them.

The two kids fell asleep early, but Abby was too keyed up to rest. She went through the remaining supplies, cataloging what they had and what else they might be needing soon. She planned to go to the spring tomorrow to wash out some clothing and blankets. Anything to keep busy, to stop obsessing over what might be happening in St. Louis.

Chapter Thirty-Six

Things were indeed happening in St. Louis. Brad and Alison, and Jules, had made it to the railroad bridge but there was no need to creep beneath it, hidden by the near-darkness. The barracks across the wall was deserted.

They made their way up Broadway and walked down Cherokee Street, arriving just as Mario's men were changing guard duty. Mario himself was the first to spot them and he broke into a smile when he saw Jules. He quickly reached them and asked, worriedly, "Why are you here? What has happened?"

Brad filled him in on the death of Walt and the capture of Elizabeth and Johnny. He explained that Abby and David were at the camp tending to EJ, who was recovering.

"Now," he said. "We need your help. Can one of your men take us north, to where they are holding the prisoners?"

"But of course," said Mario. "George!" His friend emerged from the doorway of the brewery. "Gather your men and meet us in the conference room." George went back inside, and Mario continued, "Please, come in and eat. We will talk more, and decide how best to infiltrate."

Jules was overcome with shyness, much to her mother's amusement, as they sat around the large table after breakfast. She kept gazing at Mario, until he turned his head in her direction, then quickly studied her hands, the map, the wall, anywhere but Mario himself. Brad tried to hide his smile.

It would take several hours to reach the facility, by roundabout fashion, and they had to wait until dark. This was the only area of the city in which they needed to be concerned about patrols. George and his men knew the route well, from previous expeditions, and Mario said that he, too, would be going with them.

"Come," he said, "I wish to show you what we have. . . accumulated." He took them into a nearby office.

They gaped in astonishment. Lining two of the walls were racks of Kevlar vests; the third was stacked with boxes of ammo, to the ceiling. And in the center were crates of weapons.

"You've been busy," remarked Alison, casually walking over to an M107.

"Well," said Mario deprecatingly, "the soldiers were in a hurry to vacate. And, of course, some of this was. . . liberated. . . before they moved out." He motioned to Jules, who reacted as though she'd just now noticed he was present.

He pulled down a vest and helped her into it, fastening it snugly. She wanted to look anywhere but into his eyes, but the nature of the situation prevented that. Then she wanted to close her eyes, but didn't want to look like she was expecting. . . something. At last, he stepped back and turned her around to check the fit.

"Perfect!" he announced. Then he whispered into her ear, "And now you will be much safer." Jules felt light-headed, and she blushed.

Thankfully, Alison was busy checking the M107 while Brad examined a rocket launcher, an M72LAW. Both had weapons aplenty, but these were too good to pass up, even considering the size and weight. Jules, they decided, should stick with what she knew best, her rifle and her knife.

After lunch, they had a brief rest, then met again in the conference room to finalize the plans. Mario nodded at Jules, and she blushed again, ducking her head. After the session, the men filed out along with Alison and Brad, who was talking animatedly to George.

Mario put his hand on Jules' shoulder and she stopped. "So you couldn't wait for me to come back, eh?" he teased. He put his arms around her, and leaned down to kiss her. For a split second, Jules thought her legs would melt, but then she lost herself in his embrace.

All too quickly it ended, and they hurried to catch up with the others.

They followed Chouteau to the west, then Kingshighway north. They stopped for a breather on the far side of Calvary Cemetery. Jules stayed close to Mario, but neither Alison nor Brad appeared to notice the proximity. They kept checking to make sure she was nearby, but were focused on the mission itself.

Cutting through the small city of Jennings, they moved north at a slower pace; it took perhaps two hours to reach Black Jack. They crouched in the shadow of a falling-down church on Parker Road, George and his dozen soldiers taking up defensive position. The others prepared to sneak across to the road to the well-secured concrete building.

Mario led them. Sweeping lights arced through the air, but no guards could be seen. He approached the wire-topped wall and packed two bricks of C4 into a hole. Setting the charges, he fell back with the others into the trees and pressed the remote.

BAM!

No sirens. No shouts. But there was enough of a hole blown that they could, with some effort, wiggle through into the dark yard of the prison.

As Alison climbed to her feet, she warily looked around. Strange. No one had come running, there were no sounds at all. Just the sweeping lights, high above the razor wire. They moved into a circle, backs together, weapons held at the ready.

"What the hell?" whispered Brad. "Where is everyone?"

They moved across the yard to the building. Jules jimmied the door, which wasn't particularly secure to begin with. She guessed that the government thought the wire and wall and sirens and guards would keep out those who wanted in, and keep those inside from getting out.

The hallway was deserted too.

They moved along one corridor after another, single file, Brad in the lead. Nothing. No one.

Mario clicked his radio. "George, move in. Tell me what you see." They waited.

George's voice came through clearly: "Nothing out here, boss. Nada."

Mario looked at Brad. "Well? What do you think?"

"I think we've been set up—or they've all left."

"They're gone," said Jules. "Or they would have shown up by now. This place is deserted. And creepy," she added. "Mom?"

Alison nodded. "Yeah, Jules is right. I think."

Mario clicked the radio again: "George, open fire."

"What, boss?"

Mario grinned. "Open fire. On the wall."

"Sure thing!"

They heard the muffled racket of automatic weapons, then silence. George's voice came from the radio. "Nothing and no one out here, boss! Weird."

"Alright then," said Mario. "Come on in." Within minutes, George and his men were inside the prison and everyone fanned out to finish clearing the building. Jules took off too, but Alison grabbed her arm and kept her close.

"Stay with me," she said. "Until we're positive."

The two of them went down a hallway that appeared to hold offices of some sort. The last one they came to, on the left, was the largest. It was empty except for a mahogany desk. It looked familiar, but Alison couldn't quite place it. On the desk was a single sheet of paper.

Jules turned it right side up so they could read it. Alison gasped when she saw the words.

"Dear Alison, I see you made it this far. Too bad it was for nothing. I win!"

It was signed "Kat."

Robin Tidwell

Chapter Thirty-Seven

Abby was tossing and turning, unable to sleep now that she finally had the chance. Alison and the others had been gone for just three days, and EJ was recovering nicely. David had been a big help and he, too, was back to his normal self.

That night, she dreamed about Chicago.

In the morning, she was awakened by voices. EJ was chattering away to Jules, telling her about her bullet wound and how much it had hurt, but how brave she'd been: "I didn't cry, not even once!"

Abby dragged herself out to the fire, pointed and mumbled, "Coffee." Brad obliged her and Alison looked her up and down.

"Rough night last night?"

Abby merely nodded. She was in no mood. . . what the dickens? Oh, yeah. That weird dream. Chicago. She'd never been there, had no real desire to travel up that way. She couldn't remember the details, the hows and the whys, but she did remember clearly seeing the city skyline from a great distance, from somewhere flat. Huh. She drained her mug, held it out for a refill and mentally exorcised the dream. Clearly, she had quite an imagination.

"So, talk," she told Brad and Alison.

"I see," Alison sniffed. "Still a woman of few words. So we got there okay, and Mario and his gang were all at the brewery. No sign of soldiers or anyone. In fact, we just walked across the bridge. What a concept, huh?"

Brad picked up the story, telling of their trip up north and the discovery that the holding facility was empty. "Well, for all practical purposes." He handed her the note that Alison had found.

Abby read it in silence and handed it back. "So she didn't die."

"Tell me again what happened that day, with you and Stefanie, when you were with Kat," Alison said abruptly.

"We walked with her entourage to the Federal Building. We went inside with her, and up the elevator, then down the hall to her new office." Abby stopped for a minute, remembering. "There was some conversation, not much, and she was clearly afraid of us. Well, Stefanie was being a bit, um, threatening.

"Then she put some kind of capsule in her mouth and bit down. She was gasping for breath, but said something about not killing her. I assumed that whatever she took was the same thing we used to have around here, a just-in-case remedy that. . . someone. . . once told us to use if we had to—to avoid capture." She looked squarely at Alison.

"Anyway, the bombs started falling and the building was shaking, so we got out and ran."

"Oh, things have progressed since then, Abby," Alison assured her. "If this note is from Kat, and since it was addressed to me I'm sure it is, then she took something else—

very similar in chemical properties, but it's not as strong, not lethal. It just looks that way.

"And she knows I'm around here somewhere."

"What about the kids?" asked Abby, glancing at EJ.

Brad gazed off, over the hills, and avoided the question until Alison nudged him in the arm. "We did some checking, before we left St. Louis."

"Obviously," said Abby. "Where else would you look? Get to the point, please."

Brad took a deep breath, and said, in a rush, "They took all the children to Chicago. They killed everyone over the age of sixteen."

Abby gasped. Her hands trembled, briefly, and she clasped them together tightly. "Sixteen?"

Brad was looking at Jules and David, sitting together, talking quietly and trying not to pay attention to the adults. "Yes," he said heavily. "They assume the older teens will be more resistant to their programs.

"We found the graves. . . if you could call them that. Just a ditch, really, and they didn't spend much time at it either."

A profound silence fell up them. Jules shivered at the memory.

"Chicago's a big place," Abby pointed out, unnecessarily. "How, exactly, are we supposed to find the kids up there? Like a needle in a haystack," she added bitterly.

"Not entirely," Alison said. "I know Chicago. And I know how they operate up there. Not saying it would be easy, but. . . it's possible. Maybe."

"Brad, how long do you think we have?" Abby was concerned about EJ's recovery and the timing could be critical.

"Well," Brad answered. "When they, um, worked on me, it took a long time. Seems like, best I can piece it together, I was in the hospital 24/7 for close to a year. The so-called rehab phase took almost as long; that's when they'd take me out and parade me around like a show dog, to see how I'd react to certain things.

"Based on all that, and considering my physical condition when they got me, well. . . maybe a year, probably less. We're talking about kids, after all. They're probably a lot more suggestible. And maybe more easily bribed."

"Probably less stubborn, too," added Alison. "Look, Kat issued me a direct challenge. One which I can either accept or reject. If she knows I'm here, and knew I might see the note, what else does she know?"

"Yes," said Abby. "But the real question is how does she know it?"

"Simple," Brad told her. "The files. The file on Abby, in particular. Pops knew that Abby was around, and that I defected, and he knew that Alison was with me. And of course, he had to have updated those before he died. Heck, Alison, Kat probably knew that Jules was your daughter too—maybe even before you knew it."

"I am going to kill her," Alison said. "I never really liked her, anyway." She gave a sardonic smile.

"So, I guess that means you're accepting the challenge?" Brad knew she would, anyway.

Abby sighed. "And I guess it means we're going to Chicago. Damn. Can we talk about this later? I need to think."

"Fine by me," said Brad, yawning. "Come on, Ali, let's take a nap. Jules! Go on, kiddo, get some sleep."

The weary travelers went to bed, which left EJ to her book. David and Abby sat by the fire, lost in their own thoughts.

"Abby," said David quietly. "I really want to go west. But I know you might have other ideas, so I'm willing to do whatever's needed. I just wanted to throw that in there."

She smiled at the young man, understanding exactly what he meant. "David, you'd planned to go, you took time out to take Walt and the kids down south, and now that you're back you've been a huge help. Really and truly." She laughed. "Besides, you know, saving EJ's life and all!"

"I do understand, David. It's your call, you're an adult now. And a very capable one," she added.

"Then I'll be going," said the young man decisively. "I could be ready in two days, I think."

Abby thought for a moment. "Yes. Come on, I'll help you plan your route." The two of them spent the rest of the morning poring over maps and discussing what else David would need to take with him.

After lunch, David and Jules went for a walk. They meandered back to the spring, then hiked up Purple Mountain. Looking out over the valley, David told her he was leaving soon.

Jules was torn. She knew how she felt about Mario, but now that David was leaving. . . . "When are you coming back?" she asked quietly.

"I don't know, Jules. Maybe not ever. Hard to say what's out there."

"I'll miss you," she said.

"Me too," David told her. "I like hanging out with you, Jules."

And then she knew. "Come on, I'll race you back down to the fire!" Jules took off, David right behind her.

Alison was waiting for them, foot tapping impatiently. Abby had just told them that David was leaving, going west, as had so many generations before him. She was not amused. At all. And Brad was on David's side too. He said he "understood." Huh, thought Alison. Sure he did.

But when she saw how carefree David appeared as the two teenagers reached the bottom of the hill, how he grabbed Jules from behind and swung her around in a brief hug before letting go, when she really looked at him. . . .

She knew it would be okay. He'd become a young man, a confident one, and he knew exactly what he was doing. She'd seen, firsthand, that he was knowledgeable, and his skills were more than sufficient. Walt had taught him well.

But most importantly, she knew he wasn't breaking her daughter's heart.

Chapter Thirty-Eight

They waited until June to leave. David, however, had been gone for two months already, sent off with hugs and handshakes and not too many tears, on the part of those he left behind. He promised to come back someday, of course, but they all knew it might be a promise he couldn't keep.

He spent a lot of time with Abby in the few days after he announced his departure and, as he walked away from them for the last time, she whispered in his ear.

"What did you tell him?" EJ asked curiously.

"Nothing for nosy little girls to hear," answered her mother, tweaking the little girl's braid. "I just gave him one word, the name of one person for whom he should look when he gets out there." Abby gazed after the figure, getting smaller in the distance. For a moment, she looked as though she'd like to be going too.

They stored whatever they couldn't carry far to the back of the cave. Brad and Alison brought the trucks in from the other side of Sunnytop. One remained near the spring, suitably camouflaged, and the other was packed for the trip. They planned to leave it with Mario and travel through Illinois on foot; activity in the area across the Mississippi was largely unknown.

Just before they left, they blew the entrance to the cave. Abby herself placed the charges. Too much, and their cache would be buried forever. Too little and at best they'd get a cloud of dust and a potentially dangerous blast.

As they drove away from the camp gates, EJ looked longingly out the back window of the cab. She didn't like the city, as she told them over and over, all the way to St. Louis. It made no difference to her that she'd never been to one, she just didn't like it. Jules finally told her to knock it off, and the adults had to hide their relief as EJ complied.

But then the little girl responded with, "You just want to see Mario and probably kiss him again. Yuck!" And the mostly calm ride turned into a thunderstorm.

Jules turned beet red and shrieked, "How did you know he kissed me?"

Alison's eyes grew wide. "What? He kissed you? How dare he!"

Brad laughed aloud, and even Abby smiled, a little. She was concerned for Jules, because Mario seemed so much older and more worldly. He was just two or three years older than Jules, chronologically, but had seen and done so much more than she. Still, the reaction to EJ's statement was quite comical.

"Okay, everyone, settle down! Brad, shut up. Alison, relax already, okay? She's almost eighteen for heaven's sake. Jules, chill.

"And EJ?"

"Yes, Mom?"

"You are the ever-loving limit! How did you know about this anyway? I'm assuming she's correct, Jules?"

Jules looked out the window as if her life depended upon it and let silence be her answer. EJ gazed raptly out the other window, looking at things she'd never seen and being enchanted by it all.

"What? Oh. . . I followed them that one night." EJ went back to watching the scenes moving past the truck, having lost interest in the subject immediately after she dropped her bombshell.

Silence ruled the rest of the trip, and Abby stopped the truck when they arrived in Forest Park. Brad radioed Mario and told them of their arrival, and he responded that he would send a crew to meet them. The protocol had been determined when they'd last been here. Even though the wall was no longer guarded or maintained, it served as a potential barrier should trouble arise from nearly any direction. As it was too large to be torn down, it remained in place.

Mario himself arrived within thirty minutes, to Jules' delight and Alison's dismay. He cheerfully waved as he climbed out of a black SUV with darkly tinted windows. "A gift," he told them, "from the lately departed government officials."

He then walked directly to Alison, took her hand, and bowed. "With your permission, I would like to ask your daughter to ride back with me."

Alison stammered and stuttered, and finally managed, "Um, sure. Okay. I guess."

Brad grinned and waved Jules off to the SUV. "Behave yourself!" His grin deflated a bit when Alison glared at him.

The rest of them followed Mario in the truck back to the old brewery. Abby wondered why they didn't find somewhere more comfortable, but Mario explained that they had made many changes on the inside and besides, this place was more than large enough for everyone.

When they arrived, Abby could see that this was true. Mario himself had a spacious apartment, and his lieutenants were quartered off the same hallway. The rank and file members of his group, the soldiers, had carved out small pockets of space nearby, each to his own taste. Or her own taste. Mario had many women in his group who were treated with a certain deference, but who also were equal members of his organization. He assured them that he had long grown past his childish outburst from a year or so ago, when he claimed that some situations were too dangerous for a mere woman. He looked rather embarrassed at the recall of that meeting.

Jules was uncharacteristically subdued when she arrived; Abby wondered exactly what they'd discussed on the short drive to the brewery, but she was quickly sidetracked by the logistics of finding where they would be staying, and unloading the truck.

Brad had gone to speak with George, and Alison was herding EJ from room to room, trying to answer the many questions that the little girl kept firing at her. Worn out, she finally found Abby, and dragged EJ into the room. "Your daughter is quite the chatterbox, Abby. Whew, I'm beat!"

Abby laughed. "Yes, she can be, at times. Where's Jules?"

"Huh. I don't know. Thought she was here with you." Alison stood back up and walked out the door, calling over her shoulder, "I have a pretty good idea, though!"

So did Abby.

But Jules was not with Mario. Alison found her in the rooms of two of the women who were part of his organization, chatting companionably. She rose gracefully when she saw her mother and followed her back to their quarters without question. Alison looked at her daughter closely, but Jules said nothing and serenely began unpacking her things.

Over the next few days, Brad met with George, who gratefully accepted the use of the truck until, or if, they returned. He was particularly interested in the hidden compartment beneath the bed and examined the additional after-market features closely. In spite of the age of the vehicle, it had held up well under Abby's comprehensive maintenance.

Alison and Abby kept busy making lists, repacking and reloading, and browsing Mario's armory, to which he gave them free access. And tracking down the kids. Unbelievably, there were other children here; fewer than half a dozen, to be sure, but plenty to keep EJ entertained. That is, when she wasn't underfoot asking a million questions.

By far, the biggest problem was monitoring Jules. Her mother made it clear that she was not to be alone with Mario, and that was that. Abby, however, knew that Jules managed anyway. She hadn't lived with the girl for twelve years and learned nothing. She might not talk about him, but Abby could practically read her mind.

On the first night after their arrival, Abby was still awake when Jules quietly opened the door. Unknown to the girl, she'd seen her leave too. Abby glanced at her watch. Two hours. She hoped Jules hadn't done anything stupid. She said nothing to anyone, but resolved to find a few minutes to talk to the teenager.

Jules had not, in fact, done anything stupid. She was a smart girl and, while head-over-heels falling for Mario, she had great self-control. She would have been shocked to discover that anyone might be concerned about what she may or may not be doing.

All they had done was talk. Well, okay, a little more than that, but not much. Really. And Mario wanted her to stay here, with him. Jules was wavering. She had her family, and there was Mario. Truth be told, her reticence these days was due to the swirling thoughts in her head, not any particular adherence to Alison's mandate that she not be alone with Mario.

She finally fell asleep, knowing that her time here was coming to an end and that she needed to tell Mario that she'd made her decision. For now.

Chapter Thirty-Nine

Jules slipped in the door before the rest of them were up. She shivered at the unexpected coolness of the room and began to pack her bag.

Abby was the first to awaken. "You're up and moving early, Jules." She looked closely at the young woman but said nothing else. They cleaned and reloaded their weapons, and finished packing while the others began to stir.

Chicago. It was time.

Having said their goodbyes the night before, due their early start, they left the brewery and walked up DeMenil Place to the big house. Brad heaved open the cellar doors and they descended into the dampness, shivering at the temperature change.

They crept through the tunnel, all the way beneath the Mississippi, and emerged into the daylight. No one looked back at the ruins of St. Louis, except Jules, who paused briefly as she gazed to the west. She quickly caught up with the others, and they continued through the flat Illinois countryside.

Following the old railroad tracks, the group came to the old East St. Louis rail yards and made a wide berth. Hard telling what, or who, was hidden behind the rusty doors and graffiti-covered sides of the boxcars.

The sun beat down on them. It had been particularly dry lately, with no sign of any incoming rain to provide a margin of relief. They stopped for a quick break near Collinsville, but pushed on within half an hour. Conversation was desultory; the terrain was unfamiliar, and the tension was thick.

By the end of the day, they'd passed through Edwardsville. Brad went off to find suitable quarters for the night, with EJ tagging along. After seeing not a single person or animal for the entire trip, the danger here appeared to be minimal. Abby reluctantly gave her daughter permission, and EJ happily danced off down the gravel road.

They returned within an hour, and EJ raced ahead to tell them the news. They'd found a barn, still standing. "And," EJ said, "it doesn't smell that bad. Honestly!"

Getting comfortable in the barn was easier said than done. They chased out a small flock of birds and cleaned up a space as best they could. At least they were out of the sun for a while. It was too hot and they were too miserable to attempt a fire, so they snacked on some jerky. Eventually, the temperature began to drop enough to make movement bearable.

EJ went to help Brad and Jules with dinner while Abby and Alison looked over the maps. Tomorrow, hopefully, they could make it to Beaver Dam. It would be a good spot to get their bearings and maybe stay for a day or two. Depending, of course, on whether there were any current inhabitants. And how receptive they might be to strangers. Or even if the lake was still a lake—there had been too many surprises over the years, and most of them not very nice ones.

They started early the next day or, as Jules put it, "For heaven's sake, Mom, it's the middle of the night!" Alison wasn't thrilled either, but it was a lot cooler than walking in the heat of the day. Who knew there were so many farms here and hardly any trees? Even now, years after being abandoned, the fields grew nothing taller than a few feet, and those were mostly scrawny shrubs.

EJ held up remarkably well for an eight-year-old, and they made good time traveling before dawn. They stopped near the dam early in the afternoon. Finding a grove of actual trees, they hunkered down and waited and watched. Jules scouted the immediate area and reported back that there were no signs of anyone. Still. The entire state seemed to have packed up and left.

Or been taken, thought Abby darkly.

Alison secured a shelter while Brad took EJ down to the water. They saw a few minnows swimming around and EJ immediately decided she must learn to fish. Brad cut her a pole and they dug around in the mud near the shore for worms. EJ was not fond of worms.

They returned an hour later and EJ had caught her first fish. She was so proud of the tiny thing that Abby insisted that was exactly what they'd been wanting for dinner. Thankfully, the bite-sized portion it provided for each of them was supplemented with some MREs.

After an extra day at the dam, they traveled on. They stopped just southwest of Springfield, far enough outside the former state capitol that they decided it would be safe. If, indeed, there really was anyone around. It was very strange, but then Missouri had been similar in lack of population. At least there, the territory was familiar. This was almost like walking in a dream, the same dreary scenery, over and over, and seemingly going nowhere in spite of distance traveled.

Two days later, they were, according to the map, near the old Spring Lake State Park. This, declared Abby, was it. They were stopping, they were staying, and she, herself, wasn't moving an inch until she was good and ready. No one argued. They were all exhausted, physically and mentally. And mostly just plain tired of walking.

They checked the area, saw no one and nothing, as usual. After camp was set up, EJ insisted on more fishing, so Brad and Jules took her down to the lake. Abby and Alison discovered, not far from the site, a deep blue pool, surrounded with drooping green tree branches that formed an overhead canopy.

Looking at each other for a moment, they quickly stripped down and lowered themselves into the cool, clear water. For a long time, they just lay there, floating, looking up at tiny patches of wispy clouds between the leaves.

Alison broke the silence. "Maybe we should just stay here. Absolutely no one around, nothing to think about, nothing to do. . . ."

"Yeah, right," Abby told her. "Even if we did stay here, and had nowhere to go, you'd either get bored—or something else would happen. Thought we were okay down at the camp, too, you know."

Alison sighed. "I know. And you're right. Besides, I need to find Kat. That witch. And the kids, too. Speaking of. . . ." She sat up and looked through the trees. "Here come ours."

Jules and EJ made their way along the path to the pool. EJ's eyes widened and she asked, "Can we come in too, Mom?" Jules was already pulling off her t-shirt.

The four of them splashed and hollered so much that Brad came running up from the campsite. He grinned when he saw them. "Can I come in and play?"

"No!" shouted a chorus of voices.

"Turn around," Abby said, "And give us a few minutes." She and Jules and EJ climbed out and hurriedly dressed, but Alison remained the water.

"I think I'll stay a little longer," she told Abby, winking. Before Abby and the girls were out of sight, they heard a big splash and Alison's shrieks as Brad cannonballed into the pool.

They stayed there for three days before packing up. Still at least 200 miles to Chicago. They tried not to think about the distance and simply continued walking. The town of Canton was deserted, and mostly destroyed. The downtown historic district was barely recognizable but, curiously, the clock tower in the old square was still standing.

In two days' time, they'd reached an interstate. This, Alison told them, must be near the old campground where her friends, Eric and Marta, had had their camper.

"Well, it sounds familiar," she said, when pressed for details. "But usually one of them was driving and I didn't pay much attention. I'm sure we were on this road, though. Probably. No other reason for me to be out in the sticks here!"

Rained poured down that night, a welcome respite from the heat, and they sheltered beneath the overpass. The next day dawned hot and muggy, with more clouds to the northwest. With a late start, they trudged on, damp and sticky and miserable, until they came to the Spoon River around noon.

Dark clouds still threatened, closer now, and they could hear very faint rumbles of thunder. Fortunately, the river was running quite low due to the recently ended drought and they managed to safely cross. Abby pointed to a small stand of trees near the bank, and they trudged towards it as the rain began to come down. Suddenly, the thunder was no longer faint but loud, rolling booms, one after another.

Abby had just grabbed EJ's arm to help her along, when the ground gave way with a loud sucking sound, audible over the now intermittent claps of thunder. Both of them tumbled into the sinkhole, and as the others tried to reach them, they, too, disappeared into the earth. The last thing Abby heard was a loud scream as she frantically tried to hold onto EJ.

Chapter Forty

The explosions echoed, over and over, and walls of water came crashing down upon them. Abby gasped and struggled to surface, fought for oxygen. She lashed out, grasping for EJ's hand, for anyone. A large rock bounced past her head and she ducked.

The next time she emerged, she managed to stay above the water. She made her way, slowly, towards an outcropping and pulled herself up. Thousands of gallons of water continued to rush past her as she searched in vain for the others.

Miscellaneous items flowed past her: sticks, smaller rocks, a tree trunk; then a hat, a backpack. They were gone so fast that she couldn't tell to whom they'd belonged. She huddled there for nearly an hour before the water level began to drop, then began to make her way along the underground river to a faint patch of light.

She finally climbed out of the ground, nowhere near where she'd gone in. Exhausted, she lay down on the hard ground without removing her pack or anything else. She simply breathed. Then she slept.

Gradually becoming warmer, she began to wake. Her eyes still closed, she swatted at hands and began to kick. She suddenly jumped up and grabbed her knife, holding it out, focused on the threat.

"About time," said Alison. "Thought you were going to sleep all day. Come on, time to go."

"What?" said Abby, still groggy. She shook her head to clear it and immediately said, "EJ. Where is she?"

"Relax, it's okay. Everyone's waiting for us. Come on." Alison looked at the sky. "Brad and the girls are upriver from us. Here." She handed Abby an energy bar and a bottle of water.

Abby sagged in relief. She wordlessly took the food and ate, finishing off the water too.

"I came out right behind you, but you were already out like a light. Jules got here a few minutes later, said that EJ and Brad would wait for us. She said they were fine, and then took off to let them know about us.

"Sheesh, Ab, slow down!" Alison scrambled to catch up as Abby began to walk.

"No," said Abby. "This is it. I'm done. I'm getting EJ and we're going. . . we're going somewhere! I don't know where and I don't care! These people have tried to kill me for years and years and I've had enough!" She kept going, swiftly, surely.

"Dammit, Abby, you can't quit now! We need you. We have to keep fighting!" Alison grabbed her by the shoulders and spun her around. "Abby. Listen to me."

"No. I won't. I'm done. Now let go of me."

Alison dropped her hands at the threat in Abby's voice. "Fine. But you're out of your mind. In a minute, I was going to slap you. Not like I haven't wanted to already, once or twice."

Abby almost smiled. "Good. You got it. Come on."

An hour later, they'd reached the rendezvous point. EJ came running to her mother and Abby looked her over, relieved beyond words that her daughter was safe.

"Sheesh, Mom. I'm not a baby," EJ grumbled. She stuck her knife in its sheath and led Abby to a large rock. "Sit down. You don't look so good."

"I'm fine," Abby said testily. Kids. They thought they knew everything. "Just c-cold. That's all." Abby made an effort to sit up straight, then decided the heck with it. She slumped down, leaning against the rock.

"Mom?"

"She's okay," Brad said. He put a heavy blanket around Abby and told EJ to stay with her until she fell asleep. He walked over to Jules and Alison and sat down heavily. They were all exhausted, and hungry, and cold. They needed to find some kind of shelter, something more concealing than this stand of trees.

"Got it!" exclaimed Alison, snapping shut her compass. "I know where we are—we just have to get to where we're going!"

"No kidding," said Jules. "And where might that be?"

"See that ridge over there? That old campground I used to go is right there, on the other side."

"Yeah," said Brad. "Okay. But what else is there? Or rather, who else is there?"

"I'll go!" Jules jumped up and picked up her pack and started walking before anyone could object.

"Jules, wait a minute!" Alison ignored her aching muscles and went after her daughter. "Come back as fast as you can with your report. It'll be light soon and the trip might take longer for all of us." She glanced over at Abby. "Be careful."

"Always, Mom." And Jules disappeared in the darkness.

She was back in just over an hour.

"It's there all right. Just like you said. And no one's around, at all."

"What's there?" asked Abby, who had joined the others.

"The campground. Like Mom said. A bunch of campers and trailers, I don't know, maybe twenty? Lined up on two streets. Some of them have broken windows, and a couple were off their blocks. There's a little building too, but half the roof has fallen in."

"Okay then. Let's go." Abby shouldered her pack and the Mossberg and the rest of them gathered their things as well. It wasn't a difficult hike, through the flatlands of Illinois; most of this area, too, had once been farmland, but was now covered with scrub growth. They arrived at the campground just as the sun broke fully over the horizon.

After a good night's sleep, or day, as it were, and a quick meal prior to that, everyone was in much better spirits. EJ was nose-deep in a book she'd incredibly found in the old camper they'd chosen. Jules was busy cleaning her guns while Abby and Alison sat at the table and talked in low tones. Brad was still asleep.

The camper was musty and disheveled on the inside, but at least there was a roof and walls. And now they had time to think, and to plan. The conversation was becoming heated as Abby still insisted that she and EJ were going. . . somewhere. She had been quite serious: she was done.

And then Jules spoke.

"I can hear you, you know." She finished putting her .44 back together with a snap and went into the kitchenette, pulling out a chair and propping up her feet.

"I'm going back."

"Back?" asked Alison, dumbfounded. Abby was speechless.

"Yes, back to St. Louis. I'm going to find Mario."

"But—but—you can't!"

"Yes, Mom, I can. I'm eighteen years old now. I know the way. I want to be there, with him." Jules was adamant. She wasn't asking, she was telling them. Both of them.

"But. . . ." Alison burst into tears and Abby took her hand tightly.

"Jules, your mom is just. . . upset right now. Can we talk about this later?" Abby spoke quietly, but Jules knew that tone.

"Of course," Jules answered, rising gracefully and going back into the bedroom, glancing back for a moment. "But I'm still going. Soon."

Alison dried her tears and she and Abby sat in silence for some time.

Brad finally got up and joined them. "So, did I hear that right? Or was I still dreaming? Jules wants to go back?"

"Yes," Abby told him. "You heard it right."

"Oh," said Brad, rubbing his eyes.

"Oh?" asked Alison. "That's all you can say?" She was drumming her fingers on the table, looking about wildly, and seemed on the verge of crying again. "I don't want to lose her again!"

"You're more likely to lose her if you tell her no. Besides, she'll probably go anyway. We've both seen her like this when she's made up her mind. Can't imagine where she gets it." Brad tried to lighten the moment, but failed.

"Dad, I can still hear you guys. And yes, I'm going," came a voice from the back of the camper.

"What?" said EJ, looking up from her book. "Did I miss something?"

"Yes," Abby answered. "Jules wants to go back to St. Louis. Alone."

"Oh," said EJ. "Guess she wants to be with Mario. Besides, I can help with your, you know, the mission." And she turned back to her book.

"Huh. Was I the only one who didn't know about this?" demanded Alison.

"Come on, Alison," Abby said. "You had to have seen it when we were there last. And all the other times. She's right, she's not a child anymore. What were you doing, at her age?"

"I don't know!" wailed Alison. "Um. . . getting married and having a baby? No, I was older than eighteen!"

"Not by much, I imagine. And look how she's lived, what she's been through, compared to us. I was in New Mexico, by myself, backpacking over the whole state when I wasn't much older than she." Abby looked at her friend. "You have to trust in Jules, you have to let her go gracefully. She'll not only leave anyway - but she won't come back."

"Oh, I trust her," Alison retorted. "I just don't trust all the crazy people that may or may not be out there. And. . . and I don't know when I'll see her again!"

Abby looked helplessly at Brad. "That's all I've got. Your turn."

Brad shook his head. "I don't know what else to say, Ali. She's left and come back before, and you've found her again too. No reason either of those things won't happen a second or third time. And like Abby said, if you tell her no, well. . . ."

Alison finally nodded.

"Jules!" hollered EJ. "Your mom said you can go!"

Jules ran out of the bedroom and grabbed her mother, pulling her to her feet. "Thank you!" she cried.

"Hey, settle down," said Alison ruefully. "I said it was okay, I didn't say I was happy about it."

"Of course," said Jules. "I'm sorry, really I am. But I have to go. And I will be back."

She left as soon as the sun set.

Epilogue

They stood on the edge of what used to be a small lake. As far as they could see, all around, the earth was scorched and blackened. No cover, no concealment. The place looked, Abby guessed, much as it had back in the coal mining days long ago. Barren.

Two hundred miles to the northeast lay Chicago, the last great city in the Midwest, filled with government spies and thugs and mercenaries, murderers, thieves, and all manner of disreputable and hedonistic criminals. That was the path they would take: from the inside, instead of merely looking through the window.

Days of travel lay ahead of them; dangerous, uncertain. Abby fervently hoped they'd make it, and succeed in this last mission.

The most important one of them all.

She shouldered her pack and the Mossberg, and they began the journey towards Chicago.

Robin Tidwell

ABOUT THE AUTHOR

Born in St. Louis, Missouri, Robin graduated from Parkway Central at the end of her junior year and went on to college . . . five times. Nearly 30 years later, on a whim, she looked over her transcripts and re-enrolled, completing not quite sixty hours of credit in just over one calendar year. Her degree, from Columbia College, is a combined major of psychology, sociology, and criminal justice.

Robin's writing career began at the age of eight, when her grandmother insisted she read Gone With the Wind before taking her to see the movie. Inspired by Margaret Mitchell, she began scribbling little booklets of stories, and was the editor of her elementary school newspaper and a columnist in high school. She submitted a short story to Seventeen magazine and was promptly rejected, but still keeps a copy of the manuscript in her desk.

Robin has worked as a snack bar cook, a salad prepper, a camp counselor, a waitress, a receptionist, a housekeeper, a freelancer, an editor, and an employment consultant and manager. She's also been in car sales, skin care sales, cookware sales, advertising sales, and MLM. She's owned and operated an entrepreneurial conglomerate, a cleaning service, an old-time photography studio, a bookstore, and a publishing house.

Six years ago, Robin and her husband Dennis moved back to St. Louis, after many years in Columbia, Sedalia, Colorado Springs, Durango, and Granbury and Tolar, Texas. They live with their youngest son, a dog, a cat, and a puppy.

Robin Tidwell